D0405562

THE RED LEDGER RECALL

VOLUME TWO
PARTS 4 - 5 - 6

MEREDITH WILD

This book is an original publication of Meredith Wild.

This is a work of fiction. Names, characters, places, and
incidents either are the product of the author's imagination or
are used fictitiously, and any resemblance to actual persons,
living or dead, business establishments, events, or locales is entirely
coincidental. The publisher does not assume any responsibility for third-party
websites or their content.

Copyright © 2018 Meredith Wild
Cover Design by Meredith Wild
Cover Photographs: Shutterstock

All Rights Reserved.
No part of this book may be reproduced, scanned, or
distributed in any printed or electronic format without permission. Please do
not participate in or encourage piracy
of copyrighted materials in violation of the author's rights. Purchase only
authorized editions.

Hardcover ISBN: 978-1-64263-029-9

THE RED LEDGER RECALL

VOLUME TWO
PARTS 4 - 5 - 6

MEREDITH WILD

WATERHOUSE PRESS

TABLE OF CONTENTS

For Jonathan
I could easily dedicate every book to you.
But this one, for sure, would not exist without you.

THE RED LEDGER

part 4

1

ISABEL

New York City

Millions of lights pay homage to the night. Lamps lit for those who live in the dark. Together, the silent pinpricks across the sky create a subtle glow in the one-room apartment. I'm sitting in the living room of Mateus da Silva's East Village *pied-à-terre*, content with the view but not the solitude.

Tristan's been gone an hour. I've counted every minute. He insisted he had to take a meeting alone with a man named Crow—a man like him, who takes lives without hesitation.

I still don't know what Tristan plans to do…about us or Company Eleven or the leash they're planning to put on him again. I doubt he'll tell me. He's been his usual cold self since we made the journey from New Orleans in an exhausting two-day jag. But when he's cold, he's working. I've learned that. He's calculating and planning, too focused in his mind to show me the softer side I've successfully coaxed out a time or two. Doesn't make the temperature drop much easier to accept, but acceptance is the only way through this.

Jay's invited him back into the Company to resume his role as a trained killer—the best of them. I've accepted this, at least to the degree that I would follow him in that direction if it kept us together. He could have left me at Halo with Martine and the others. For his part, he seems to have resigned himself to the fact that I won't give up on us. At least not without a fight.

Yet I find myself missing the mansion on St. Charles now. I miss Martine's air of quiet confidence, like a mother's watchful eye over the house and everyone in it. Skye's unexpected friendship. Even Noam's merciless training, because it came from his heart. My time with the people attached to Halo wasn't exactly a fairy tale, but I enjoyed a moment of stability there. Or at least a taste of it.

I pick up my phone and chance a late-night call to Skye, hoping I don't wake her.

"About time you called." Her voice is scratchy with sleep when she picks up.

I smile against a strong pang of emotion. We didn't have much time for goodbyes before Tristan and I took off for New York. As I packed my bags quickly, she was tearful and apologetic for leaving the hotel with Zeda so swiftly. Martine, watching the scene play out remotely, had pulled them out as soon as Tristan blasted onto the scene, gun in hand, ready to use it on the man who'd viciously beaten me. Vince Boswell had a twisted idea about foreplay, but it was enough to collect what we needed to have him call off the hit on my life. At least that's what we hoped.

"Where are you?" she asks.

"New York. We got here a couple days ago. We're staying at a friend's apartment in the city while Tristan does whatever he has to do."

"And what's that?"

I trust Skye, but I can't share Tristan's business with anyone. Not when he's in the business of killing people, or at least tied to it for the foreseeable future. She knows what he does, but that's about it.

"Meeting with an old associate," I finally say.

She chuckles softly. "So you're in knots."

"Basically."

"You can always come back, you know."

"He needs me, whether he chooses to admit it or not."

She doesn't need to say anything. Her inherent distrust of most men extends to Tristan, and her skeptical snort on the other side of the phone confirms it.

"I know what you're thinking, but I'm his only reason to stop doing what he's been doing. If I'm out of the picture, I'm afraid he'll go back to it, and I'll never see him again."

"You sure you're not just prolonging the inevitable?"

I wince. I don't like the sound of that. I refuse to accept Tristan returning to a life of killing people for money. Will I fight as hard as I can to keep him from going there again, at the risk of my own safety?

"I'm not losing him again," I say with finality.

I'm not spending another six years wondering where he is or what he's doing, my heart never healing, just breaking a little more with every passing day. No. I'd face death and danger over the almost carefree life I left to run away with Tristan. I'd make the same choice all over again if I had to. A thousand times over.

She sighs on the other end. "All right then. You know we'll always be here for you."

"Thank you. And thanks for picking up. I needed to hear a friendly voice."

"Anytime, hon. Come back soon, okay?"

"I'll try."

I hang up and feel the loss of her daily companionship even more acutely. Living in limbo, not knowing our next stop, is excruciating at times. New York decidedly isn't a place to hide away without purpose. The soul of the city seems powered by an unending rush to handle matters at hand. And if I stay idle in this apartment much longer just to wait for Tristan to find a way out of his commitment with Company Eleven, I'll soon be climbing the walls.

I stare at my phone and think about texting him. He won't answer anyway, so I go to the bedroom instead. In the corner beside my emptied suitcases is a black bag. A little ripple of worry goes through me that Tristan will find me going through his things. But he's gone and not likely to come back for a while. So I take a seat on the floor, unzip the bag, and begin to unpack it, one item at a time. Rolled-up T-shirts and clothes. Weapons that don't scare me as much as they used to. Guns and knives and extra magazines. An entire pack of zip ties. I let those drop to the floor without care, because him using them to tie me to the bed the night we reunited is not yet a distant memory. Of course, if he used them now, I probably wouldn't mind so much.

I continue unpacking until there's nothing left. I check the smaller interior pockets and find his passports and a few bricks of cash. American dollars. Money that no doubt was obtained carrying out the work of a mercenary. Then the red leather notebook that holds the record of his wrongdoings. Names of the unfortunate. I unwind the leather strap and go through it, somberly, like the pages of a program at a funeral. Most of the names are masculine, some feminine. Round numbers are beside them. Fees earned.

Each one is a bloody story. A story that started with a wish or a grudge or a vow that was made maybe years ago. Maybe decades ago. One thing is certain. Each name holds its own secrets. I run my finger over the faint indentations on the paper made in Tristan's messy script.

I want to shut the notebook and tie up everything this book represents. Burn it. Toss it into the river to live with the sludge at the bottom and be forgotten. But that won't make what Tristan did go away. And this ledger has value to him. He calls it insurance, and I wonder now if this could be the insurance we need to get him away from the Company.

Surely they have their own ledger. But what if we unraveled enough to scare them into leaving us alone, once and for all? Because I lived, we could track down the people who wanted me dead. The dead don't have a voice, but their families do. Their friends do. What if we uncovered enough to buy back Tristan's freedom?

Keeping the notebook out, I begin returning his things to the bag, when a sliver of white catches my eye. It's barely noticeable, sticking out behind the rectangular piece of plastic that lines the bottom of the bag. I peel back the barrier to reveal a thick file folder, and as I pull it out and open it, several glossy photos slip out among the papers. The first one paralyzes me.

The pale, wounded body of a man with dozens of sutures across his torso. I touch the photo, leaving my fingerprints on the surface. Tristan. My beautiful Tristan. Marred with the wounds of war. I press my hand to my mouth. Then, slowly, I go to the next photo and the next. His legs. His profile. Shots taken from every angle, like a crime scene. One that, miraculously, he lived through.

Fighting nausea, I push the photos away and sift through the other paperwork in the file. High school transcripts, military forms, and briefings filled with terms I don't fully comprehend. I pause on a letter with the CIA insignia centered on the page.

I scan the letter quickly and land on one sentence that I read again and again until my eyes blur.

Please accept my highest recommendation of Tristan Stone for placement in the Striker Special Forces training program.

Then the illegible scrawl of my father, signing off on Tristan's future.

TRISTAN

"I'm here to see Crow."

The tall, brawny bouncer gives me a cursory glance, lifts the velvet rope between the entrance to Topaz 31 and me, and murmurs into the microphone hidden in his sleeve cuff as I head for the front door of the club—an upscale gentlemen's lounge in Midtown. I half expected Crow to lure me into a seedy bar in South Jersey where he and his mob family hail from. To talk to me or kill me, who knows.

Inviting me here instead may have been his way of putting me at ease, but I'm as on guard as ever. I nearly killed him last time I saw him, a circumstance I'm sure he's not forgotten.

Once inside, the main area seduces the senses with blue lights, clinks of glass from the bar, and several rows of leather crescent chairs swiveling as patrons casually follow the leggy blonde crossing the stage. She pivots near the edge where a man in a suit peers up at her bared assets.

"Can I get you a drink?"

A topless waitress approaches me from behind. She's petite, short even in her stilettos. Pretty enough with brown eyes and tawny skin. I'm not interested in this woman's tits, but for about a half a second, they're hard to ignore. Unnaturally full but attractive. Just not the set I'm into right now.

She pushes her chest out proudly but wilts a little when I ignore her preening and look around the club for Crow.

"No, I'm here to meet someone."

"Are you Red?" she asks, drawing my attention back.

"That's me."

"Crow's in one of the suites in the back. He's expecting you. This way."

I follow her around the side of the stage, taking in details as I go. The thin Thursday night crowd. A dozen or so men and one couple whose gazes are fixed on the show. A handful of servers offering massages and bottle service. Nothing obviously suspicious.

The waitress leads me deeper into the club, stops in front of an unmarked door, and opens it without knocking. Dimly lit like the one we came from, the room is small but not claustrophobic. Crow lounges casually with his feet up on a black leather couch that wraps around the base of a narrow runway-like stage. Another beautiful girl is on it, gyrating around a pole in the middle and shooting furtive glances at her only client.

Crow. The big, cocky guy I shot up a few weeks ago. He doesn't look too sore about it when he notices my arrival. He waves me closer with a hand wound in a flesh-toned bandage.

I take a seat on the opposite side of the couch.

"We meet again." He pops some peanuts into his mouth and smirks. "We're just a couple of world travelers, aren't we?"

He laughs loudly. "Yeah. It's good to be home though."

I glance at the stage briefly and back to him. "I thought Jersey was home."

He shakes his head a little. "I could be a king there, you know? I want to be a king here."

I almost laugh at his lofty dreams. Being the king of Manhattan would require wealth beyond anything we could ever make knocking off important people. Even a king's ransom wouldn't be enough to be the king here. But I'm relying on Crow's delusions of grandeur to get me closer to Soloman, so I let him dream.

The waitress returns with two bottles. A bottle of scotch and an eighteen-year-old Dom Pérignon chilling in a bucket of ice.

"Are we celebrating?"

"It's not for you, asshole." Crow nods toward the bottle of scotch. "You can help yourself to the Macallan, though."

"I'm good."

"Suit yourself." He takes the neat pour from the waitress before slipping her a twenty and sending her on her way. "I'm in pain every day, thanks to you, but I refuse to take the shit my doctor's pushing."

"Sorry about that," I lie.

He grimaces over his next swallow. "Thanks, Red. Means a lot."

"You said you wanted to meet. Here I am. What do you want to talk about?"

"How's it going with Jay?" Something glimmers in his eyes.

"Why do you ask?"

He smirks. "I don't know. She's offering a nice bounty to bring you in. Pretty fucked up since you didn't kill the bitch when you had the chance, huh?"

Something tightens in my gut. An unexpected blow of resentment that I left Jay alive only to have her turn again so quickly. I don't know why I'd expect anything else. Maybe my ego or pride in my job superseded the obvious.

"Interesting," I say thinly.

"Yeah, she said you agreed to come back in, but she's not sure you'll follow through. Said if I got to you first, to hold you and she'd make it worth my while. One more job to fatten up my retirement account."

"So you're allowed to bow out of the Company, but I'm not?"

"I didn't botch a job."

"You couldn't manage to kill me. Fucked that up pretty good, didn't you?"

He frowns a little, downing the last of his drink and setting it on the table. "That's different."

"Why?"

"Because you're you. That wasn't an easy job."

"Even with all your backup? I'm flattered."

He blows out a breath. "Listen, Red. I didn't ask you to come here to see who could piss the farthest. And even though part of me wants to, I'm not going to kill you."

Good luck trying, you clumsy fuck.

"That's really sweet of you. What do you want?"

"I want to work with you."

"I'm not interested in a partner," I say quickly.

"You've got Isabel now."

I don't answer. Isabel is none of his business. I don't even like the sound of her name passing through his lips.

He seems to know this because he grins. "Relax, Red. If I'm not coming for you, I'm not coming for your girl."

I clench my fist and unfurl it a few times, silently calming myself. "If you have a proposal, I'd suggest you lay it out now."

"How many hits do you have under your belt?"

"Plenty." I know the number, of course, but like he said, this isn't a pissing contest.

"Me too. And what's an average hit? Like, twenty to fifty K, right? The really important ones are more, of course, but—"

"Get to the point."

He smiles again. That same smug, glittering smile that could almost be endearing if it came with a good plan to take Jay and her operation down. I really wish he had one, but he's probably just wasting my time.

"If someone can afford fifty thousand dollars to kill someone else, what's *their* life worth?"

I pause and wait for him to continue. Because if he's proposing what I think he's proposing…

"I know you've got a list, Red. So do I."

"And you want to turn the tables and come after the people who did the hiring."

He nods. "You know the kind of clients who hire Soloman. Heads of state. CEOs. Princes. The top of the food chain."

"Maybe so. But if you do this, Company Eleven will bring an army after you, and whoever you fuck over is going to bring their army too. Good luck with that."

"I've got my own army."

I barely refrain from rolling my eyes. "I bet they're a real loyal bunch too. The kind of clients you're talking about would turn anyone close to you for short dollars. You'd have a bullet in your back in no time."

He swings his legs down and straightens into a sitting position, wincing slightly. "You're wrong."

"Because they're your family?"

"Fuck no. Because once we pull off one big job, we can buy loyalty. And when we've pulled off enough of them, they won't be able to touch us. We'll be hands-off—the way Soloman is now. Tug a few strings here and there, get things done, and trigger the payments after. And the best part?"

I'm not sure I even want to hear the best part.

"Company Eleven implodes. We won't even have to dismantle them. They'll dismantle themselves. Credibility ruined. They'll never get another job again. Hell, they'll be lucky to get out of this business alive."

I rake my hands through my hair and blow out a breath. Crow's plan is terrible. Fraught with potential pitfalls. Dangerous ones that would leave both of us dead. Still, I'm strangely interested in talking it through.

"Okay, let's ignore for the moment that your plan is basically impossible on a large scale. We'd be on everyone's most-wanted list before we could even think about reaping the rewards. For argument's sake, though, let's say we could target one job strategically. One client. How would you collect the intel you needed?"

"The hard way or the easy way. The hard way? We do our homework. Research connections and sniff out whatever shit triggered the hit."

"And the easy way?"

He smiles broadly. "We snatch Jay and squeeze her for all the details. Talk or else. Plenty of basements in Jersey. Then we pop whoever we need to on the way. Easy."

"Jesus Christ, you're a bull in a china shop." And suddenly I feel like his level-headed life coach trying to turn the pieces of his insane plan into something that could work.

He slaps his hands together and rubs them greedily. "But you're still here. So I've piqued your interest."

"Which raises the question, why do you need me with this so-called army of yours?"

"Because you're Jay's pet project. Poor little grunt who lost his memory. Maybe she wants you dead, but she's got a soft spot for you. You're probably the only one who can lure her out. Plus you're smart as fuck, and I can use you. I think we'd make a good team on this."

I stare at him in disbelief. He's a maniac—more than I ever gave him credit for. Then again, what kind of idiot leaves a crime family to kill people for a living? An ambitious one, I suppose. I can't tell him this, of course. Saying no closes the door to whatever he learns about

Soloman's operation along the way. And Crow's being friendly now. All that could change in an instant. If I give him a good enough reason, he's greedy enough to try to snag me in return for whatever Jay's offering. Not that I'd ever let him.

"What do you know about Soloman?"

"I know how to find him. That's about it." He points his finger at me. "*Correction*. I know how to get a meeting with him."

"How?"

"It's a one-shot thing. We'd need someone with enough legitimate bank to be taken seriously. He doesn't mess with people who are small-time. Find that person, and I know who can set it up."

I run through scenarios, but there's not enough to work with. I know nothing about Soloman or what motivates him. Unfortunately, I don't think Jay knows much either. If she did, she would have told me more when I was ready to crush her windpipe. She knows what I'm capable of.

"I have people who could get a meeting, but it'd be a huge ask," Crow continues. "If we don't get what we want out of it, game over."

"I have someone too, but you're right. It's not worth pulling favors until we know more."

Mateus would do it in a heartbeat, and he's got enough money to fund a thousand hits. Doesn't matter. I wouldn't put him in that position unless I could put a definitive end to Soloman and Company Eleven and give Isabel the freedom she deserves.

"I'll think about it," I finally say.

Crow's distracted when the music changes. A new girl takes the platform. She's got raven hair down to her waist. Her face is heavily made up, but her patented seductive pout relaxes into something more genuine when she sees Crow.

He looks to me, suddenly serious. "You know where to find me."

I take the hint and get up just as the girl begins her dance.

2

ISABEL

I jolt awake at the sound of the door shutting. Then Tristan's footsteps drawing closer. I blink and glance around quickly. The tableside lamp illuminates the contents of Tristan's bag scattered across the bedroom floor. The clock reads three a.m.

Tristan halts when he sees me. Looks around at the evidence.

The silence between us is heavy. My heart speeds up, and I brace myself. His belongings are few, but going through them is an invasion of privacy he doesn't seem to be taking lightly.

His jaw tightens. "Did you find what you were looking for?"

I cycle through any excuse that would justify my behavior. Then I see the letter that I'd read at least a dozen times before dozing off. Tristan follows my gaze. He picks up the piece of paper and lets it float back to the bed a moment later.

"Why didn't you tell me about it?"

"Because it doesn't matter," he says, his tone clipped.

"It matters. You wouldn't be this way if it weren't for what he did.

I'll never forgive him."

The letter was penned so professionally, so convincingly, like my father was trying to get Tristan into his top choice of colleges. No. My father was nominating Tristan for the front lines, where he could have died and likely should have.

Tristan doesn't seem to be dwelling on it. He shoves the paper back into its folder, tucks it into the bottom of the bag, and starts packing the rest of his belongings on top of it. He grabs the notebook last.

"Wait," I say.

"What?" He looks down at it, then back up to me. "Were you looking for this?"

I nod.

"Why?"

I don't answer, because he already seems to be in a mood. Perhaps not the best time for me to start pitching new ideas on how to get him out of the assassin business. That and he's historically not a huge fan of my plans.

He tosses the notebook into the bag without another word, zips it up securely, and disappears around the corner into the kitchen. I follow and find him bent toward the refrigerator, pulling out day-old pizza.

"Where were you?"

"At a strip club," he mutters.

My jaw falls. "Seriously?"

He slams the refrigerator door shut and takes a bite of the slice that probably tasted a lot better when we bought it off the street vendor yesterday. "Does that piss you off?"

I grind my teeth at his challenge, instantly plagued with visions of beautiful, busty women crawling all over him. "What do you think?"

"You going through my stuff pisses me off. Don't do it again."

I take a deep breath and attempt to calm my nerves. "Did you at least get a lap dance?"

"No." He chews in silence a second. "Just a half-cocked plan to take down Company Eleven."

I still. "What's the plan?"

"There is no plan."

I roll my eyes. "Okay, what did you talk about?"

"Supposedly Jay made him an offer to bring me in if he got to me before she did."

"He told you that?"

"Yeah, but Crow's got his eyes on a bigger prize. He wants to track down more people who hired the Company. Blackmail them like we did Boswell. I don't know. His logic is if they can afford to knock someone off, they can afford to protect their reputation. Or their lives."

I bite my lip.

He stares at me. "What?"

"I think that's a good plan."

"You're kidding."

"I mean, I'm sure it's a lot more complicated, but the idea has legs, right? If Jay wants you out of the picture, it's probably because the things you know are a liability."

"And if I go unraveling every job, we'll all be dead long before we can collect and disappear. Not that we could ever run far or fast enough from the people we piss off."

I exhale a sigh and pace to the wall of windows. I can see the faintest reflection of myself. I'm not the person I was a month ago. So much has changed.

"Now that you've met with Crow, there's no reason we can't go back to New Orleans, right?"

"It's easier to hide here."

I turn. "I want to go back."

He works his jaw. "Like you wanted to go to Brienne's?"

A cold stillness comes over me. I walk past him toward the bedroom, but he's on my heels.

"I'm sorry," he says. "Isabel."

He catches my arm, halting my retreat. I let him because I have nowhere to go anyway. Not at this hour. Not in this little sliver of living space. I wrestle free from his embrace though.

"I was hiding at Brienne's. I was alone, and I was scared. You sent me off on my own at a time when I couldn't have been more vulnerable." My voice cracks as the last words spill free. Words I repeat in my head every time I battle with my guilt over my friend's gruesome death. If I'd never come back into her life, she'd be alive. If I'd chosen to stay somewhere else, maybe someone else would have died. Or maybe the Company would have hit their mark and I'd be gone.

I close my eyes and try to ignore the same thoughts running the same track. Around and around they go. Never giving me any solace. Never granting me the forgiveness I probably don't deserve anyway.

"I know," Tristan says quietly, coaxing me into his arms. "I don't know why I said that. I'm sorry."

I lean against him, fighting the relief that inevitably comes when I'm this close to him. I inhale, expecting to smell perfume or the scent of another woman. But it's just Tristan. I soften into his soothing caresses down my back, realizing he's barely touched me since we got here. We've been close. Sharing the same bed and the same space but emotionally adrift.

"Why haven't you touched me?"

I look up and search his eyes, noticing the flecks of gray among the pale blue. His unshaven jaw. The tired lines.

"Because it makes me want you, and wanting you is torture."

Something sparks in me when I remember how I affect him. I slide my hands under his shirt and graze the warm, muscled flesh beneath.

"Then why don't you just take what you want?"

His eyes darken before they close. I glide one palm higher so it rests over his heart. Its silent beats thrum under my fingertips, steady at first, then faster. My own heart races as energy hums between us. Belonging… Me, to this one man and all his broken pieces. Him, to all of mine.

He opens his eyes, his features a mix of fight and surrender. "It's not that simple and you know it."

I shake my head because I can hear his doubts as if he's said them aloud. He's hardened against the world and still finding his heart, but we're tied together in this way whether we like it or not. Through our passion. Our past.

"We'll never be perfect, Tristan. Not even close. We can only be who we are."

If he doesn't believe me, I intend to sway him. So I lift on my toes and press my lips to his. I twine my arms around him. Melt into him until we both surrender to a moment that feels like forgiveness...acceptance. Soft and slow like we're holding each other's hurt and imperfections too. The whole ugly, beautiful life that's ours to chart.

I swallow over the knot in my throat, overwhelmed by how much space Tristan's always held in my heart. If only life hadn't erased the space I held in his, maybe all of this would be easier somehow.

"I wish you could remember me."

He's quiet a moment, gliding his fingers through my hair. "I do sometimes."

"You do?" I look up, hopeful.

"When I'm touching you. Or kissing you. When we're together. Sometimes it'll trigger little flashes of memory."

"Like what?"

He shrugs a little, touches my cheek. "It's mostly...intimate. It's how I know we were real though."

My cheeks heat a little. I miss his touches and kisses. I miss the way we move together when there's nothing between us.

But just as I start to follow more of those thoughts, he pulls away.

"Come on. It's late. Let's get some sleep."

TRISTAN

The French doors are slightly ajar. Through them, I can see Morgan working at his desk. The house is quiet. We're alone here. And even though everything about this house highlights the inadequacy of my own, I find myself crawling into Isabel's window as often as I can to spend more time here. In her bed, tangled up in her sweet-smelling sheets, making the most of every minute we can steal.

But when Morgan looks up, barely masking his disdain, I remember that

I'm hardly welcome here.

"Tristan. Come on in."

I enter without a greeting, closing the door behind me. I know why I'm here, and it's not to exchange pleasantries. I take the seat across from his desk, and he gives me a short nod of approval.

"How did the meeting with the recruiter go?"

"Fine," *I say in a clipped tone.*

He nods again. "Do you have any questions? Any hesitations I could help clear up for you?"

"Your intentions are very clear, Mr. Foster."

His grim stare matches mine. "I don't think it serves anyone for me to be vague. We all want what's best for Isabel, right?"

If only I were stupid enough to be able to convince myself that I am what's best for her. I'm clearly not. I know I can make her happy, but I also know she's giving up dreams for me. That, and I'm not who I was when I met her. Something broke when my mother died, and I don't know how to fix it. Even the girl I'm desperately in love with can't seem to make me whole again.

"When will you tell Isabel, then?"

I clench my jaw hard at the veiled hopefulness in his voice. "I guess I'll tell her when I make a decision."

"When will that be?"

"I don't know. I'm not sure I want to spend the next four years being a glorified grunt on the front lines. I know you think I'm worthless, but I actually value my life."

"I don't think you're worthless. I know you're highly intelligent, and you would bring valuable skills to the program I've nominated you for." *He pauses, softening his tone slightly.* "I just want Isabel to have a chance to follow through on the dreams she had before she met you. In four years, you can both reevaluate where you want to be, and whatever you choose at that point, you'll have my blessing."

I don't buy any of it. He's never supported our relationship. Four years won't change that. Doesn't matter what degree she's holding in her hand.

"The signing bonus was significant, wasn't it?"

I hold back a glare. The five-digit financial incentive the army recruiter offered isn't a deciding factor, but the money won't hurt. My mother's funeral expenses wiped out what little savings we had. I have no idea how I'll manage a move to California with Isabel when I barely have enough to make rent on the shitty house I can't seem to give up because it's the last link I have to my dead mother.

Morgan's quiet offer to get me onto an elite Special Forces team if I agree to enlist is something I should shove back in his face with a resounding "fuck you" before I drive off into the sunset with his daughter. But as much as his disapproval burns me, the enlistment opportunity is a path that makes sense. It's an occupation. Stability when I have none. Without it, I'm just a broke, emotionally wrecked orphan who's somehow managed to win an incredible woman's heart. One day she'll figure it out, and I'll have to live with the resentment that I held her back. I don't deserve Isabel, but I can try to change that. I can start by letting her have the dream her parents want for her—an Ivy League education and four years of a normal college life that I would have stolen by following through on our UCLA plan.

The truth is I'd likely end up dropping out to support myself anyway. Then she'd have a degree and a job worthy of it, and God knows what I'd be doing trying to catch up.

"What do I have to do to convince you?" Morgan presses.

"It's not up to you," I say, enjoying the anxiety my indecision is giving him.

He clears his throat, pausing a moment. "I'll match the bonus if that would help. You couldn't tell Isabel about it, of course."

I shake my head with a disgusted grimace. "I don't want your fucking money. I want her. She's the one I'm doing this for, not you."

His lips form a thin line. "So you'll do it then."

Something roils deep inside me. An agonizing sound that has no place to go, so I bury it. I shove it down with the rest of my pain. The rest of the blows I've had to take in this unfortunate life. Walking away from Isabel is just another one I'll have to learn to accept.

"I'll do it."

I jolt awake. My breaths come rapidly. I swallow hard, because I haven't had a flashback like that since we were back in Brazil. Except this one was completely new and vivid. Rich. Almost as if Isabel asked for it when I held her last night and my brain delivered.

Faintly ill, I replay the moment I'd decided to let her go, surrendering our dreams to Morgan, the overprotective father who sealed my fate with an offer I couldn't refuse. I wasn't surprised when I read the letter among the other documents in the file after I'd retrieved them from Jay's apartment. Morgan had the most incentive to get me out of Isabel's life. And why wouldn't he want to get me away from her?

My groggy thoughts drift to the dingy house in Baltimore. The dark room where we'd spent who knows how many hours hiding away from the world, planning our life together. All our planning, and I still couldn't go through with it, knowing I didn't deserve her.

Not much has changed. She's still in love with me, is too eager to run away together, and now all I have to offer her is a bank account full of blood money. I exhale a heavy sigh as my heartbeat slows to a normal rhythm. Late-morning light seeps in past the edges of the blackout shades covering the bedroom windows. It's enough to highlight the lines of Isabel's body under the sheets. The shadows of her messy hair framing her face as she sleeps. The hues of the fading bruises on her cheek and jaw.

I push up onto my elbow to see her better and feather the faintest caress over the discolored skin. She doesn't stir. Seeing the bruises eats away at me daily. Every time, I relive the moment where I was forced to watch Vince Boswell land those few vicious strikes before she decided to fight back.

I still don't deserve her or her love, but every time I think I can turn away from her, something turns me back.

My life used to follow a straight line—an arrow pointed at someone who needed to die. My interests always aligned with the job that had to be done and the people who paid me to do it. Now everything is a vicious tangle of lies and secrets and splintered memories.

I lean down, inhaling her scent. Vanilla, hints of cocoa, and something else—something so deeply familiar that it releases a shockwave of faceless memories every time I taste her. I slide my lips over her smooth skin…giving in…knowing the moments we shared once upon a time live beyond the barrier of my broken brain. If I could unleash them, would the path forward become more clear? Would it mean I could never turn away from her again?

I'm too tired to hold back. So I taste her. A flicker of tongue against her collarbone, then her neck. She moans softly against me, her hot hand dragging lazily down the front of my chest. I should stop now while I'm only a sensation in her dreams. Let her breathing take on its sleepy rhythm again. Keep her at a safe distance the way I have been.

But I can't. Not when the memory of us is still pulsing like adrenaline through my veins. So real…

Her body undulates faintly as I glide my hand up her inner thigh. All silk and warmth. Her eyelids flutter open with a sigh. I nip and roam as she slowly wakes, answering my touches with more of her own.

"I need you," I murmur against her ear.

"You're burning hot." She lifts her shadowed gaze to mine and rounds her hands over my shoulders. "Did you have a dream?"

Something knots in my stomach. Vulnerability I'm not used to. I silence her questioning with a deep kiss and more eager slides of my palms across skin I'm in a hurry to possess. I knead her through her panties until I can feel her arousal seep through.

Her needy whimpers signal my last shred of willpower disintegrating. I strip her quickly, settle between her legs, and claim her mouth again. She drags her hands down my torso, urging me tighter, closer. Then deeper as I roll my hips and join us. Her awe-filled gasp echoes between us, rushes into all the empty places inside me like a storm rolling in. When she opens her eyes, they hold that drugged kind of haziness I recognize when I'm inside her.

She brings her hands to my face, raking her blunt fingernails along my unshaven jaw. "Tristan," she whispers. "Tell me."

This isn't the time to talk about it. But I can't escape her or the feelings. I'm overwhelmed by her. By how much I need her. How much I worry I'll always need her. My lips part. I don't know what to say, though. How to explain how the dream ripped me open a little more but how lost I still feel in the fog of my memories. How she's the one clear thing. Her and this love between us that barely makes sense but can't be denied.

I hush her with a kiss. Hold her tightly. Rock into her slowly. Take. Feel. Revel in her. Mold against her as she wraps around me. Consumes me. Accepts all of me.

My heart twists as my body climbs, tight and fevered. Words clamor and lodge in my throat until she glides her fingers into my hair. Soothes my burning skin with her healing touches. And for a fleeting moment, the darkness becomes a safe shroud around the truth. The union of our bodies opens the door I keep closed, beckons for the words that finally leave my lips as I lower my forehead to hers.

"I want what they took away from us. I want it back."

Our gazes lock in the darkness. Her eyes glimmer. A mirror of hurt and loss.

"Me too." She brushes her fingertips over my lips. "We'll make it right. I promise."

I don't know how we ever can, but her words make a vow for both of us. And I believe her.

3

ISABEL

Midafternoon light floods the apartment as I get dressed. Through the sliding-glass doors, Tristan leans over the brick-lined terrace with his coffee. The wind ruffles his hair and T-shirt. The horizon is thick with buildings that pierce the hazy layer of sky between the city and the wispy spring clouds. Tristan barely moves, as if he's deep in conversation with the world beyond.

Or maybe with his demons... The ones who crept into his dreams this morning. He won't talk to me about them, but I can't fight the inexplicable desire to wrap my arms around his pain. His words earlier might haunt me forever. Recognizing all we've lost. Acknowledging that he feels that emptiness too...

I'm angry for him and everything we've endured. When he shows me his heart, something changes. I want to fight for him the way he fights for me. There's so much wrong to right, but I'm nowhere close to giving up trying.

I go to the kitchen for coffee. I hear the door slide open and closed again, and Tristan joins me a moment later. I pour myself a cup, and he comes behind me, wrapping his arm around my middle as he tops up his own.

"Hi," he says, kissing me on the cheek.

I smile, warmed by the affection he's so adept at holding back when he wants to.

When he goes to the living room, I follow. We sit across from each other on opposite couches. The apartment is silent except for the distant sounds of the street below.

"Did you have a nightmare last night?"

He purses his lips. "More like a vivid dream. A memory."

I straighten, instantly curious, but also concerned because he seemed troubled despite the way he woke me up, with his hands everywhere, his need palpable.

"Do you want to talk about it?"

"Not really."

I exhale through my nose, trying not to appear as frustrated as I am. "It might help, you know. Talking it through might trigger something new."

He looks over his shoulder through the window and then back to me. "I don't get to pick and choose what memories are going to hit me. I want to remember, but then no matter what it is, I'm never really ready for it. It's a setback. It's jarring when I have other shit I need to think about and focus on. Like us. Figuring out our next move."

My frustration fades, replaced with empathy. I can't imagine how uncomfortable it must be for Tristan to process everything he does. To parse true memory from whatever his imagination serves up beside it. To not completely lose his shit every time he gets a particularly troubling dose of truth about his old life and everything we lost.

I'm ready to go to him when he leans forward, dropping his notebook onto the center of the coffee table between us. I glance between it and him, because the ledger's mere presence is a taunt. Bait that ultimately I can't resist.

"What are you going to do with that?" I finally ask.

"You mean, what are *we* going to do with it?"

I don't answer, but he has to know my silence is agreement. We're in this together, and if his little red notebook is the key, I'm all in.

"You've gone through it," he continues.

I nod. "A little."

"Crow's plan won't work. He's in it for the money, and it's going to get us killed. I don't care about money. I just want to get us out of this mess."

"So how do we do that?"

He drums his fingertips on his knee, looking pensive. "We do it carefully. Strategically. Like a good hit, it should be well planned, quick, and fatal."

I swallow, because this is definitely his area of expertise, not mine. "What's your plan?"

"We reverse engineer a hit. Once we figure out who did the hiring, we target them. Blackmail if necessary. But whatever we do, however uncomfortable we make them, the intent will be to make Company Eleven the culpable party. Then we hope it's enough of a blow to either take them out of the game or—at the very least—send a clear message that if they don't leave us alone, I'll keep going down the list, making their operation a living hell one name at a time."

I set down my coffee and consider Tristan's plan. I pick up the notebook. Its contents will probably haunt me the rest of my life, but if one of these names could free Tristan from this life…then the red ledger could mean something more. Give us a path to follow.

"Where do we start? Who do we pick?"

"We could look at the high-profile hits. Those would have the highest risk of scandal if exposed. Or someone rich. All the Company's clients are flush, but more money means more power, and that power could be a valuable weapon to punish the Company's fuck up. Or we pick someone dangerous. Someone who played without rules and whose friends won't hesitate to mete out their own kind of justice."

My thoughts jump around the possibilities—all of them thrilling but scary at once.

"That's a lot to consider. You know these people better than I do."

I go to open the book.

"Don't."

I lift my gaze.

"I've got them all memorized, Isabel. Every name. Every detail. It's all in my head. I don't want you going through the list and researching every one on your own."

I frown. "Why?"

He pins me with a pained look. "A lot of these people weren't good. I know that. But some were like you. Innocent." He hesitates. A hint of remorse shadows his eyes. "I can't undo what I've done."

I set the book down and slide it to the center of the table once more. His words settle between us, taking up space I wish didn't exist. The reality of what he's done and the life he lived before won't ever be something that doesn't cause me pain. It's like grief. Heavy and relentless. An invisible but ever-present burden. Maybe with time it won't hurt quite as much.

Either way, I know I have to find it in my heart to forgive him no matter what I discover along the way. There's no undoing the past, and neither of us can waste more time wishing for the impossible. We can only do our best with the time we have. Be better and do better.

I shake my head because what I'm thinking now seems foolish to say out loud. Quixotic even.

"What?" he presses.

"There's no erasing these names…but what if we tried to make it right somehow?"

His brows knit. "How? Take out the Company and then put a bullet in my head?"

I flinch. "No. Don't say that."

"Well, that would look a lot like justice. I don't know what else you have in mind."

"Forget it. I don't know what I'm trying to say."

I rest back on the couch and release a frustrated sigh. I roll the conversation around in my head, trying to find the path we were on before we derailed. High profile, rich, or dangerous. Every possibility is a Pandora's box and scary as hell when I really start to think about it.

"What about a live target?"

He lifts an eyebrow and takes a sip of his coffee. "Explain."

"Ask Jay for a job. If she gives you one, it'd be easier to trace something back with a live subject."

"That's not a bad idea."

I can't mask my smile. "That's possibly the only time you've ever said that to me."

He grins. "Well, the catch of course is that I don't know her end game. I can't trust any information she gives me."

"Never hurts to ask."

He shrugs. "Suppose not."

He reaches for his laptop and opens it. I get up and take the seat beside him, leaning in so close our sides touch.

He types in the password to the computer faster than I can guess the keys he's hitting. It's a long one.

"What's your password?"

He shakes his head slightly. "No way."

"What if it's an emergency and I need to get into it?"

"Like you got into my bag yesterday? Was that an emergency too?"

"No, I was curious. If we're in this together, we shouldn't really be keeping secrets, should we?"

He pulls up a simple chat terminal with an unfamiliar gray and black screen that looks like something a hacker or programmer might use.

I tuck the password argument away for later. "What's this?"

"An SSH chat. It's a command-line utility that works well when you have a small group you talk to. Basic, untraceable. It's how Jay and I communicate."

"You don't have her cell? You can't just text her?"

He chuckles. "No. You know how easy those are to trace?"

Our eyes lock, and I can read his thoughts in an instant. "You track me through my phone."

He only hesitates a second. "I need to know where you are."

I think about arguing, but I get it. This is about life and death, not personal space and privacy etiquette.

"Don't you think it should go both ways? What if we get separated and I need to find you?"

Ignoring me, he looks back to the screen and types Jay's name into the chat terminal. "Then what? You're going to swoop in and rescue me? Trust me, if you're trying to find me, you're probably headed for trouble and better off not knowing."

I frown, offended at the insinuation. "You don't know that."

He hovers his fingertips over the keys, blows out a breath, and begins to type.

> **RED: Ready when you are.**

The cursor blinks for several seconds before a new message appears with a ding.

> **JAY: You have a debt.**

I look up at him. "A debt?"

"For the intel on Boswell. For fucking up and getting away with my life. It's all bullshit anyway. Test of commitment. Or pretending like I can be a good little soldier again."

He taps out a response.

> **RED: I'm aware. How much?**

> **JAY: Three jobs. Soloman's price.**

> **RED: Fine. Where to?**

> **JAY: I'll prepare the details.**
> **You'll have the dossier tonight.**

JAY: Welcome back.

"I hate her," I mutter, suddenly furious that she can speak to him with such ease, such rapport, when all she's doing is arranging for him to take more lives.

Tristan closes the laptop with a click and sets it aside. "She's not worth your hate."

I rear back a little. "After everything she's done to you? She's the murderer here. For years she's taken advantage of your vulnerabilities to use you as a weapon in this sick game of theirs."

"And there's a murderer above her and probably another above her. Who knows how high it goes? That's what we need to be focused on. Hate is distracting. It's basic, and you're better than that."

I pause, trying to talk myself out of the emotion that feels too overwhelming to rise above at the moment. I can't manage it, at least not right now.

"I'm allowed to hate her for what she's done to you."

He falls quiet and reaches for my hand. Our fingers glide and hook. The simple connection offers more relief than he probably realizes.

"Just don't dwell on it too much," he says. "We've got bigger fish to fry."

I huff out a sigh, very much dwelling on the woman I despise, realizing too that jealousy lives somewhere inside my hatred for her. I resent that she's known him and been in his life, even in this limited and strange capacity, when I've been shut out this whole time. If I had a list of people who'd wronged me in the worst possible way, Jude McKenna's name would be at the top of it.

"Flanders Fields."

I blink a few times. "Huh?"

"It's my password."

"Oh." I pause. "What's the significance?"

"Look it up sometime. And if it makes you feel better, I'll let you track my phone. Just in case you need to rescue me sometime."

I lean in. "Maybe I already have."

He begins to smile, but it fades as he brings his hand to my face, tracing over the tender skin along my jaw. "You're probably right."

TRISTAN

We spend the afternoon milling around Midtown. It's busy and hectic the same way it always is, which drives me crazy and gives me solace at the same time. I don't know how to absorb less of what I see. The details come in a deluge, but over time, I've come to terms with this being normal. Because crowds are camouflage, and even though I don't think anyone's looking for us here, I rule nothing out.

The stores get pricier the farther up Fifth Avenue we go, which doesn't matter much because we've been window shopping most of the time. Neither of us has room for superfluous things.

"Do you want to go back? Maybe we can catch lunch somewhere on the way," she says.

I nod toward the hotel tucked into the next block just before Central Park.

"Let's grab a drink in the Plaza."

She looks me over and then down at her simple clothes. Tight jeans and a dark sweater that hangs off her shoulder a little. "We're not dressed for that."

"Nonsense." I take her hand, and we start walking that way. "The trick is to walk in like you belong there. Don't make eye contact with the bellmen. Just walk straight up to the bar like you've got a suite reserved for the week."

"That simple, huh?"

"Bet on it."

We stroll in that way, swiftly bypassing the man in the hotel uniform. Isabel lifts her chin confidently. Her pretty lips are pursed proudly as we walk hand in hand up the marble staircase to the Rose Bar. We take two stools, and the bartender with the Irish lilt is none the wiser.

As I watch her peruse the menu, I'm hit with something so much more powerful than desire or affection or this unending urge to keep her safe. It's…*gratitude?*

She was joking about rescuing me a few hours ago, even though I could tell it burned her to think that she never could. The truth is she already has. If it weren't for her blind faith in us, I'd never know what it's like to love a woman. To know that, against the odds and everything that should have kept us apart, we're heading down this uncertain path…together.

The *together* part has my chest struggling to expand. Because someone could rip her away from me in an instant. If I fuck up. If I lose her… It'll be like losing my memory and my past and my freedom and everything that's ever mattered. Except it'll be so much worse because I won't have the benefit of amnesia to mask the pain.

We order drinks and a few small bites for lunch. When my phone vibrates—the burner one I told Crow to contact me through on short notice—I pull it out of my pocket and answer.

"Hello?"

"Hey. It's Crow."

"What do you want?"

Is everything okay? Isabel mouths the words silently.

I nod, get up, and pace a few steps from the bar.

"Wanted to know if you gave my proposal any more thought," he says.

"That was twelve hours ago. I told you I'd let you know."

"So let me know now. I'm anxious. I need something to do, and I'm ready to put this into action. I've got a hit list mapped out. Recent jobs from the last few months that should be fresh in Jay's mind. No excuses for being forgetful."

I look back to Isabel, who's sipping her drink and shooting nervous looks my way.

"Listen, Crow, we've both got issues with the Company, but we're in this for different reasons. I can be a resource. I can't be your partner."

He sighs loudly. "All right. I figured you'd say something like that. I'm not sure I can work that closely with you and not fucking shoot you anyway."

"Great, so we're in agreement."

"If you want to be a resource, I need a favor before you ride off into the sunset with the girl."

I halt my pacing. "What do you want? And what are you offering?"

"We working together or we negotiating, Red? You do me a favor, and when you need one, I'll do you one." His voice is unnecessarily loud and tinged with his Italian roots, more than usual.

He may be delusional and inept, but I'd rather he focus his anger on Jay. Unfortunately he's not likely to live long enough to repay any favors, but I figure I'll hear him out. "What do you need?"

"I need you to get me Jay."

I haven't forgotten the details of my last encounter with her—one I'm not thrilled to repeat. "I'm playing nice with her right now. It's not good timing."

"Listen, just set up the meeting, and I'll take care of it. You don't even need to show up."

Unwelcome concern for Jay needles me. "I don't think she knows as much as you think she does."

He laughs loudly. I yank the phone away from my ear until it fades out.

"Red, she's been the manager for years. Trust me, she knows plenty. Anyway, I just want to pump her for some info, and then I'll throw her back when I don't need her anymore. Or not. I'll have to see how it goes."

I think how my strategy changes without Jay in the picture. She's my line into the Company. She's as deceitful as they come, though, so it doesn't really matter. My history with her is an impediment to getting to Soloman and shutting the rest of this shit down anyway.

"Fine," I say. "I'm expecting to hear from her with some information tonight. I'll send you the details when I set something up."

"Perfect."

"Listen, Crow. I showed her mercy last time. Barely. She'll be expecting trouble. She had someone else from the Company with her and half a dozen others on her heels ready to act."

"Sweet-talk her into traveling light, Red. I'll do the rest. Don't worry. I won't fuck it up."

"Don't," I say with force before hanging up.

I return to the bar, slide onto the stool, and down a few gulps of my beer. Fucking Crow. He'd better be more help than hindrance or I'll kill him myself.

"Who was it?" Isabel's voice pulls me out of my aggravation a little.

"Crow."

"What did he want?"

"He's pressing me to make a decision on the 'plan.'"

"And what did you tell him?"

I take another swallow of my pint to avoid answering her right away. A few hours ago, I all but promised transparency with Isabel. I'm not sure she's ready for the cold, hard truths of how I work, though. I can't tell her I'm about to set up a kidnapping of a not-so-innocent woman that could very likely end in her death.

I can't say that, because it'll show her the monster she's trying to save.

"I told him I'm still thinking about it. Just stalling him until we get a name from Jay. He'll wait," I lie.

I offer her an easy smile and hope to hell she buys it.

4

ISABEL

Something's changed since Crow called. Tristan has an edge about him that didn't exist this morning. He was softer before. When he looked into my eyes, I felt like he was really seeing me and I was seeing him.

Now, after one conversation with someone from his old life, he seems hurtled back into it. He tries to play at being normal with me, but I'm beginning to know him better. I can decode the absent touches. The distracted way he engages when we talk, like he's somewhere else.

"Any word yet?"

It's almost midnight. He's lying on the couch with his computer on his lap. He clicks around the track pad a few times. "Not yet."

I can't see his screen but trust that Jay still hasn't reached out.

I'm curled up on the opposite couch, scrolling through my phone. The waiting game is killing me. So I decide to search for the password he told me earlier. The results return a nineteenth-century poem written by John McCrae.

Breaking the silence, I read it aloud, drawing Tristan's attention to me once more.

In Flanders fields the poppies blow
Between the crosses, row on row,
That mark our place, and in the sky,
The larks, still bravely singing, fly,
Scarce heard amid the guns below.

We are the dead; short days ago
We lived, felt dawn, saw sunset glow,
Loved and were loved, and now we lie
In Flanders fields.

I stop before the next stanza because what I'm reading is gradually tearing me apart. Haunted visions of the fallen take up space in my thoughts. Soldiers brought to battlegrounds to fight wars they didn't ask for. Tristan was one of those soldiers once.

"Keep reading," he says quietly.

So I do.

Take up our quarrel with the foe!
To you from failing hands we throw
The torch; be yours to hold it high!
If ye break faith with us who die
We shall not sleep, though poppies grow
In Flanders fields.

A long silence stretches between us. I reread the words, new meaning resonating each time I do.

"A field of red poppies is one of the things I remembered from my old life," he finally says. "Blood red, as far as the eye could see. In the nightmares—dreams, whatever—it's the last thing I see before I die."

"But you didn't die."

"I should have." He breaks eye contact and stares up at the ceiling. "Anyway, I used to read a lot right before Jay started keeping me busy. Stumbled across that poem and it stuck with me, I guess."

"I can see why."

He refocuses on his computer, and I stare out the window at the city lights twinkling. Several minutes pass before his voice cuts through the silence.

"It's done."

Tristan closes his laptop and sets it aside, straightening as he does.

I blink a few times until I catch his meaning.

"She gave you a name? Who is it?"

"Devon Aguilera."

It's late afternoon before I step out of the nearest Krav Maga center and onto the busy sidewalk. I head toward the apartment several blocks away, thoroughly wiped out but driven by purpose I didn't have before. Because now we have a name.

Going up against the Company this way is intimidating but undeniably thrilling. My adrenaline hasn't stopped pumping since Tristan got the message last night.

Devon Aguilera is an associate professor at Florida State University who's been causing enough trouble for someone to want her dead. Jay made a specific request when she sent the file on Aguilera. Her death is to be made to seem accidental, which means a homicide will have too many people finger pointing, likely in the right direction. For this reason, I'm confident Jay's supplied us with a prime lead. Someone who likely already knows her enemies and can lead us right to them.

Tristan has one week to show results before she'll give him his next job. Little does she know, he'll never get that far.

I'm near the apartment, ready to pack up and hit the road with Tristan as soon as we can, when I stop in my tracks.

An old man is leaning against the building. He's short in stature, slender and unassuming except for the dark suit he's dressed in. When he glances up, his dark eyes brighten. "Isabel."

I'm momentarily speechless as my mouth falls open. "Papa!"

My grandfather comes to me and pulls me into a tight embrace, sighing as he does. He whispers my name once more and cups his hand at the back of my head like he did when I was a little girl.

"What are you doing here?"

He finally releases me, his eyes shining with emotion. "I came back for your funeral, Isabel. And to speak with your mother. She's worried for you." His silver brows furrow.

"There's nothing to worry about," I say, not really believing my own words. "I told her I was fine."

I curse myself for not calling her sooner. Unsure how to explain the shift in plans that brought us to New York, I only sent her a brief message that I was in the city and would call soon.

"She was trying to give you space to start fresh. But she's worried about this man you're with."

I glance across the street to a café. Taking him up to the apartment to meet Tristan may not be the best choice right now. "Do you want to get some coffee?"

"All right," he says and then follows me across.

There we snag a little table that's set uncomfortably close to others but will have to do. Everyone seems too absorbed in their own conversations or devices to bother with us.

"I'm safe with Tristan, Papa. You don't need to worry about that," I finally say.

"I tried to reassure Lucia. Perhaps it takes a dangerous man to protect you from dangerous people."

"He is, and he does."

He nods, but his expression is tight with concern. "I think she's also worried about driving you closer to him when it's not meant to be."

As I consider his words, an unwelcome thought presents itself— the possibility that my mother too had encouraged Tristan's enlistment plans without my knowing. I sigh and rub my temples. It's too much of a betrayal to wrap my head around right now when nothing can take me off my current course—one that involves Tristan and ends with him being in my life indefinitely.

"So she tracked my phone and sent you here instead, hoping to reason with me?"

His eyes soften. "You've been given a new life. A chance to start over. The path is yours, Isabel. I came because I haven't seen you."

My shoulders relax. "I'm glad you did. I'm sorry."

The barista calls out an order loudly, and the door to the street opens with a jingling sound. No one here has any idea what I've been through. That on paper, I'm a dead woman.

"How did you do it, Papa? How did you fake my death?"

He takes my hands, holds them between his, smooth and wrinkled with age. "I will do anything for my family. I would give my life for yours. I would have given it for Mariana's in a heartbeat if I'd been given the chance."

Sadness sweeps between us. The faintest memories of Mariana are tainted with what I know about her death now. Without a doubt, I've inherited the grudge he and my mother have been holding on to for years.

"You heard about Vince Boswell?"

"Martine told us what happened. Sadly, he's not the worst of them."

I flinch involuntarily, haunted by visions of what went down in the hotel room in New Orleans only days ago. "That's hard to imagine."

"It takes a diabolical man to raise his children to act as they have."

"Vince's father?"

"Kristopher. I worked closely with him. He was the one who insisted I skew my research so it would pass the regulatory tests. Once I saw the depth of his greed—really understood how little concern he had for the welfare of others—I knew I had to come out against him publicly. I couldn't stomach that the work I'd done to help people could be used to hurt them. He cared only about the momentum he could gain and stopping any impediments to growing the company as large as he possibly could." He's quiet a moment. "He's won. Their wealth, their reach… It's everything he wanted. We've done so little to slow their progress. The inevitable, it would seem."

I squeeze his hand in mine. "Papa, no." But I fear he's right. Whatever my mother and Martine have done to handicap their growth hasn't been enough.

"It's all right. The way I grew up, and your mother too, we understood fear and also the power of resistance and fighting back. But this war with their family…" He shoots me a hollow stare, his voice broken with defeat as he speaks again. "I'm so sorry, Isabel. For everything this has brought upon you. Of all people, you're the least deserving of their malice. And yet, that's how they strike. They knew exactly where to hurt us, and over the years, we've become complacent."

So complacent that Tristan was sent to kill me.

"You're certain about Mariana? They definitely knew what they were doing?"

Papa's lips thin. "We haven't been on this journey without certain cause, I promise you. We've fought long and hard for justice for Mariana, but the time's come to admit defeat. Protecting what we have left is more important than anything else right now."

I don't know what to say. Because I still have fight in me. In fact, nothing but blind determination to take down the Company and people behind it have fueled my thoughts for days. This same fire has been burning in my mother and grandfather for years, yet I'm not sure I'm as capable of giving up as they seem to be.

"Tristan… What kind of man is he?"

I'm not sure how to describe Tristan, especially if my parents have already poisoned Papa with their own opinions.

"He's…"

Broken. Scarred. Dangerous.

Mine.

I manage a small smile and meet Papa's eyes. "He's the only reason I'm alive right now."

"I'd welcome the chance to thank him one day."

I nod but don't reply. The prospect of introducing him to Tristan feels oddly like worlds colliding, especially if my parents are still eager to drive us apart. That realization triggers my need to protect what Tristan and I have at any cost. For now, my grandfather's world is theirs. He belongs to a life I had to leave behind. Ironically he's had a big hand in that coming to pass.

"Don't worry," he says. "Today doesn't have to be that day. I plan to stay in the States for a little while. I have business with Martine that needs attention."

"If you're ready to let things go with the Boswells, what's left to work out with Martine?"

"Mariana's been gone for over twenty years. We've been helping each other ever since. Halo's mission has been far-reaching, well beyond the misdeeds of Kristopher and his heirs."

I think back to the day Martine welcomed me into Halo and her speech about illuminating the truth and shining light on those who would do us harm. I remember how her words comforted me then, even as I questioned how she carried out her mission.

"She told me as much. But she's been vague. I guess I didn't stay long enough to truly understand what it is that Halo does."

Papa hesitates, as if he's contemplating whether to tell me more. He frowns a little. "Will you go back?"

I shrug. "I've thought of it. We have to take care of some other things first."

"What kinds of things?"

I chew the inside of my lip. The new plan is exciting but dangerous enough that anyone who truly cares for me would worry for my well-being. Still, Papa has come all this way, and he doesn't seem to be a stranger to risk.

"We're trying to get more information on the people Tristan used to work for. It hasn't exactly been a clean break."

"Information is something we could help with."

I consider his offer. The web of information Skye claims Halo is banking is something I've thought of since Aguilera's name came up. But Martine's the last person Tristan would go to for help after what I went through with Vince. He doesn't need to say it. I can see the rage burning in his eyes every time he lingers on the bruises that I can finally hide with a little makeup. He'd never tolerate something like that again.

"I'll keep that in mind, Papa. Thank you."

"You don't trust me?"

"It's not that. I'm not opposed to help, but I think Tristan wants to fight this battle on his own. The things that happened with Vince broke his faith with Halo, I'm afraid."

"You were hurt." Pain flashes behind his eyes like a parent who feels every pang of a child's suffering.

"I'm fine now. But he saw everything. He doesn't forgive easily."

He exhales a sigh. "Martine shouldn't have used you as a pawn. She takes risks…" He shakes his head, glancing away for a moment. "If I'm telling the truth, sometimes I don't entirely trust her. Tristan might be wise not to either."

TRISTAN

Isabel wants to leave as soon as possible, but something has me tethered here. Uncertainty about Crow's plan. Uncertainty about Jay and the job. I've been watching the scales tip back and forth in my head, trying to figure out what and whose interests have the most weight.

Is the job a ploy to take another shot at me? Devon Aguilera could be a decoy for all I know. Who knows how badly Jay wants to reel me in—to kill me or teach me a memorable lesson so I never stray from the Company again. I have no idea. The job could be perfectly legitimate too. My gut tells me it is. The only way I can game-plan is to know more, and it's up to Crow to set it all in motion.

Until he does, Isabel and I can't take off in any direction.

I look at the time on my phone. I was supposed to meet Jay outside Philadelphia at an inconspicuous but well-frequented diner hours ago. Unbeknownst to Isabel, when I accepted the Aguilera job, I did it on the condition that I get a meeting first. To clear the air and reestablish trust that had been broken—as if trust could ever exist between us. Regardless of whether she bought it or not, if Jay wanted to snag me, now would have been her chance, except I'll never show. How Crow planned to intercept her, I'm not sure. I just hope he did it right.

I should wait for an update, but I'm sick of the waiting game. Plus, Isabel will be back soon, and I have no idea how I'm going to explain all this to her, if I do at all. So I call him. He picks up on the second ring.

"Hey," he answers brusquely.

"How's it going?"

"I have her."

I enjoy the briefest hit of relief. It's quickly diminished because Crow doesn't sound like his usual jovial self.

"And?"

"She's not talking. And trust me, I know how to get people to talk."

I curl my hand over the edge of the counter. "Are you sure she knows—"

"She fucking knows! Don't you, sweetheart?"

The rough sounds of footsteps. A woman's anguished cry.

Fuck. Fuck. Fuck.

I don't know why I care. I *don't* care. Crow should kill her and be done with it. Do what I couldn't do. Cut the most critical tie that's bound me to this sick life for too long.

"Why don't you tell Red what you told me? You want to tell him how you don't know anything? You think he'll buy it?"

"Tristan." Her voice is garbled and distant.

The voice in my head is screaming at me not to feel the things I do. Everything inside me wants to hang up and forget this happened. But he has her now. He's set things in motion.

There's commotion on the other end of the phone. Crow's voice, low and angry but indistinguishable. A punctuated shriek. Then a moment later, a slammed door and Crow's labored breathing.

"Crow. What the hell is going on? Where are you?"

He cusses under his breath. I can hear other voices in the background. Laughing and hollering. No doubt others in his crew who don't understand the danger everyone's in.

"Crow," I press.

"You fuck her or something?"

"Excuse me?"

"You know what she just said to me? Said she'll talk to *you*. No one else." He lets out a caustic laugh. "I'm just surprised because I'm not exactly making her comfortable right now. You must have really made an impression on her."

I should leave this on his lap. Let him test Jay's resolve until she gives in. But this is my mess as much as it's his now. I gave him the go-ahead, and his best efforts aren't getting the job done. He can't see it through. Deep down, I know he can't. Not without my help.

"Fine. Send me the location."

"Come alone," he says.

"Obviously." I hang up and wait a few seconds for the next text to come through. A pin about thirty miles southeast of Philadelphia city limits. I zoom in and see nothing but empty fields around the pin.

The door squeaks open and Isabel comes in, interrupting my cycling thoughts. She's dressed in her workout clothes, but something about her countenance seems off. Serious, even.

"Everything okay? You were gone a while."

She drops her wallet onto the counter. "I ran into someone."

My heart stops. "Who?"

"My grandfather, Gabriel. He came to DC for the funeral and decided to come up to see me."

I pause. "How did he find you?"

"My mom gave me a phone before I left DC. I guess you're both on the same plan with keeping tabs on me."

"Fuck," I mutter.

Wasting no time, I move to the bedroom and riffle through her things until I find the device. I rip the battery out and smash it on the bureau.

When I turn, she's there.

She crosses her arms. "Was that really necessary?"

"Anyone knowing exactly where we are is a potential problem. You could have told me about that, you know."

"Sorry. It wasn't top of mind with everything we've been dealing with. It's not like my mother's trying to kill me."

I ignore her comment and grab my bag. I put it on the bed and toss out the Glock and a couple of magazines for Isabel to keep. The rest will come with me.

"What's that for?"

Her earlier sarcasm has melted away, replaced by fear I wish I never had to witness in her again.

"I have to run an errand," I say, knowing it won't satisfy her.

"An errand? What kind of errand?"

I shake my head. "Don't ask me questions."

Her fear morphs into indignation, her eyes wide with it. "Don't ask you questions? What about being honest with each other? Being on the same team?"

She'll never accept evasion, so I come out with it. I straighten and level my gaze to hers.

"Crow kidnapped Jay. He's holding her at some remote hideout outside Philadelphia. She won't talk to him, and he's not exactly going easy on her. It's time for me to step in."

Her jaw falls. "Oh."

"I can be there in a couple hours. Maybe I'll get lucky and get information on Aguilera while I'm there."

"No. You're taking me with you."

I pinch the bridge of my nose. "Isabel. Please. Let's not do this."

She doesn't answer. Only starts moving around the room and packing her things.

"I'm not bringing you into this," I say firmly.

She doesn't slow down. "You already have."

"Not like this. Crow is…" Dangerous. Ruthless. Not that different from me. "I'm not introducing you to him and his goons, okay? I know you think you're tough now, but—"

"Go to hell, Tristan." She shoots me a narrow-eyed look.

"I'm confident that's where I'm headed if it makes you feel any better."

She flies around the apartment like a woman on a mission, my panic at her determination climbing with every passing second. I catch her coming back from the living room with some clothes and haul her against me. Her breath rushes out, and I don't give her any room to budge.

"You're not listening to me."

She sets her jaw, determination gleaming in her eyes. "Maybe you're the one who's not listening."

"I'm not going to bring you into a dangerous situation for no other reason than to keep us together. I'll be back—"

"I'm not letting you leave me behind. You don't want to take me right into the thick of it, okay. I get it. I'm scared too. But I can be close. Maybe you can drop me at a hotel nearby or something. Talk to Jay, and when you're done, we'll be that much closer to our next stop."

Some of the demand has slipped from her tone. She's trying to be reasonable, and I'm having a hard time holding my ground. Especially when she's this close. Because like every other time we've had to go our separate ways, by circumstance or one of us deciding to go it alone, I've hated every minute of it. Deep down I knew it was wrong even if my sense of logic argued it was right.

I consider her proposal and decide it's reasonable enough. Even if it weren't, we don't have time to argue. The clock is ticking. If Crow can't get what he wants, all we've done is make targets of both of us. The whole Company will be looking for us. And Isabel.

5

ISABEL

The Mullica Hill Inn just over the New Jersey border is a sobering reminder that this new life—on the run and on the road—is not always destined to be comfortable. I insisted we stay here since the next closest hotel to the pin Crow sent Tristan was another twenty miles down the highway, and I'm in a panic about any unnecessary distance between us right now.

The parking lot is largely empty. The staff are wholly uninterested in who we are past the sixty-one dollars plus tax we owe them for the room. Once inside, the salmon walls and garish magenta and navy-blue comforters on the two double beds welcome us. A thick red drape hangs over the window, giving the room privacy. Tristan hasn't followed me in, though. He hesitates in the doorway, his lips thin. His posture is stiff, as if he's coiled tight and ready to strike at whatever dangers are ahead.

"Is there anything I can do? I feel useless here," I say.

"Why don't you map the rest of the trip? Figure out some good places to stop."

"Really?" I slant my head because I know he's placating me. The trip from New Orleans was anything but leisurely, and I'm certain getting to his next assignment will be no less urgent.

He smirks a little. "I'll be back as soon as I can. Watch a movie or something. For what we paid for the room, I think we can afford it."

As if a movie could take my mind off whatever is going to go down tonight. I step toward him and curl my fingers into his shirt, my anxiety ratcheting up as the seconds slip by. I think back to Mateus's house in Petrópolis and how Tristan insisted on staying back to face off with a Hummer full of mercenaries. He was up against Crow then too. Tristan found his way back to me all the same. I lean my forehead against his chest. Focus on his even breath. The strength of his arms folding around me. Faith that feels easier to reach for when life gets this desperate.

"Every minute you're gone, I'll think the worst," I whisper. "I'm going to be a mess. I can't help it."

"You don't ever need to worry about me. This is what I do, remember?"

I look up at him, hoping to find some magic in his eyes that will make me believe it. "This may be what you do, but the game has changed and you know it."

He's quiet. So quiet that I know I'm right. Our enemies have multiplied. Tables have turned. Alliances have formed and broken.

He touches my cheek. "It has changed, but it's nothing I can't handle."

I exhale the breath I've been holding, willing myself to believe it. He'll be okay. He'll come back.

Still, I can't let go. My fingers won't unclench. My feet won't take me a few steps away to signal that he's okay to leave. Because every other second is the devastating realization that he might not come back. That someone will be more ready than he is and take his life.

"Isabel, I have to do this." His voice is determined but laced with understanding.

I shake my head, unready.

He cups my cheeks and tilts my face up. His gaze is so intent I'm convinced he can see past my skin, right down to my aching heart.

"Isabel. Listen to me. I love you, and I'm coming back to you."

My breath rushes out. My heart surges in my chest. I'm ready to say it back to him a thousand times, but he slants his mouth over mine before I can. He silences the reciprocation and an ounce of my worry with a kiss that means even more than the echo of his words.

And then he's pulling away. Leaving me. The thud of his boots fades down the concrete path to the car. The engine hums to life before he drives away. The red glow of his tail lights trails toward the highway on-ramp until he's completely out of sight and I'm alone.

I don't know how long I stand there until the sound of car doors slamming jars me. Two young men get out of a two-door sedan with faded red paint and head toward the front desk. I duck back into the room and shut the door soundlessly.

I let go of a heavy sigh. I'm wary to sit anywhere but decide the vinyl leather chairs around the tiny table in the corner are likely safe. I send up a silent prayer that Tristan's business is swift so we don't need to spend the night here.

I think about pulling up Tristan's location on my phone but decide to wait until he gets there, and even then, I'm not sure I should.

TRISTAN

I drop my speed as I pass the sign for Fawn Hollow Farms and the few short buildings behind it. Glancing down at the GPS on my phone, I cut my headlights and pull off onto a dirt road a few yards ahead that will take me just a little closer. I can see some lights in the distance, then the faintest outline of a barn-shaped building against the darkened sky. That has to be where Crow's keeping her.

I park on the side and kill the engine. Roll down the windows. Listen. There's laughter coming from the barn. The lazy whine of a windmill rolling through the light breeze. Nothing from the house or the farm buildings I'd passed. The road is quiet too.

My phone buzzes, and a text from Isabel lights up the darkness.

Please be careful. I love you.

I know she's a wreck already. Very likely pacing a hole in the carpet of that roach motel room. That godawful place will probably be singed into my memory for all eternity now, since ten minutes ago, out of nowhere, I decided to tell her I loved her on one of its fine thresholds.

Something I didn't think I'd ever do. Something that's going to make it a lot harder to let her go if I ever need to. Because now I can't deny it, and nothing but death can make me forget the look on her face when I said it. Pure emotion. A crashing wave of joy as if she'd been waiting on a precipice, praying and hoping to hear only those words for the past six years. Perhaps that's exactly what it was.

A woman's shriek cuts through the night. Jay.

I get out of the car, shut the door quietly, and make my way through the field. Gun in hand, I approach. A black SUV is parked along the building, but no one seems to be on the lookout. They probably figure it's too remote to need to.

A man's voice inside floats through the air. "You used to be such a pretty girl. Now look at ya." Metal on metal. A muffled squeal. "How about we cut the rest of these clothes off and make some designs. How about that? Should we do that, or you wanna talk and I can put the knife away?"

I've never been into torture. I've had to get creative in the past. Sometimes taking someone out wasn't as straightforward as putting a bullet in their brain, but I've always tried to make it quick. I may be a killer, but I've got limits. I don't get off on this kind of shit.

I nudge the barn door open with my foot. The huge structure is bathed in a dull golden glow coming off a few lights hung from the rafters. Bales of hay and rusty tools line the walls.

I can only make out Jay's legs and bare feet on the dirt floor several feet away, because the round silhouette of the man speaking to her completely blocks the view.

"Hey!"

In my periphery there are two other men about my age standing several feet away. I keep my gun low and obscured behind my leg.

"I'm Red. Where's Crow?"

"He's good, guys. Crow said he was coming," the big guy says, turning away from Jay and coming my way. He walks with swagger, mostly due to his size, I suppose, a long hay knife dangling from one hand and a shorter, undoubtedly sharper hunting knife in the other. "You wanna talk to her?" He smirks and gestures over his shoulder with the shorter knife, finally out of the way enough that I can see her.

I swallow over the disgust spidering through me like a disease and mask any signs of it in the calm expression I return. I even manage to match his shitty smile with one of my own, like we're definitely on the same page. "That's the plan," I say.

"Good luck, brother. She ain't talking to us, and as far as I can tell, there ain't much left to do but be done with her."

"Give me ten minutes. Do you mind?"

"Nah. Come on, guys. Let's give the man some space to work."

He waves the others out of the barn. Then we're alone save their mindless chatter that gets farther away with every passing second. I walk toward Jay, my jaw so tight I feel like I might crack a molar.

I stop in front of her, drenched in self-loathing. The only thing that possibly can make it worse is the fact that I can't let on to any of it. If I'm going to save her... If she's going to feel mercy ever again...she has to believe that I truly don't give a shit that her face is so bloody and bruised that I might not recognize her if I hadn't seen her so recently.

"I'm sorry," she says over a sob.

"Don't cry. You're swollen enough. It'll make everything worse."

She bobs her head a little. "You're right."

"How'd they find you?"

"State trooper pulled me over on the way to the diner. Said the rental was reported stolen. He cuffed me and brought me here. Probably on Crow's family's payroll."

"You didn't have protection?"

"They were staked out near the diner, waiting."

"That was a mistake," I say.

She nods again. "Lots of mistakes," she mutters.

Mistakes that I wouldn't have made if the tables were turned and the people who came for me had a chance to get what they wanted. The irony isn't lost on me that I could be the one bound and bloody if things had gone differently.

"Why won't you talk to Crow?"

"Because he's going to kill me as soon as I give him what he wants. It would almost be worth it now. I can't..." She swallows and winces like she's fighting the tears again. "I'll tell you what you want to know, Tristan. Then please just be done with it. I can't give them the satisfaction. I'd rather be dead."

I lower to my haunches and study her. Her ripped clothes. The telltale glaze of blood and come smeared along her thigh that's obvious now. Rage lights up like a firestorm in my veins. Where the *fuck* is Crow? Because he will surely be answering for this disaster of an interrogation as soon as I see him again.

"They raped you?"

She doesn't answer. Averts her eyes, her chin trembling.

"Which one?"

"The one with the knives. After Crow left, he...he—"

"Don't. You don't have to say anything else."

My thoughts start spinning wildly now. The layout. The plan. Two paths and the sudden recognition that I could go down one more easily than the other. End this poor woman's torture and the torture she's inflicted on me over the past three years. Or take another path. One that feels wrong and right at the same time.

"What do you know, Jay?"

She lifts her head, her bloodshot eyes still a piercing blue against the rainbow of abused flesh. A single tear travels down her cheek and drops onto her dirtied pencil skirt.

"I know everything."

The hum of an engine grows louder and closer. In my bones, I know it's Crow. The fork in the road is minutes away. Seconds away...

"This is what we're going to do, Jay."

She blinks her eyes slowly.

"I need you to listen very carefully. And do exactly what I tell you to do."

"I will," she whispers. "Just don't let them—"

"No. That shit is over. Come with me."

I coax her upright just as Crow's voice bellows from outside. The door swings open, and his round comrade saunters in.

"Hey, boss is back." He lifts his eyebrows at Jay's upright figure. "What's up? You gonna give her a ride? She's not half bad."

I force a laugh and give her arm a firm squeeze before letting her go. She stiffens, sways a little with her hands bound behind her, but manages to hold herself upright as I walk toward the man.

"I just had a quick question."

I meet him in the middle of the barn, and now I'm smiling for real. As soon as I'm close enough, I swing and stab my knuckles into his larynx. The damage is nearly soundless and clogs his next breath. Grabbing the collar of his cheap polo shirt, I drag him to the other side of the barn and loop a hanging length of chain around his useless neck, tethering him there.

His eyes are wide with horror, his thick arms flailing, but all he can do is clamor at the chains and gasp for the air he's not getting.

"Do you know why this is happening to you?"

He shakes his head, with more gasps and soundless words I don't care about.

"You're a disgusting sack of shit, that's why. Just in case your buddies get you out of this jam, I'm going to teach you a quick lesson."

Sadly he's without his knife, but I see something better hanging on the wall.

"Perfect," I say with lightness that probably has him shitting his pants.

After unhooking it, I take a moment to appreciate the sickle's antique wooden handle. I run my finger along the long curved edge, grateful that it's not too dull for my intentions.

I lift my stare to his panicked one. He's fervently shaking his head. I smile. This shouldn't be so satisfying. I'm not into torture. I am into revenge, though, and what he's done to Jay makes me sick. And when I think about it, all the rage it inspires moves me. Swiftly and directly, I hook the blade into the flesh between his thighs. He makes a choked sound, and his eyes and mouth go perfectly round.

"Don't stick your dick in a woman without asking permission."

"Red, what the fuck!"

I turn to see Crow hovering near the barn door. The other men flank him and draw their guns. I keep walking toward them, undeterred.

I point to Crow. "You and I need to talk. Outside. Now. Call off the dogs."

He's huffing, his face red with irritation. "That's my cousin."

"Sorry," I say flatly. "He's going to need a tracheotomy and probably some therapy. Why don't you guys go help him out."

Crow hesitates a moment longer. We both stare at his cousin, whose trousers are saturated with deep crimson. Finally Crow nods to the guys, who run over to the man and start unwrapping the chain around his neck.

I cuff my hand around Jay's arm and face him. "The only thing you managed to get right was snatching her without anyone in the Company following you. The rest of this is a nightmare. Now I'm going to fix it."

His face falls as understanding dawns. "Wait. You're not taking her. No fucking way, Red. I brought her in."

"Yes, I am taking her," I reply calmly. "And you're going to let me. Because she's going to tell you what you need to know right now."

Crow blinks as if he's just figured out that he's about to get what he wants after hours of pointless torture.

I lift my chin toward the door. "Let's walk."

We walk a ways into the field until we're almost back to my car. Crow finally halts and turns to me.

"We going to talk or what?"

"What do you want to know? Do you have a pen or something to write this down?"

Jay's muscles go lax in my grip, the relief rippling off her in invisible waves.

He withdraws a receipt out of his back pocket, and I fish out a pen from my jacket when he can't find one.

"Hurry," I say. "Your cousin needs an ambulance, and I don't trust those idiots not to call one."

"All right. Wait a sec. Shit." He palms his forehead. "Starla Velasquez."

A few seconds go by, and for a moment I worry Jay won't do it. She wouldn't hold out... Not after all this.

"Her husband, Angel Velasquez," she begins, her voice weak. "He runs a multimillion-dollar gun trade operation from Miami to Mexico. She was threatening to expose him if he didn't give her a divorce and a huge settlement."

Crow scribbles the details down in messy scrawl. "Got it. What about Bill Wheeler? That insurance guy from Indiana."

"The order came straight from the top of his company. He had a twenty-year track record of manipulating claims to screw his clients and move himself up the ladder. Started drinking and talking about it at conferences. A journalist overheard him at the bar and did some digging. Then his company got wind of it."

Crow smiles broadly. "Don't tell me that was the chick from Chicago I took out right after."

"Justine Collins. You got to her right after she got the go-ahead from her editor to start writing the piece."

"Love it. How about Adriane Avitia?"

She takes a deep breath like she's bracing herself. "There's a group... like a life coaching, motivational group. They recruit a lot of people from New York and LA. Adriane had been with them for a while. She inherited a lot of money, and they convinced her to bequeath it to the group in her will. They hired us to speed up the distribution, I guess."

He frowns. "Who's they?"

"It's called the Masters Fellowship. Sam Burgess is the ringleader."

"Interesting. Anita Eschweiler. Revenge hit? She was hot."

Jay shakes her head. "A warning shot. Her uncle was poised to beat the sitting Chancellor in Germany's last federal election. He wouldn't back down. Wouldn't take bribes."

Crow makes a sound and scribbles more onto his receipt.

"Is that enough?" I say.

"I guess it's got to be. We don't have a lot of time, do we? Too bad we wasted so much of it." The look he shoots Jay is pure disdain. Then he shifts it to me. "So now what? You going to add her to your collection of people who should be dead?"

I groan inwardly because I just wish he'd disappear. I can't remember a time I've disliked him more. "I haven't decided yet. I'll let you know."

Jay starts to shake.

Crow seems to notice and huffs out a weak laugh. "Let me know how it goes."

6

ISABEL

After several minutes of anxiously pacing the motel room, I decide to call my mother. As soon as she realizes my phone isn't pinging my location anymore, she'll worry.

"Where are you?" My mother's panicked voice cracks through the phone as soon as she picks up.

"Mom, calm down." I get up and start to pace again. "I'm fine."

"Calm down? You're with a man who kills people for a living, and you're asking me to *calm down*? I just buried you, Isabel. I endured a wake, a funeral, a burial, and a reception in my home with all of our friends and family. For days I've pretended in front of everyone that you were dead and being lowered into the ground. To pull that off, I had to make myself believe it, and then suddenly your phone is off and I can't reach you."

The hysteria in her voice is unlike anything I've ever heard. "Mom, please. I'm sorry, okay? Please calm down. I promise you, I'm fine."

"Are you still in New York?"

I sigh, embattled over this tug of war between her and Tristan that

I don't expect will ever go away. He craves anonymity, and she's going to lose her mind if she doesn't know where I am.

"Not anymore," I say. "We're just outside Philadelphia."

"What are you doing there?"

"I… We had to see someone. And then I think we're heading to Florida." I rub my forehead vigorously because I'm not sure how to explain all of this, but I'm not sure she'll give me any choice.

"What's in Florida?"

"There's a woman Tristan's been hired to take care of. Obviously he's not going to do that, but we're going to talk to her and see if we can maybe figure out who might want her dead."

I can only hear her breathing on the other end of the phone. Calming down, I hope, though this news could have the opposite effect.

"This is a dangerous game you're playing, Isabel. Trust me, it almost cost me you."

"I know that. But it's a game Tristan knows. This is his playground. His kind of people."

"Which is exactly why you shouldn't be along for the ride. I sent you to Martine's to keep you safe. Not so you could throw yourself right back into danger with him."

I'm quiet a moment, contemplating what she's done. Never mind these choices are mine now. None of this would have happened if it weren't for her vengeance. If Tristan hadn't left to begin with…

"Did you know about Dad's involvement in recruiting Tristan into the army?"

She pauses. "What are you talking about?"

"I found a letter that Dad wrote, recommending him for a Special Forces team." I pause. "Did you know about it?"

Silence stretches between us.

The anger and resentment I felt the night I discovered the letter is compounded now. "I can't believe it. All this time, you knew. You watched everything fall apart between us, and that was exactly what you wanted." I bite my lip hard, consumed with disbelief, utterly betrayed.

I hear her sigh through the phone.

"Morgan came to me with the idea, and I'll admit that I didn't oppose it. We were worried about you, Isabel. We did it out of love. You were becoming inseparable. After his mother died, we barely saw you."

"He needed me!" I halt my pacing. "He was alone and we were in love, and you couldn't even come to the service. You did nothing to support us, and all we wanted was to be together. Thanks to you, nothing's changed except we've lost time we'll never get back."

"You were meant for more than to be some boy's emotional crutch at that age. He would have held you back terribly, and you would have grown to resent it in time. I didn't want to see you go through that and miss out on opportunities you'd never have again. We did it for *you*. Don't you see that? You mean everything to us. We'd give our lives for you."

"Yet Tristan and I are the ones who've given our lives because of the choices you made. You set us on this path, and now you're going to have to deal with where it takes us. Don't call me again."

I hang up and drop the phone on the bed. I'm tempted to turn it off. Sever the last lifeline she has to me as punishment for a betrayal so painful I can barely process it right now. But no matter how angry I am with her, I can't stoop to her level. Maybe she and my father held no reservations about strategically cutting Tristan out of my life, but I can't manage to cut her out of mine knowing the anguish it would give her.

I stare at the phone, half expecting her to call back, when I hear shuffling outside. Then the rattle of keys, the twist of the knob, and a face I never thought I'd see again. I bring my hand to my mouth as Tristan guides the beaten woman through the doorway and shuts the door behind them.

I look between them, grasping for an explanation. But no one says anything, and the longer I look at Jay, the more panicked I become. Tristan couldn't have done this. It had to have been Crow. Why else would Tristan have brought her here?

"Does she need a doctor?"

I doubt it's an option, but she looks like she's ready to drop.

"No. I'm fine," she whispers, sounding anything but fine. "Just a shower would be nice, if you don't mind."

"Of course."

I lead her to the dingy little bathroom and turn on the shower. When I face her again, her arms are wrapped tightly around herself like she might unravel if she lets go.

"I can bring you something clean to wear."

"Thank you, Isabel."

The last time I heard her say my name in her office at Trinity House, things had been very different. I didn't know then that Jude McKenna was the woman who pulled the strings and had managed Tristan's life as an assassin for as long as he could remember. All I knew was that her presence was unsettling, bordering on frightening. But any power she held over me then has swiftly diminished.

The woman before me is someone else. I feel for her, but knowing what she's capable of, I'm afraid to give her all my compassion.

She slowly begins to unbutton her soiled blouse with trembling fingers.

"Do you need help?"

"I'm fine. Thank you."

With that, I leave to give her privacy. I find a shirt and some pants in my bag and sneak them onto the bathroom counter for her once she's hidden behind the shower curtain. When I return, Tristan's sitting on one of the beds with his head in his hands.

"What happened?"

He lifts his gaze to mine, his mouth a rigid line. "I couldn't leave her there. Not when I set this up. Part of it, anyway."

"They did all that to get her to talk to them?"

He closes his eyes and scrapes his fingers along his scalp. "They did all that and more."

I frown. Then his meaning dawns on me. "They didn't…"

"They did. Well, one of them had his way with her, anyway. Don't worry. I took care of him."

My eyes go wide. "Tristan."

He stands up abruptly and faces me. "What do you want me to

do? Tell me what you want me to do, because I have no idea anymore. I used to trust my instincts, and now I don't trust anything. I hate this woman." He points to the bathroom where the sound of the shower spray goes on and on. "I *hate* her. I know you do too. But when I saw her there, tied up and ready to get sliced up by those idiots, all I could register was guilt and rage. And when I taught the guy who touched her a lesson, it felt like justice. So tell me, Isabel, what would you do if you were me? Should I have left her there for them to finish her off?"

"I'm not saying that. I just…" I swallow over the uncomfortable thought of Tristan killing—for hire or for circumstance. None of it sits well with me. "It's hard for me to think about you…*ending* someone's life."

He paces back and forth. "He might be all right. I don't know. I don't have it in me to care."

I try to push the disturbing thought away. More important things are at play. We have Jay, a dangerous but badly beaten woman on our hands. "What are we going to do now?"

"We can't stay here much longer," Tristan says. "Between Crow and whoever from the Company knew about our meeting, there are too many people looking for us."

"Your meeting?"

He walks away, pauses with his back to me. "Crow wanted me to lure her out. So when she sent the info on Aguilera that night, I asked for a meeting with her I never planned to take."

I set my jaw tightly. "And you never told me."

He turns back. "The look on your face when you saw Jay walk through the door is exactly why I didn't. Because I knew things could get ugly, and if they did, you're the last person I wanted to know about it. You don't have the stomach for this kind of shit, Isabel."

I ball my fists, riled at his routine underestimation. Also because he's right. "Apparently you don't either since you couldn't leave her there."

He narrows his eyes. "Should I have left her there to die? Should I have let the rest of Crow's guys take their turn with her?"

I wince, disgusted by the prospect of her enduring more than she already has. "I didn't say that. But don't act like I'm the only one who gives a shit. You obviously care about this woman."

"Then why did I give her to Crow if I care so fucking much?"

I feel the uncertainty in the question despite the angry way he delivers it. Like he's asking himself why the same way I am. Could he have predicted that Crow's men would act like such animals with a defenseless woman? Did Tristan expect her to live through whatever interrogation they'd planned? I don't know, and I'm not sure I want to. But I trust that when faced with the results, he got her away from there because he's not the soulless person he believed himself to be for so long. And maybe even more because of the important place Jay held in his narrow existence.

Just then the shower stops. A few tense minutes pass before Jay emerges in my black shirt and yoga pants, her hair wet, her skin pink where it's not discolored everywhere else. Her feet are bare. Narrow and feminine. She crosses her arms around her slender torso again and looks between us.

"So what's the plan, Jay?" Tristan asks, his tone less heated than it had been a moment ago.

"You're asking *me*?"

Jay's voice has a little more strength than it had before. She seems fortified somehow. No doubt by the enormous relief of knowing she's not going to die after everything she's been through. Even if she knows what Tristan's capable of, she has to know that's not the kind of person I am.

"You must have had a plan when you asked Crow to bring me here and talk to you. We may as well get our intentions out in the open if any of us hope to get out of this mess alive."

"I'm at your mercy. Even if I hadn't told Crow everything I did, the Company would probably still want me dead. I can't resurface. All I can do is hide. So you can help me hide, or…" She swallows. "It's in your hands, Tristan. I'll fight for my life, but that's about all I have the energy for right now."

A long silence follows. A silence filled with possibilities, doubts, and a growing seed of worry that Jay's about to become a fixture in my world, something I never expected.

"We were heading south," Tristan finally says.

Her eyes narrow slightly, as if she's calculating something. "Aguilera?"

"That was the plan."

"It's too obvious," she says. "They'll send someone else to take care of her, but they'll be waiting for you to show up first."

"Halo… They could hide her," I say.

If Jay recognizes the name, she doesn't show it.

Tristan meets my gaze. We're homeless, rootless, and running again. The closest place to home for me was Halo, and it's been calling me back for days.

"I guess we'll find out if they want to make this their problem," he says.

I shrug. "It's better than showing up where they'll most expect us."

Jay shifts on her feet uncomfortably, no doubt fully aware that she's the problem. Her existence. The Company she represents. Everything she knows.

Except if she's given Crow information, maybe now we'll finally get some too. Learn about the Company and how we can be rid of them, once and for all. Jay is a snake. I don't trust her. But by some odd twist of fate, her survival now hinges on ours.

"What about the woman, though? If we don't get to her first…" My voice trails off.

Jay and Tristan share a brief look. I'm certain she doesn't care if this woman dies, but Tristan is beginning to. Neither of us wants her blood on our hands. But how do we get Devon Aguilera out of the crosshairs without putting ourselves in danger?

I look to Tristan, not wanting to say Makanga's name in front of a woman I still very much consider the enemy. "What about the Postman?"

He nods. "I'll have him leave tonight. Be ready to leave in five minutes."

Tristan makes his call outside, and soon after, we're on the road.

We drive for an hour and make a short stop for food and supplies. While Tristan and Jay wait, I spend more time than I probably should in the local supercenter, picking up things for the two-day journey and also for Jay, whose ordeal has me more conflicted by the minute. I'm devastated by what she's endured tonight. But I also can't ignore that she's facilitated the death of likely hundreds of people over the past several years. In the end, my instinct to comfort a woman in distress can't be overruled by the awful things she's done.

"Jesus, Isabel. What is all this?"

Back in the car, I ignore Tristan's exasperated tone as I sort through the bags.

"Here," I say, handing back a pillow and blanket for Jay and a bag of snacks and drinks that will hopefully sustain us for a while.

I don't miss her hesitation accepting the small comforts, or the gratitude in her eyes.

"Thank you," she utters, barely above a whisper.

As Tristan guides us back onto the highway, she carefully unpackages the blanket and wraps herself up tightly, taking the full width of the back seat to rest. A few minutes go by before she dozes off.

A few hours later, when I can no longer stay alert on the road, Tristan seems to notice. He threads his hand in mine and strokes his thumb rhythmically. "Get some rest. I'll wake you up, and we can switch off in a few hours."

I doubt he'll let me take a shift, but I'm too wiped out to deny the offer to sleep. So I drift off too, lulled into slumber by darkness and the hum of the highway.

TRISTAN

We drive until dawn, when Isabel wakes and insists we stop for food. Jay's in no condition to be seen in public, so we get drive-through and a more respectable room at a hotel just outside Chattanooga, more than halfway to our destination.

We eat in silence. Isabel and Jay at the table. Me on one of the beds. I catch Isabel staring at Jay every once in a while, studying her visible wounds.

"Do you want me to get you some ice?"

Jay tries to smile, though it seems like the small motion causes her pain. "That might help. Thank you."

"I can get it," I say.

But Isabel's already halfway out the door. "I've got it."

Jay drags a french fry through a pile of ketchup. "She's very sweet. Thoughtful."

I don't acknowledge her comment. I'm not about to start singing Isabel's praises to a woman who hired me to kill her. That and Isabel's qualities can't be summed up with common words. Nothing could capture the soul of her or the thousand perfect, maddening things that make her the only human being in the world I'm ready to make every sacrifice for.

"Where is this place you're taking me to?" Jay's question disrupts my thoughts.

"A safehouse of sorts. They've been at odds with the Boswell family for years, though. So I'm not really sure how this is going to work."

A few silent moments pass before she speaks again. "There's someone else who might be able to help me."

"Who is it?"

She closes her eyes and exhales softly.

"Jay, you're going to have to start talking eventually."

"I realize that. It just goes against every instinct."

"I can relate."

She looks up. "You've changed, haven't you?"

I take a big bite of my sandwich, because I don't know how to respond. Sometimes I wonder if I've changed or if there was someone better hiding inside me all this time. Isabel seems to think so, and I want to believe her. Still, I don't want Jay thinking I won't hesitate to do whatever I need to do to keep Isabel and myself safe. She's vulnerable and completely dependent on my good will now, but that doesn't mean

I have to put her totally at ease.

"Maybe I just did bad things because that's the only life I knew."

A sad smile lifts her lips, but she doesn't say anything more.

"So who's your lifeline, other than me, of course. Family?"

She shakes her head. "I don't have any family."

"Boyfriend?"

"Honestly, Tristan. If I had anyone I cared about, I couldn't do what I do. It'd be too risky. The only life I can take responsibility for is my own." She takes another bite of food and swallows it down. "It's Townsend."

I pause. "Townsend?" I know his name from the files I snatched from Jay's office, long since destroyed but burned into my memory all the same. If it's the same Townsend, he's a British-born spy, an enemy of the state on more than one count and reclusive enough that I've never crossed paths with him.

"I don't believe we've met."

"He doesn't like to be met, generally."

"Then why would he take you in?"

She collects her hair, a dark auburn, and twists it to lay over her shoulder. "Sometimes connections are made."

"So he's your favorite." I can't help the teasing in my voice. "I was beginning to think I was."

She smirks. "You're the best. That's different." She looks up, her eyes more somber. "I'm in your debt for what you did back there with Crow. I haven't given you a lot of reasons to show me mercy."

Isabel returns with a bucket of ice before I can respond, which is fine because I don't want to. I'd rather not contemplate the uncomfortable attachment I have to Jay, which has kept me from ending her life not once but twice.

We finish eating, and even though the sunshine is pouring in through the windows, we pull the drapes closed and resign ourselves to a few hours of rest before we get on the road again. I take the bed nearest the door and tuck Isabel against me. Only when I hear the two women's soft snores do I let myself drift.

I jolt awake at the sound of loud voices outside the room. I sit upright, blinking away sleep as the voices get quieter. Just other hotel patrons passing by the room. I check the digital clock on the table, noting that more than a few hours have passed. Jay is obscured under the blanket on the other bed.

I rub Isabel's shoulder gently until she wakes. Her eyes widen quickly, and she glances around the room. "What is it?"

"Everything's fine. It's just time to get back on the road."

She relaxes against her pillow with a heavy sigh. I straighten the pendant at her neck that's slipped to the side in her sleep and talk myself out of kissing her, knowing it'll lead to things I'm in no position to finish. Her sleepy gaze locks with mine, and our hands fold together.

"Do you think they'll hide her?"

She's talking about Halo, and I've asked myself the same question about a hundred times since we left New Jersey. Because I can't spend the rest of my life babysitting Jay, and I obviously can't kill her or leave someone else to do it. She's my responsibility now until someone else can take her in. I hope to hell Martine is that person.

"If Martine's still in the business of soul saving, I can't think of a more desperate candidate."

7

ISABEL

Halo is unchanged. The house still smells like spices and home. Except its friendly faces aren't focused on me. Each set of curious eyes is trained on Jay. She's the burning question in the room. The stranger with an aura of mystery whose stolid expression still holds a hint of pleading in it. For our part, Tristan and I are silently pleading too, or at least we will be once Martine shows up.

We're waiting in the dining room of the mansion on St. Charles. The sun has set, and the chandelier above the table casts a dazzling pattern of lights on the walls. Zeda is across from us, silently studying Jay when Skye walks in with a few glasses of tea and sets one in front of each of us.

"Can I get you anything else?" Skye may be opening the offer to everyone, but she's looking directly at Jay.

Skye doesn't have to say it. I can tell she's reliving the horror of what she went through with her old pimp the second we walked in. She's been all nervous energy and questions and fussing since we arrived.

Finally the front door opens with a groan. The click of heels on the hardwood floor ends with Martine's presence filling the room.

Halo's own fairy godmother is dressed in a white shift dress, emboldened with loud streaks of color as if she'd walked through a narrow gauntlet of ready paintbrushes. Her cheeks are tinted with their usual rouge. Her yellow hair coiffed for whatever business she was attending to today is still held nicely in place.

She stands at the head of the table, paused beside the chair reserved for her.

"Isabel. Tristan. You've come back." She smiles warmly. "With a friend, I see. To whom do I owe the pleasure?"

"This is Jude McKenna," I say.

"Welcome to our home, Jude. You'll have to pardon my very bold assumptions, but you do look as if you're in need of a soft place to land, child."

Still Jay doesn't speak, and I know now I'll have to be the one to do it. For a moment, I worry that explaining the situation with Skye and Zeda in the audience is wrong, but then I remember what Skye once told me about there being no need for secrets. How it puts everyone in danger. And if they decide to accept a manager of mercenaries in their midst, they deserve to know the extent of it. Especially Skye, who looks like she's ready to take Jay under her wing the second Martine gives the okay. At the moment, she has no idea what kind of person Jay really is.

"She goes by Jay and has been working with Tristan for several years," I begin. "She was the one who confirmed the information about Vince Boswell when we needed it. She was also the one who arranged for the hit on my life."

Silence descends on the room. A heavy, tense silence.

"By a series of unfortunate events, she's been disconnected from that organization. Not by choice but by circumstance. And now…"

"The people I work for are not the forgiving type," Jay says, her voice steady and almost businesslike. "I've been compromised. If I'm found, they'll kill me. No questions asked."

"So you're the reason why Isabel's been on the run?" Skye interrupts.

"I'm one cog in the wheel. I'm not blameless, but I'm hardly the mastermind of the operation who doles out assignments to men like Tristan. I can assure you, there's a lot more to it."

Skye grimaces, conflicted, as if she's pissed that I let her feel sorry for such a soulless woman. I offer an apologetic half smile.

Martine drags her chair back, its feet moaning along the floor before she lowers into it. She leans back and cocks her head slightly. "This is a safehouse, you realize."

"I'm not a murderer."

"And yet you've murdered," Zeda adds coolly.

Jay sighs. "If it's not obvious already, I'm not especially adept at defending myself. I wish no one here harm. I'm only here by Isabel's invitation in an attempt to protect my own life. If you can't help me then don't."

Martine purses her lips, still carefully studying her would-be charge. "Who do you answer to?"

Jay hesitates and glances to Tristan.

"I'm curious about that myself," he mutters.

"Are you wanting to barter?" Jay asks pointedly.

Martine lifts the corner of her mouth into a coy smile. "I don't ask for payment from those who stay with us. I ask for an open mind. I ask for loyalty and trust. I don't imagine you can give us much of that, so perhaps I can, in this case, ask for something more specific. An offering in exchange for *our* trust to hold you here among us."

Jay's breathing ticks up. She stares down at her lap, twisting her fingers. The information she carries is her true lifeline. Once it's gone, it's gone. Then she's just a woman who's betrayed the strictest confidence, a certain death sentence.

"You may stay here tonight. But I can't have an enemy residing inside these walls, Miss McKenna. You've struck against one of our own, so you'll need to prove some semblance of loyalty to us if you hope to have our protection. I see no other way around it." Martine rises. "We can meet again in the morning, once everyone's had some rest. Skye, please show Miss McKenna to a room and whatever she might need to be comfortable for the evening."

With that, Martine leaves and everyone slowly begins to move. While Skye gets Jay settled upstairs, Zeda follows us to the foyer.

"You staying here?"

"I didn't know if it was an option," I admit.

Zeda laughs. "If she can stay"—she gestures toward the stairs—"you can stay."

Tristan stiffens. "I'd rather not."

I glance up at him and take his hand. "Just one night, okay? It's been a long drive."

Zeda doesn't wait for him to relent. "Come on. There's a second master this way."

She walks us to the east side of the house through a hallway that leads to a large corner bedroom with an adjoining bath and bay windows that face the street.

"Most people who come are on their own, so this room rarely gets used. I'm sure Martine will let you stay as long as you want."

I step through the doorway and survey the space. White carpet stretches across the floor, meeting the bottoms of the floor-to-ceiling drapes, which are rough, creamy silk. In the center of the room sits a four-poster iron bed, bracketed by lavender velvet head- and footboards and covered in matching decorative pillows.

"Will this work?"

I turn to her. "It's perfect, thank you."

"Get some sleep," she says, lifting her chin toward Tristan as if some camaraderie exists between them.

"What was that about?" I ask when she shuts the door.

He goes to the windows and draws the curtains closed. "We got to know each other a little when we were prepping things at the hotel for your rendezvous with Boswell."

I tug off my shirt and toss it to the floor. "You're quite the pair for confidences."

He turns to me. "She doesn't trust Martine's soul-saving bullshit, and neither do I. That's as far as the confidences go." He strips down to his briefs and tears back the silky duvet before sliding atop the sheets.

Undeterred by his mood, I slip off my jeans and the rest of my garments until I'm naked.

"I was just asking. You can bring your guard down now."

I move to the foot of the bed and lift my knee to the mattress. He's still, following me with his eyes.

"What do you think you're doing?"

Slowly, I crawl up the bed and sit astride him. "Reclaiming all of your attention."

He brings his hands to my hips, taking firm hold as if to keep me there.

I smooth my hands over his pectorals and down his rippled abdomen, admiring and savoring the feel of him, a luxury I've been denied for too long. "I feel like I can't touch you or say what I want to when she's around."

He grasps my roaming fingers, squeezing them gently.

"You're wise not to. You can never trust her. No matter how humble she may seem all of a sudden."

I know it, of course, but his reminder is one I'll have to keep fresh in my mind. Jay is smart enough to play on my kindness if it suits her agenda, if her agenda is anything past staying alive.

"Do you think she'll talk to Martine?"

"If she doesn't talk to her, I think she'll talk to me. And if keeping Martine in the know means taking Jay off my hands, at least for a little while, then I'm on board with that. I just need to find out who's behind the Company."

"I guess we'll find out soon. Until then…" I brush my lips over his, flickering my tongue along his lower lip.

When I pull away, he cups my nape and guides me back, holding us together as our mouths reacquaint. He trails his lips from mine, drawing hot kisses down my neck and over my chest, teasing my nipples into aching points.

"We probably shouldn't be doing this here," he mutters without much conviction.

"It's a big house."

He groans. "We should have gotten a room."

"Tristan?"

"Yes?"

"I need you to shut up and fuck me…please."

He exhales roughly, his eyes darkening. My heartbeat ticks up. Something about the dangerous fusion of lust and challenge swimming in the depths of his look prickles my skin and wraps me in a welcome heat. Like he's a stranger capable of the darkest deeds wrapped in a lover I know. The lover I need…

I roll my hips. Slowly and deliberately, making no mistake of my desire against his. "I don't want to think about anything except how you feel."

With a low growl, he shoves me to his side and quickly takes the advantage, holding his weight above me and using it to pin me to the mattress at once. He nips at my collarbone. Rakes his blunt nails down my thigh until I'm bucking against him. "My dirty little saint. Now I want to make you scream."

Clawing the sheets, I silently beg him to. I don't want to alert the rest of the house to all the ways I need him, but when he kicks away the last barrier of his clothing and slides into me, I cease caring.

We move together, grabbing and holding on to each other like one of us might slip away. But the world only seems to contain the two of us. Two lost souls climbing toward that one pinnacle moment when everything that haunts us can fade into the darkness. I'm torn between the journey and destination, but the climb is too fast.

I'm trembling at the edge of release when my name slips off his lips. Then a needy groan that disappears into his next savage kiss. His thrusts speed up. "Come for me. Need to feel it…"

I whimper into the electrified air between us, tumbling into the pure possession of his movements. Then, as if his words alone had the power to summon it, a fierce climax like none other rips through me. He swallows my screams, extends the feeling when he pounds out his own fevered release, pulling me further into the drowning wave. Until slowly the wave flows back out to sea, leaving us to our racing hearts and humming skin.

He rolls to the side, bringing me with him so there's no space between us. I catch my breath and trace the planes of his ribs and stomach. I close my eyes, letting my fingertips memorize the scars I wish I could take away.

He stills my restless touch, threading our fingers together with a sigh. "I think you officially reclaimed all of my attention."

I giggle and nuzzle against his skin, wrapped in contentment I know can't last.

TRISTAN

The morning is lively—an almost surreal contrast from the tense meeting the night before. With an apron cinched over her sunshine-yellow dress, Martine is the captain of the kitchen, tending to the pans on the stove and directing everyone else. Zeda is cutting up fruit and placing it into little bowls while Skye arranges place settings in the dining room. Jay joins from upstairs just as Isabel and I are noticed.

Martine lifts her eyebrows. "Miss McKenna. You showed up just in time. I have toast that needs butter."

"I can do it," Skye offers.

"Nonsense. Your hands work, don't they?"

Jay glances nervously between Martine and me. I bite the inside of my lip, holding back a laugh at the hilarity of it all. After a moment of hesitation, Jay comes to the island and wordlessly starts in on the task.

Martine turns down the burners and waves me over. "I need you too. Take this to the table for me, please."

She arms me with mitts to relocate a cast-iron pan of fried potatoes that might weigh as much as she does. And after several more minutes of fussing and directing, she calls everyone to sit. We dig into the hearty breakfast in unison. I'm not especially at ease here, but I allow myself to accept the normalcy of it. Too, I recognize how the comforts of the home Martine's created draws her tenants in and keeps them here long enough to brainwash them into loyalty and glorified servitude.

If I weren't convinced Martine kept a mountain of secrets hidden under all that light she pretends to spread across the land, I might become a willing follower, with my stomach full and my basic needs more than met after weeks on the run. But I know better, and I suspect Jay soon will too.

Conversation is thin, limited to small talk about the goings-on in town. A street festival coming up soon. A small mention of Noam, who will no doubt be relieved to see Isabel back in the studio again.

Then the dishes are cleared and Martine's proposition lingers, unspoken but ever present. She pushes back from the table, crosses her legs at the knee, and focuses on Jay.

"Miss McKenna, how did you sleep?"

Jay smiles politely. "Very well. You've been more than hospitable."

"I appreciate that. We're all fresh now and our appetites are satisfied. Seems as if this might be a good time to settle the matter of whether you'd like to stay here with us."

Jay clears her throat and lifts her chin. "What exactly are you offering? I'd like clear terms, if you don't mind, since my life is on the line."

"Certainly. You may stay here at the house as long as you wish. Rent free, obligation free, save a few household to-dos that we all chip in with."

"I don't care about buttering toast. I'm more concerned about what happens if my whereabouts become known." Jay's silver tongue is revealing itself. Once more she's the calculating manager who's lethal behind a desk, even if she can't hold her own when faced head-on with the men she uses as weapons.

"I know many others who would bring you under their roof without hesitation," Martine says. "If it's a matter of protection, you have my word that we will provide. Keeping our sisters safe is of paramount importance."

The muscles in Jay's jaw tense and release. She shakes her head slightly. "I'm sorry. I'm certain you have the best intentions, but I'm not sure you realize who you're up against."

Martine's face lifts into an easy smile. "Child, I've brought governors to their knees. I've faced off with bankers and lawyers and the worst kinds of men, here in our city and all over the country. I keep a rather colorful range of people in my acquaintance—some well-meaning and others not as much. This is all to say, I know very well where I sit in the grand scheme of things, both in the hierarchy of the world we read about in the papers and the real one that exists in the underbelly of our society. I'm certain you work for some powerful forces, but if that sort of thing scared me, I'd hardly be in a position to help anyone."

Jay pauses, seeming to take that all in. "And if I were to tell you more about those powerful forces, in detail, what do you intend to do with that information?"

I lean in to speak. "You said you know everything, so what's the difference if you're already marked?"

If Jay starts revealing information based on what she thinks we'll do with it, we'll only get a fraction of the picture. And I want the whole thing. Every piece of the puzzle.

She narrows her eyes. "Because, Tristan, if you or anyone else here take action against them using the information I give you, you have no idea how aggressively they'll maneuver to destroy you. You have *no* idea."

Martine and I share a look. A hungry glimmer of anticipation.

"Martine's given you her word that she can keep you safe. Why don't you just tell us what you know, Jay, and let us worry about the rest?"

Jay takes in a deep breath. Wrings her fingers in her lap. And for a few tense moments, her choice hangs in the empty silence.

8

ISABEL

"I take my orders from a man we call Soloman."

Jay's pallor is evident, her expression notably grim, as if someone has just handed down her death sentence. Her gaze zigzags around the table, like there's a map drawn on it.

"What does Soloman do?" I ask, hoping to urge her forward, lest her anxiety keep her from divulging the details we so desperately need.

"Soloman is a broker. He used to deal in precious stones. Blood diamonds. Rare finds. He facilitated deals between private buyers until he was so well connected that he realized he could broker other things. Artwork, black-market items." She pauses. "The real money came with the brokering of favors, though. Arrangements that needed to be handled discreetly. To protect his clients and keep his dealings under the radar, he soon realized that he had to keep a very small roster of clients. The richest of men, the most powerful, and sometimes the most dangerous."

She brings her hands to the table and draws lines in the wood grain with her fingertips. "Favors started to overlap. One favor could benefit one client and gravely hurt another. So the list got smaller. The favors got more expensive. Not because they were worth more but because the people who could make these requests were so few." Her voice grows quiet. "So they formed a group. A small circle of men and women whose power and influence outrank their competitors'. When a favor is requested, it's put to a vote. Unanimous decisions are preferred but not required. Matters are always up for debate. All alliances must be considered. This is how things are decided."

"How does Vince play into this?" Tristan asks.

"His father, Kristopher Boswell, was invited to a seat. His company has grown exponentially in recent years. The Chalys Pharmaceuticals footprint on the economy is substantial, and their influence can already be felt among the other members. Of course, membership is both a privilege and a concession. Members must learn to yield to the same power they wish to wield in a room of giants."

Tristan frowns. "You're saying you kept all of us busy with a handful of clients? How many people could they possibly need to take out?"

"It doesn't work like that. Requests are made by members but more often through them. Jobs are considered from their extended network, accepted in return for favors that would benefit others in the circle. Sometimes money alone is accepted, though that rarely will instigate a hit."

She looks to me. "Naturally, a request made by a member of the circle is of the utmost importance. That's why Tristan was sent for you. That's why Crow was nearby, on standby, from day one. I was to leave nothing to chance. Not because you were a danger to anyone but simply because a man of the highest order wanted you dead, and it had to be taken care of no matter what."

"No one knew that he might recognize me?"

She shakes her head. "I research every job as thoroughly as I can, but the details had to do with your life in Rio and the history between your family and Boswell. I wouldn't have dug that deep into your past relationships. Unfortunately, or perhaps fortunately, I failed to recollect your father's involvement with Tristan early on. I vet every contractor for the Company before they're onboarded, but it had been years since I referenced those files. It was pure chance and possibly one of the worst times for Tristan to fail."

"I didn't fail," he says.

"In their eyes, you did. You didn't exactly have a vote."

He ignores her reply and pushes on. "If Boswell is so precious to the operation, why did you give up information on Vince and his nephew?"

"We underestimated you. Vince had his tickets booked for New Orleans nearly the minute I told you. We planned to beef up security at his residences and work once he got back. I had no idea you'd maneuver so quickly."

One glance at Martine and I recognize the hint of satisfaction in her eyes. Tristan may hate the way the situation went down, but there's a touch of glory in having gotten to Boswell first.

"So how do we get them to forget about us?" I ask.

"The good news is that Crow will likely be making a mess with the names I gave him. Even his family ties won't save him when he crosses the Company. The bad news, of course, is they'll know the information came from me. But as long as we all stay out of the way for a little while, I think we'll be safe here." She looks to Martine. "If you or this place was never on my radar, it shouldn't be on theirs."

Tristan rises and paces to the window. "That's reassuring, but until they find the bodies—yours and mine—they won't stay satisfied with us being out of sight for long."

She nods, starts tracing the lines in the wood again. "If you go after them, they'll kill you, Tristan. Their power and influence have no bounds."

"They're expecting *him*," Skye says. "Like you said, we're not on their radar."

Jay's skepticism doesn't need to be uttered aloud. It's palpable.

Zeda smirks. "You don't know us, and we're just getting to know you. We took care of Boswell in less than three days. What makes you think we can't do worse?"

"That was you?"

"It was all of us," Zeda says.

Jay shoots a questioning look to Tristan.

He shrugs. "I didn't exactly give my blessing, but yes, it was a team effort. Unfortunately Isabel sacrificed the most. Boswell was lucky to leave with his life after what he did to her."

"Even so, he was unguarded. The people in this circle are not," she says.

"Then you tell us. Where are their weaknesses?"

"Together?" She lifts her brows. "They have none. They're impenetrable. Individually, of course, everyone has vulnerabilities. How and when you choose to take advantage of them is another matter."

"And that is something we will carefully consider, Miss McKenna," Martine says. "Thank you for your trust in us. We'll honor it by treating this information with great care, and I believe that together we can devise a plan that will protect you and others they wish to harm."

Jay sighs heavily, though she looks anything but unburdened.

"For now, let's get you well. I have a private physician who can come by this afternoon to see you and tend to your injuries. Skye, would you be so kind as to help outfit Miss McKenna with some basic necessities? I'm sure she could use some clothes of her own."

"Of course."

Martine smiles serenely and stands. "I'll be in my office for the next couple hours if anyone needs anything. If you'll excuse me."

With that, she leaves and the others disperse. Tristan lingers at the window, seemingly lost in thought. I go to him.

"What now?"

He shakes his head. "Let's get out of here."

TRISTAN

The sky is a murky gray as we walk through the park. Manes of Spanish moss hang from the live oaks that line the broad path. The scenery is picturesque and moody. Romantic even. But I'm only physically here. The rest of me is retracing dozens of hits knowing what I know, replaying the conversations with Jay, and trying to make connections that could be useful.

The original plan to track hits back to their instigators isn't out of the question, except now everything is complicated by this extra layer of interest—the mysterious circle of deciding members. If money isn't a motivator, everything is a power play. To protect it, threaten it, or further it.

"Look." Isabel points ahead. An egret launches from its nearby perch and sails over the pond with a squawk.

I follow her gaze, trying to pull myself back into the moment. She's patient and thoughtful by my side, her hand in mine as if it's always belonged there. Being with her is beginning to feel that way now—like it's been this way forever. Part of me wonders if it's my latent memory lending to the feeling or if it's simply an evolution of our brief time together. It's been a month. Already I'm possessive and consumed in ways that should require more earning of those emotions. But we've also faced death, which quickly condenses quality of life into the space of a moment.

She leans her cheek against my arm. "What are you thinking, Tristan? Talk to me."

"Ten thousand things. I'm having a hard time narrowing it all down into a coherent thought. My head can be a hectic place to be sometimes."

"Do you think Jay will be okay at Halo?"

"I have no idea. It's definitely not her style, but I think her tolerance of the situation will depend a lot on how Martine chooses to use the information Jay gives us."

"And how do *you* plan to use it?"

I shrug. "The plan hasn't changed that much. Except I'm starting to get a better idea of who we're up against."

"The way Jay talks about them… She's scared to death."

"She has good reason to be. The secrets she's privy to are more valuable than anyone's life. They'll go to great lengths to protect them. She knows this better than anyone."

Isabel's quiet a moment, as if she's taking that reality in.

"Have you heard from Makanga yet?"

"He sent me a message this morning. They're safe. He has Aguilera tucked away in a little town south of Atlanta where he has contacts. Figured out that she was having an affair with the senator."

She looks up at me, her eyebrows high. "Oh."

"The bigger 'oh' is that she's three-months pregnant, and she won't give it up. She'll be due right before the midterm elections, which I'm guessing won't be great timing for the campaign."

"Makanga can't keep her hidden forever. What are we going to do?"

"The easiest way to erase the dot on her head is probably to go public. She wasn't intending to. Says they're in love, I guess. Which makes me wonder if it's the senator's call or someone else's. Someone who's invested in a candidate who can't fail right now."

"That would make sense."

I slow to a halt and turn to her. "It's time to set up a home base. Working our way out of this mess isn't likely to be straightforward or especially quick. We'll have to follow the trouble as we find it, but living on the road will probably drive one of us crazy before we find what we're looking for."

She nods, her brows crinkling. "I mean, Halo—"

"No way. I'm going way outside my comfort zone working with Martine in any capacity. I need autonomy, and that's not really her thing."

"You can have autonomy and take advantage of an empty room in her house. You're not taking an oath of fealty or anything. I think she knows you're well beyond her reach."

"Yeah, but I don't trust her."

"You don't trust anyone."

I sift my fingers into her hair, guiding her closer to me. "I trust you, Isabel."

She sighs and settles her palms against my chest. "I think we'll be safe there. It's a safehouse, by definition."

"Run by someone with enough power to be dangerous. We need to be able to maneuver. I can't do that under her roof."

Resignation shows in the slight slump of her shoulders. "Then where? Can we stay in New Orleans?"

"Is that what you want?"

She nods, a hint of pleading in her eyes. In that moment, something new and strange reveals itself within me—an instinctive desire not only to keep her safe from bodily harm but to give her a life that will make her happy. I've ripped her from the life she knew in the most traumatic way possible. The least I can do is offer some stability. And if this is where she wants to be, this is where we'll stay. For as long as we can.

"Then we'll stay. And I'll tolerate Martine's incredibly addictive home-cooked meals until we find the right place."

She smiles broadly, lifts onto her toes, and seals the deal with a kiss.

We spend the rest of the afternoon and early evening roving the city. Some areas are familiar to me. Everything is new to Isabel, whose eyes light up at nearly every turn. We eat well, pick up some fliers for local real estate and rentals, and steal enough kisses in courtyards and alleyways that I'm eager to get back to Martine's, if only to find more ways to put our four-poster bed to good use.

But when we get back to the house around nightfall, Jay is in the sitting room just past the entrance. She's curled up on a couch with a book in her lap, a faraway look on her face.

I pause and look to Isabel. "Give us a minute?"

"Sure," she says and steps away.

"Mind if I join you?"

Jay offers a tight smile, which I accept as a tentative yes. I sit on the adjacent chair and rest my elbows on my knees.

"What did the doctor say?"

She lifts her shoulder. "Nothing of consequence. Gave me the morning-after pill, just in case I wasn't uncomfortable enough. He says I can get other tests done eventually. Obviously a rape kit was out of the question."

A tense moment passes. "Were we right to bring you here?"

She blinks a few times, as if she doesn't understand the question. "I had no choice."

"I don't want you to feel like a prisoner."

She laughs. "Tristan, my life is a prison. I'll know freedom in death. Probably sooner rather than later."

I frown. "Things aren't that dire. Not yet at least."

"Everything is out of my control. Nothing is in order. I'm a bystander in my own life, forced to sit idly while others make the decisions knowing a fraction of what's at stake."

"Then why don't you tell me so I know. Show me the minefields."

She looks away. "I've told you all I know."

"That's bullshit, and we both know it. Martine cut things short. She wants to needle it out of you herself."

She meets my gaze. "You don't think I know that already?" She looks me over. "You're doing the same thing, by the way. I'm beginning to feel like the courted prom queen."

I smirk, and she can't mask her own.

"Listen… I don't fully know what Martine's intentions are. She's shrewd and cunning. But she's built a network of supposed do-gooders who tear down the bad guys and bolster the good guys."

"Is that why you dislike her?"

"No. I'm just not much of a joiner."

She cocks her head.

"If the Company's work required group projects, I would have been done for long ago."

"And now you have a partner," she says, the irony like honey on her lips.

I tighten my jaw, unable to deny that she's right. Isabel might be ill-equipped for the life of an assassin, but we've managed fine together. For the most part, our intentions align. They seem to more and more as the days go by.

"I never wanted this life," I say. "You gave it to me. Why, I'll never understand. I wanted to be free of it before Isabel, even if I refused to fully admit it to myself. You don't understand it yet, Jay, because you still yearn for your old life. You wish you could wind the clocks back and make different choices so everything could keep humming along the way it always has been. Pretty soon, you'll just want out of this prison no matter what it takes, no matter what you have to leave behind. That's the prison you and I both live in—the prison the Company and all these fucking people created."

Her eyes glisten, but her gaze is steady on me.

"I want to break out, and you will too. You and me? We deserve everything we get. Isabel doesn't. She's innocent. She has more heart than we ever will. So when I'm asking you to tell me what you know, I'm not trying to save the world or map out a path to glory. I just want a second chance, and I want her safe."

She takes in an unsteady breath. "I have regrets too, you know. You pretend to know me, but you don't. I used to care about things. I used to want a normal life. I wasn't always this way."

A tear travels down her cheek, leaving a glimmering trail. She wipes at it, and I reach for her hand, capturing it between us. Because I need her attention. I need her trust. She tenses, her eyes going wide.

"Then let's crawl out of this shit together. Can you at least try to trust me?"

Her breathing grows shallow. I know what I've proposed is next to impossible for her on so many levels. A month ago, if someone had told me I needed to let go of the life I knew and start trusting and caring about people, I would have had choice words for them and possibly a more physical reply.

Jay's not caught up yet, but she will be. In time.

"Tristan?"

Jay rips her hand out of mine, shifting her gaze to Isabel hovering near the doorway.

"Is everything okay?"

I stand and go to her. "Everything's fine."

9

ISABEL

We don't talk about why he was holding Jay's hand or why she jerked it away as if she had something to hide. I quickly decide to place jealousy into the basket of basic emotions Tristan deems are beneath me, including hatred for Jay that is changing shape all the time. I don't want to give the moment any strength or dwell on how deep their connection goes.

Instead I fall into bed with Tristan, and for the next couple of hours, we let our bodies answer all the promises our teasing touches made throughout the day. The storm rolling in hides the sounds of our lovemaking. And our lovemaking hides the worry in my heart.

Several hours later, the sliver of night sky between the curtains reveals the rain whipping shadows against the glass. Tristan is asleep on his back, his arm crooked over his eyes. Every few minutes I'll feel the little movements of his dreams, which don't seem to be tormenting him the way others have.

They can't possibly be tormenting him the way my thoughts are torturing me. So I get up quietly, careful not to rouse him, and slip on some clothes. In the kitchen I fumble through the cabinets to find some tea and a mug to fill with hot water.

When there's a break in the storm's rumbling, I hear voices. Indistinct but then stronger, like an argument's being had. I still and strain to hear more. I recognize Martine's voice but have to venture closer to make out what she's saying.

I go toward the back of the house. An angle of lamplight cuts across the hallway from Martine's office.

"This woman is a treasure for our cause. She's only begun to open up to us about the structure behind their operation. She's got more to share, and we can use all of it to our advantage. Every morsel. Even if I can't earn Tristan's trust, I don't need to. She's a walking bible of history on him too."

"To what end? This is my question to you."

I freeze and flatten my body against the wall at the sound of the man's voice.

"To further the cause! Gabriel, this is what I've been telling you."

"This cause is no longer mine. Isabel's lost everything, and this is why. Your and Lucia's incessant meddling. You've fed her thirst for vengeance all these years, and we'll never have justice."

"You can still have it! Kristopher is sitting in the inner circle of this group."

"Which only strengthens his position."

"We've been striking at them with our fists when they've had an arsenal. McKenna is the key. What she knows gives us the power to match their strength. To build a counter-effort that will reduce them to rubble."

"You cannot fight men without hearts and expect to win this way. They will destroy you. I'm sorry, but he's taken enough from me. I won't let them destroy my family."

"Then retreat back to your village and play God," she snaps.

A few seconds go by, and I wonder if they've finished. I'm terrified at being caught eavesdropping, but I can't bring myself to move. The woman behind the door sounds like a version of Martine that she'll never show her followers.

"Martine, I have stood by you all these years. Our intentions were honest and true. But I fear this isn't about casting light in dark corners anymore. I have every reason to make it personal, but I am humble enough to know when I've been bested. You've hardly paused to consider what this has meant for Isabel. What could have happened had she not been saved by this man from her past?"

"She follows him around like a lovesick child, and she's likely never been happier. Lucia's smothered her her whole life. She may be dead on paper, but now she's finally living. She'll grow with Halo if he gives her the chance."

"The only things growing here are Halo's bank accounts and your ego, and I'll have no part of it," he shouts. Then, his voice lower, "And I'll let the devil take me before I let you lead my granddaughter any further into this plan of yours."

Tears burn behind my eyes. Soundlessly I retreat back to the kitchen and head to the hallway. I catch a dart of movement in the corner of my eye. I suck in a breath but manage to quell a frightened shriek. My heart beats wildly in my chest even though I feel frozen in my spot again.

The shadow moves again, several feet away, until it changes under a sliver of moonlight. I release a dizzying breath and then another, my terror seeping away in small measures.

Zeda's sharp profile comes into view. She lifts her finger to her lips.

When the door to Martine's office slams, I turn away and rush back to the bedroom.

I close the door with a click and try to slip beside Tristan unnoticed.

He turns his body to me when my full weight hits the mattress. "You okay?"

"I'm fine," I say lightly.

He hums and tugs me closer, catching me against his chest with a sigh. Soon his sleepy softness hardens. "You're shaking. Isabel, what's wrong?"

"Nothing. I'm just... I had a bad dream."

He lifts onto his elbow and looks down at me. He touches my

face, draws his hand down the column of my neck and finally over my racing heart.

"Why are you lying to me?"

I bite the inside of my lip, cursing myself. Asking myself the same question.

I shake my head, because I don't know why. "I'm scared."

"What happened?"

I haven't had a minute to process what I heard. I don't know how Tristan will react when I tell him…or if I should.

"Can we just talk about it in the morning?" I ask, hoping to buy more time.

"No, we can talk about it now because the longer you don't tell me, the more I'm going to worry."

I draw in a deep breath, trying to calm my nerves. "I couldn't sleep, so I went to the kitchen to get some tea, and I overheard Martine in her office. My grandfather was in there with her. They were arguing."

"About what?"

"About me. About Jay. My grandfather doesn't want anything to do with Halo's work anymore because of what happened to me. And she's… I don't know, Tristan."

Martine sounded like a woman possessed by her mission, blindly driven to it despite the threats of danger she promised earlier to heed. But is she so wrong to want to take the Company down? Is anyone more capable of destroying them? Is Tristan, alone but selfishly driven by his need to protect the two of us, more able?

"What about Martine? What did she say?" he presses.

"She's obsessed with learning everything Jay knows. She thinks she's the key to destroying the Company."

"We already know that."

"I know, but…she was different. Like she wasn't going to let anything get in her way. I've never heard her so single-minded. She was talking to my grandfather like he was worthless."

Like I meant nothing. *A lovesick child…*

I wince, remembering her cold words, and avert my eyes from

Tristan's intent stare. *If she had any idea what we've been through, what we've endured.*

"Did they see you?"

"No, I snuck away before they finished. But someone saw me leave."

"Who?"

"Zeda."

TRISTAN

Sleep is impossible. If Isabel achieves any, she's lying again.

Why was her first instinct to lie? Was the fear of getting caught by them unthinkingly transferred to me in the heat of the moment? No. She was holding something back. The longer I lie awake, the more convinced I am of it. Though for the life of me, I can't understand why. Despite my hesitations, she's always ready to give our host the benefit of the doubt. How could overhearing one exchange leave her so shaken unless there's more she's not telling me?

As dawn starts to spill light into the room, I rise and get dressed.

Isabel sits up with the sheet drawn over her chest. Her eyes are tired, her expression wary. "Where are you going? It's still early."

"Not sure. Maybe for a run."

She traps her bottom lip between her teeth. "Do you want to talk?"

I swing my gaze to her. "Do you?"

She doesn't answer, and her early evasion stabs at me a little more. "I'll be back after breakfast."

I pass through the empty kitchen and leave the house as quickly and quietly as I can.

"Tristan?"

On the porch, the sound of my name stops me in my tracks. I turn, and a man with silvering hair straightens off one of the rocking chairs. He's dressed in dark slacks and a starched white button-down that contrasts with his dark features.

"You must be Gabriel."

He smiles kindly and extends his hand. "Gabriel Martinez," he says, his accent rolling over the name.

I take it in a firm shake. "Tristan Red."

"I'm glad to finally shake your hand. My thanks to you are overdue. You saved Isabel's life."

I struggle with his statement. The truth is I simply chose not to end it. Thankfully I was chosen over anyone else who wouldn't have had a reason to hesitate. "Thank fate, I guess."

"Or perhaps God himself."

I shrug. "If you believe in that sort of thing."

"I do," he says with surety. He looks out to the street. "Would you like to walk with me?"

"Sure."

Together we descend the painted wooden steps, down the path toward the street. An odd sense of relief washes over me when the heavy metal gate clanks shut behind us. One glance over my shoulder, and I catch the movement of curtains in the front bedroom. Isabel watching us leave, which lodges fresh worry in my gut.

We take a left and head east. The skies have cleared, but the night's storm hangs like an invisible fog, clinging to my skin and thickening the air.

I'd love to ask him about his late-night meeting with Martine, but I don't know him and don't wish to upset the pretend harmony Martine likes to cultivate in the house. At least not until I get what I want from Jay.

"So, what brings you to Halo?" I finally ask.

He hums softly. "That's a complicated question." We walk a few more minutes in silence. "Lucia says you're in love with Isabel. Is that true?"

I laugh awkwardly. Way to ease into it.

He smiles. "Is that too personal?"

I tuck my hands into my pockets and hope he continues without acknowledgment of what he must already know to be true.

"I ask because I need to know that she's going to be taken care of. I can stay close for a little while, but home will call me back soon."

"Where's home?"

"La Mina. It's a village in Honduras, close to where Lucia was raised before we emigrated to the United States. I trained in medicine at the university in Tegucigalpa, and of course that's how I found a position with Chalys many years ago. A brief detour from my greater purpose."

"What's that?"

"I'm a doctor, an occupation that requires training and education. But at the heart of things, I'm a healer. There are no certificates or diplomas for that kind of work. For a brief time, I believed my position at Chalys would truly help me serve others. Cure illnesses, ease people's suffering, give hope. It felt like I'd found my calling." He shakes his head. "It wasn't like that. I do much better work in La Mina."

He winks, but I can sense his discomfort under the jovial tone. Mariana's death hides in his shadowed eyes. The lines of age and worry in his face.

He glances down at his shoes as they clip along the sidewalk. Polished tan leather. "The people you worked for, they're monsters. To bring Boswell into their ranks, they have to be."

"I have no doubt."

"Isabel must be protected."

"That's my purpose if I've ever had one."

He slows. We stop walking and face one another.

He regards me quietly. "I feel that must be true. There can be no other explanation for how you've been reintroduced into her life this way."

It was a matter of chance. An auspicious twist of circumstances as Jay already explained. But as Gabriel speaks, something inside me tries to believe that coming to Isabel's apartment that night was more than chance. That it was destined. An offering from some unknown force, that if accepted, gave her life and me a soul. At least a chance at one. But there's still more work to be done. More blood to shed...

I tense a little. "Part of keeping her safe requires neutralizing the threat. You realize that, right?"

He taps his foot absently. "I'm not a stranger to violence, though I prefer to avoid it. When it comes to Isabel, though, I want her nowhere near it."

"I'm with you on that."

"Then you must take her someplace safe, Tristan. Take her away from Halo. Martine…" He shakes his head, his face wrinkling into a pained grimace. "She'll only use her the way she's used Lucia. She is my daughter, but I can't sway her. Her need to avenge Mariana fuels a hatred no amount of justice could possibly extinguish. But Isabel is innocent. She has hope."

"I have no intention of staying at Halo. The situation is temporary. We'll be out as soon as I can lock down a new place."

His pained expression doesn't ease. "I'm torn."

I frown.

He begins walking again, back toward the house. I follow, waiting for him to elaborate.

"Martine's likely talked of her reach. Her prowess and power. Never mind her mission."

"She has."

"She doesn't exaggerate." He lifts a finger. "Except when it comes to the mission. I fear that her motivations are primarily selfish these days. Time has changed her values. But Halo *is* very well connected. The information we've collected over the years holds even more value than the wealth she's accumulated through sometimes questionable means."

"What are you trying to say?"

"Martine can fight this war for you. She could even win."

"So you're suggesting that Isabel and I lie low while she tries?"

He slows again, stops, and looks ahead at the mansion set off the street several yards down the block. "The father in me…and the grandfather in me…wants to believe that's the answer."

"But?"

He presses his lips into a thin line. "Only time will tell." He withdraws a piece of paper from his pocket and hands it to me. "This is my number while I'm here in the States. Lucia says she can no longer reach Isabel through her phone. I hope you'll trust me to keep me informed of her general whereabouts once you leave Halo. I care for her deeply, and I'm here to help in any way I can."

I accept it and consider his words and the unselfish way in which he speaks about Isabel. I nod and extend my hand to his, grasping it in another handshake, one of unspoken commitment.

"I'll be in touch."

10

ISABEL

Restless, I scroll through apartment listings on my phone while I wait for Tristan to return. What could he be discussing with my grandfather? My thoughts spin endlessly while my omissions from the conversation I overheard last night sit like a rock in my stomach.

Why did I lie to him when I've done nothing but campaign for his honesty?

Maybe because there was something I could relate to in Martine's passion to take down the Company, even if she was almost unrecognizable in her expression of it. Even if she said things that struck at my heart when I wasn't meant to hear them.

Her unapologetic desire to fight and win still resonates, even though I'm admittedly outmatched. I don't want to hide and play it safe. Yet without someone like Martine or Tristan driving the mission and using all the things they know, how can it be possible?

I toss my phone aside and get cleaned up. As I dress, I check the clock, expecting to hear the usual morning breakfast ruckus begin any time. The growling in my stomach persists as I wait for the first hints of

Martine's signature cooking smells, but the house is oddly quiet.

I venture out, but there's no one. Suddenly I hear feet rushing down the stairs. Skye appears, her bright eyes round with concern.

"What's wrong?"

"Have you seen Jay?"

I still. "Not since last night. Why?"

She goes into the sitting room and circles back without making eye contact, heading straight for Martine's office in the back. The front door opens, and I turn to see Tristan returning. He's alone, which means my grandfather likely left after their walk. I'm eager to ask Tristan what they discussed and if he learned any more.

He frowns. "Everything okay?"

I shake my head. "I don't know."

"What do you mean? Where is everyone?"

Just then Skye returns. "She's gone."

"Who's gone?" Tristan asks.

"Martine. Jay too."

An eerie silence falls between us. Though Tristan's flinty expression barely changes, I can feel him go inward and his energy turn cool. He's becoming someone else. Someone I'm afraid to know. Someone I'm not sure I can ever change when this side of him shows up. If he's waded through ten thousand thoughts, I'm certain he's now boiled them all down to one. A pure and fearsome malice toward Martine.

Skye seems to feel it too as she looks to me with more questions than answers in her eyes. Only then do I notice the letter in her hand. She follows my gaze and lifts it.

"This was tacked to Martine's office door."

I take it and rip open the envelope. It's a handwritten letter. I read it aloud.

Friends,

After careful consideration, I have decided it is in the best interests of our newest guest to house her elsewhere. Rest assured, she will be safe. I will return once the matter is settled.

Give light,

Martine Benoit

Tristan rips the letter from my grasp and reads it over before crumpling it in his hand.

I'm in disbelief. Martine took her right from under us. Did Jay go willingly?

"What do we do?" I say.

Skye points to the letter. "If Martine said—"

"We find her." Tristan's voice is steady, void of emotion, uttering the course as if it's law. He tosses the balled-up letter onto the counter and glances between us. "That's what we do. We find her."

THE RED LEDGER

part 5

1

ISABEL

New Orleans

Creamy white blossoms curl up from their leafy nests in the magnolia tree shading the stone courtyard. Those unexpected sprigs of elegance decorate the thick, gnarly branches like lotus flowers unfurled from the mud. Detached and beautiful, almost separate from their ugly roots.

In these quiet moments alone, I try to derive some wisdom from my surroundings when everything else has descended into turmoil and confusion. Our rootless, winding journey. This house and its absent host. Our search for answers, now terminally linked to Jude McKenna, whereabouts unknown.

Tristan's been pacing and plotting for hours. Meanwhile, I've disappeared into the quiet of the garden. What I can't tell him is that I'd rather commit myself to almost any other mission than join a search party for Jay, which has been his single-minded focus since she disappeared this morning.

The back door squeaks open and slams shut. Tristan emerges. The full force of his energy seems to radiate off his muscled form, extending his presence. His features are rigid—intimidating and fascinating at once. The strong set of his jaw. The aquiline ridge of his nose. His silvery-blue eyes grow darker under the shady magnolia, and his mood is indisputably distressed.

Before he can reach my spot at the wrought-iron table, I'm prickling with trepidation. Anticipation of our next step. Halo was a haven for me once, but now it's the epicenter of my uncertainty.

Tristan takes the seat beside me and rests his forearms over the ornate tabletop. "Are you hiding out here?"

"Maybe."

"What's on your mind?"

I laugh a little. "I may be as conflicted over Jay as you are."

His dark brows wrinkle. "This doesn't have to do with how I feel about her. This has to do with everything she knows. Things no one else knows. We have to find her."

I hold his gaze, remembering how Martine counted Jay's knowledge of Tristan's history among her assets. Nothing about the heated encounter I overheard with my grandfather last night sits well with me, but those words strike me now as particularly unsettling. Why would Tristan's past as a killer be valuable to Martine? Maybe she doesn't separate the transgressions of the Company from his, even though he's broken away.

I can't possibly know her true motivations, but I do know I'm still at war over Jay's role in all of this. She's not a victim, but Tristan insists she needs saving. He's already saved her once. Of course, the alternative would have been to leave her for dead or days more of abuse from Crow and his men. I wouldn't wish that fate on anyone—friend or foe. But the way he's committed to finding her now weighs on me in an unsettling way.

Finally I lob the question that's been roiling inside me for too long.

"How *do* you feel about her?"

His frown deepens. "Isabel… Don't do this."

"You saved her life. You were holding her hand just last night. You claim to hate her, yet it feels like you've grown closer. You're connecting with her in ways you never did before. Tell me that's not true."

"What do you want me to do?" He renders the question so softly, so calmly, as if the fate of the situation is somehow up to me.

I look up at the blossoms again. Anything to distract me from these fickle thoughts. My jealousy shouldn't change our course. I'm not sure what I want. Acknowledgment of something I wish weren't true? We have enough adversity coming at us without this line of thinking.

The door opens again. Zeda and Skye pass through and walk toward us.

Tristan stands. "Where have you been?"

"Out," Zeda replies curtly.

Skye's eyes are wide, her posture tense. "I found something."

"What is it?" I ask.

"Blood in the room Jay was staying in. A smear on the sink and a few drops on the floor. Barely anything. I missed it when I was looking for her in a rush this morning."

I don't miss the sudden tightness in Tristan's jaw or his cold stare between the two women.

Zeda doesn't seem to care. She lowers into the seat beside me, her tall figure folding into it with carefree grace. "I don't think Martine took her by force, if that's what you're thinking," she says. "I saw them leave a couple hours after Martine and Gabriel were arguing in the office last night. I hung back for a while after he stormed out. Martine was between her office and her bedroom for a while after. Then she went upstairs. About twenty minutes later, she and Jay left together. Right out the back door." She points toward the metal gate covered in vines at the end of the courtyard.

I shake my head. "Why would there be blood if she left without a fight?"

"We should sweep the house," Tristan says. "Every room."

Skye stiffens again. "Martine will be back soon. I'm sure there's a reasonable explanation for all this. She's never gone for more than a few days at a time."

"Which is exactly why we should search the house now," he snaps back.

Zeda sighs loudly. "Listen, we could be blowing all this out of proportion a little bit. We don't know what happened. Martine probably had a good reason to get Jay out of the house."

Tristan opens his mouth to speak, but Zeda cuts him off.

"We should let the dust settle for a while. We could probably all use a little time to decompress and think it over before we jump to conclusions. I was thinking about hitting up that festival over on Freret later. Anyone want to come?"

She shoots a look to Tristan that only lasts a second. Skye misses it. I don't.

Skye's expression brightens a little, her relief evident. "I think Zeda's right. We shouldn't be rash. And I'm in."

Tristan manages a small smile. "Fine. You're probably right. Let's give it twenty-four hours."

Something about the easy way he relents tells me he's not even close to actually giving up. When we're back in the room, I press him on it.

"It seems like you and Zeda are up to something."

He sits on the edge of the bed. "I need to get the watchdog out of the house so I can look around."

"Whether Skye is here or not, Martine's office is locked."

He shoots me a bored look, and I almost laugh. He doesn't let much come in the way of what he wants.

"Okay, what do you expect to find? I doubt she left a map."

"I'm not sure yet. But can we both agree Martine shouldn't be trusted?"

I pause. "After what I heard last night, I don't trust that she's entirely the person she portrays herself to be."

"Your grandfather doesn't think so either."

My growing doubts about Martine's intentions take root a little more. "What did you talk about? I saw you walk away with him this morning."

"He thinks Martine's ego is out of control. He wants you far away from all of this in case she decides to drag you further into it the way she did with Boswell. I think he's telling the truth. I believe he cares about you and wants the best for you."

"He's my grandfather. Of course he does."

Even as I say it, I think about my own parents' betrayal. Actions they took with my best interests in mind, supposedly. I shake those thoughts, because what's done is done. I can't dwell on it for long. "Skye and Zeda will only be gone a few hours. Will that be enough time?"

"Should be. You're going with them."

I still. "Why?"

His expression softens. "Because it'll be good for you to get out of the house. Do something normal."

I laugh. "Normal?"

"You had fun when you all went out before. It was the happiest I've ever seen you."

I walk over to him, take the space between his thighs. "Being with you makes me happy."

"It's also fucking with your head right now." He rests his hand on my hip and holds my gaze.

He might be right, but I'm still wary about leaving him alone when it feels like we're in the middle of a crisis—one I'm eager to escape. I don't know how else we'll get Skye out of the house for any extended period of time otherwise, though.

"Are you sure?"

"I'm sure. Stay on guard and stay together, obviously. But you should get out and get to know the city, especially if we're going to be staying here."

"Okay," I say tentatively.

"Don't worry about Jay, okay? Let this be my problem." He touches my cheek, traces my lower lip. "You're all I care about. Everything comes back to you."

TRISTAN

I don't enjoy seeing her walk away from me, sandwiched between her disillusioned friend and Zeda, the woman I'm putting more stock in lately. But I tell myself this is the right thing. I can't think straight when she's drilling me about Jay—supportive of the humanity I show her one minute and questioning my attachment to her the next. I can't overthink it. There's simply no time. Not when Martine's got this much of a head start.

Every hour that passes is valuable time lost. If I have to tear this house apart to get some answers, I will. I can't do that with Skye anywhere near. Unfortunately it'll take more than a missing sister of the house to shake her loyalty to Martine.

I let some time pass before I head back to Martine's office. The door is locked, but I manage to release both the doorknob and the deadbolt with some deft movements of a couple of paperclips I found in a junk drawer in the kitchen.

The inside of the room is just as I remember it. Darker and less feminine than I would have expected, since her overall look is loud and consistently feminine. Then again, Martine isn't who she claims to be. Of this, I'm certain.

I sit behind her desk and tap the keyboard, waking up the display. The computer is locked, which is fine. I pick the nearby cabinet, which reveals a monitor showing cameras strategically placed around the house. The upstairs and downstairs hallways, sitting room, and kitchen. I'm relieved to not see the bedrooms. God knows there's already enough elicit video of Isabel in Martine's possession after the Boswell ordeal.

I open the attached laptop and navigate back to the wee hours of the night until I catch movement through the kitchen. It's too dark to identify the shape of the person. I rewind the video a little further and pause it on Jay's figure walking down the stairs alone. A little further back shows Martine entering her room and leaving a short time later. Jay would have been alone for the moments before she left through the back door, Martine by her side.

Zeda's story checks out. Nothing seems amiss. No pauses. No struggles. Just a quiet march from Jay's room to the back door after a quick visit from Martine. She must have said something to get Jay to leave so suddenly. Was it a threat? Misinformation?

I navigate around the surveillance software a little more, disappointed there's no audio attached to the visuals picked up by the camera. I glance around Martine's office, knowing there's bound to be something of value hiding in her filing cabinets. I open the closest one to find mostly administrative paperwork. Bills and invoices. Another contains dozens of files associated with properties. Deeds and plots and purchase agreements. Some go back a decade or more, all now in the name of Halo Ministries. There's no sign of tax forms.

I shake my head with a silent laugh. Unbelievable. For however long Martine's been driving the Halo mission, I'd be willing to bet she's been doing it tax free. How much is Halo sitting on?

I pull another drawer but find it locked. I fiddle with the lock impatiently until it springs open, revealing its contents. A handful of folders hang in the otherwise empty drawer. The first one contains statements from a local bank. A checking account and a savings account. The former serves as the general Halo operating account, judging by the nature of the transactions and small amounts listed on the paperwork. Between the two, there's just over five million dollars combined.

The amount doesn't faze me. There has to be more. Martine's hands are in too many pots.

The next folders confirm it. Four other accounts spread across different institutions, including an offshore account, each totaling eight figures or more. The only activity on the accounts are a dozen or so monthly deposits in the tens of thousands and a couple of outgoing wire transfers for far less.

Halo is sitting on piles of cash and who knows how much more in real estate. And all of it is completely under the radar. Why would a supposedly charitable organization hold on to that much liquidity? The women in the house have every need met, but with the amount of money Martine's working with, she should be helping more people, and they should all be driving around in Bentleys. She's stockpiling. But for what?

I hit the brakes on my racing thoughts because they're leading me down a road I don't have time to travel right now. The only asset I should be worried about is Jay, who Martine's got in her clutches. It could take hours to piece this paperwork together and get a clearer picture of her game, but even then, who knows if anything will point to where she's keeping Jay.

After putting things back the way I found them, I abandon the office and head upstairs to the room where Jay was staying. It's bare beyond some stacks of clothes with tags set atop a bureau. Whatever Skye bought for Jay didn't go with her, or at least not much of it. The polished pine floors that are as old as the house lead into a bathroom. Brick-colored ceramic tile covers the floor and continues seamlessly into the shower.

I immediately notice the smear of blood on the white sink. I crouch lower and study the floor to find several perfectly round red droplets sprinkled around a two-foot radius, almost camouflaged on the flooring. What the hell was Jay doing?

Everything else is bare and clean. I rise to my feet, ready to abandon the investigation of Jay's room, when something catches my eye. A tiny black dot at the bottom of the toilet bowl, barely noticeable. I bend, submerge my hand in the water, and retrieve it. I roll it between my thumb and forefinger. I've never seen one exactly like this, but I know enough to recognize it's a micro tracking chip. This one is no larger than a pill capsule, except flatter, easily hidden under the flesh.

And I'm willing to bet the contents of Halo's Swiss bank account that it's been inside Jay until she cut it out this morning. She probably tried flushing it, but it never carried through the drain pipe. What's even more concerning is the tiny switch on one side, just big enough to move with my thumbnail. But I'm not sure if this thing is still pinging, and I don't want to be the one to set it off.

Either way, I've found one more good reason to get Isabel as far away from Halo as possible.

2

ISABEL

Freret Street is as lively during the day as Frenchmen was at night. It's another reminder of the way people come together in New Orleans— loudly, enthusiastically, and with a seemingly single-minded desire to satisfy the senses.

Jazz music blares from a concert stage nearby as Skye hooks her arm with mine. Zeda leads our way into the festival. Colorful banners stretch from one side of the street to the other. Hundreds of people flow around food stands offering local fare, all emitting aromas that are hard to ignore. Spices and various concoctions, a banquet of savory and sugary richness. If I wasn't hungry before, I am now.

"All this smells amazing," I say, unmistakable awe in my voice.

"Here. Try these." Skye pauses at a vendor manned by a gentleman with dreadlocks past his waist and a broad smile that almost distracts me from my most troubling thoughts. Thoughts we came here to escape from, at least for a few hours.

"How many you want?" he asks.

"Half a dozen." She hands over a few bills. "These are pralines.

They're super sweet," she says as we continue meandering through the crowd.

"Where's Zeda?"

Skye squints and looks ahead. "She's probably headed toward Cure to grab us a table. They have awesome drinks. We usually hang out there when we come here, but it'll be mobbed because of the festival."

"Okay." I temper my little flare of panic and take a bite of the little round dessert. I'm greeted with a textured explosion of sugar and pecan. "Holy shit, they *are* sweet." And unlike anything I've ever tasted.

She laughs and pops one in her mouth. "Good though, right?"

We stop at a few more stands before heading to the bar. We're nearly to the door when my skin prickles. I stop a few feet from the entrance and scan the crowd behind us. All walks of life fill the street, but no one is catching my eye as out of place. I exhale a sigh, trying to shake the odd feeling that's crept over me.

"You okay?" Skye asks.

I glance around again and shake my head slightly. "I'm fine. I think I'm just jumpy from not getting great sleep last night. Let's go in."

I'm relieved to spot Zeda at the back of the bar, precisely where Skye figured she would be. Tristan told me to be on guard, but I'm obviously letting my nerves and fatigue get the best of me.

She's already ordered some small bites and has a colorful cocktail in front of her. I check the time on my phone. We have some time to kill for Tristan to do what he needs, so when Skye asks me if I want a drink, I agree.

While Skye's at the bar, Zeda's gaze locks with mine. We share a quiet understanding.

"What do you think of all this stuff with Jay?" I ask.

She glances to Skye briefly and back to me. "I'm not sure. But I think we're close to finding out."

I think she's probably right. Tristan's thorough, and if there's dirt to be found on Martine, he's the one to unearth it.

"Are you from here?" I ask, figuring we should change the subject before our friend returns, lest she suspect anything about Tristan's time at the house.

Zeda nods. "Ninth Ward."

"Do you miss it?"

She laughs, and I think it's the first time I've seen her smile. She's strikingly beautiful, but she's so serious much of the time that I haven't been able to get a read on her. I get the feeling friendships don't come easy for her. Apparently Tristan has made more progress than I have.

"No," she says. "It's still a mess down there. Every boarded-up house is a reminder of what happened." She swirls her drink quietly. "Sometimes we lose things…things we'll never recover. All you can do is move on. Try not to look back too much."

"I know how you feel," I say softly.

She narrows her gaze. "Do you?"

I hold her stare, meeting her challenge with all the empathy I possess. "I do." I know the pain in my heart may not be the same as hers. I don't know what horrors she's endured. I only know my own. No doubt about it, though, we've both seen things we wish we hadn't.

Her expression relaxes a fraction before Skye returns with drinks and the brand of energy we probably all need.

"Cheers, ladies!"

I can't help but laugh. "What on earth would we be toasting to?"

She cocks her head and quirks her lips into a coy smile. "How about to homecoming? Forget all this crap with Jay. I'm just glad you're back home."

I return a half smile and raise my glass. Because my hopes for making New Orleans our home are riding a dangerous edge now. Anything could tip the scales and drive us out.

"To homecoming," I say, pretending it's not an empty celebration.

We kill a couple more rounds, until Zeda is smiling more and the problems we left at Halo seem far away. A male server comes by with another round…one we didn't order.

"These are on the house, ladies."

Skye jerks back. "Oh?"

The odd prickling I felt earlier returns and has my heart beating a little faster. Or is it the drinks?

He sets the round of cocktails in front of us and briefly points back to the crowded bar. "You've got an admirer at the bar. His treat. Enjoy." He gives us a cute salute and retreats.

Then I spot a man whose focus is trained directly on me. His eyes are serious, then crinkle at the edges when he smiles. He looks to be at least ten years our senior, his thick, muscled arms covered in tattoos.

"That must be him," Skye says.

"Not bad." Zeda trades her empty drink for the fresh one.

Skye crinkles her nose and turns away from him. "No thanks."

I laugh. "I'm going to hit the ladies' room. I'll be right back."

I push up and find the restrooms in the back. When I'm finished freshening up, I bring up Tristan's number to see if the coast is clear for us to return, but the reception inside is poor, so I step out the back entrance. Before I can connect the call, I hear a man's voice.

"Hey."

I look up. It's the man from the bar. Except up close, he's enormous. Over six feet tall, with bulging muscles that are testing the integrity of his white T-shirt. He's wearing green camouflage cargo pants and black boots. A quick circuit back to his face, and I recognize his military hairstyle too—a look I'm plenty familiar with having grown up near DC.

"Hi," I say, tucking my phone away.

"Did you like the drink?"

I laugh nervously. "I think I've hit my limit, actually. But thanks."

"What's your name?"

My lips part, but I can't quite manage a response. If he's some random guy, it shouldn't matter if I answer with Isabel or any other from the fake IDs I've accumulated. I just need to let him down gently and get back to the girls.

But the way he's boring into me with his stare makes me think it doesn't matter what I say.

He smiles and tilts his head. "Isabel?"

The *whoosh* of blood thrumming through my veins suddenly fills my ears. My throat threatens to close, and I take a stumbling step back.

He shakes his head. "Don't do that."

"Listen, I've got to get back to my friends."

His expression flattens. "Nah. I want to introduce you to mine first."

He consumes the space between us with one huge step. The hum of the air conditioners blowing out the back of the restaurant and his giant hand muffles the scream that tries to tear free. Except he's not just covering my mouth. I can't breathe through my nose when it's crushed under his palm. I tear my fingernails into his T-shirt and any skin I can reach, but he doesn't seem to care. I kick and try to aim for his groin, but he blocks me, flattening me painfully against the wall. I'm helpless against his massive strength. The more I fight him off, the more futile it seems. Tears form in my eyes when I slowly realize no one's going to rescue me. Then the edges of my vision start to go black until the hate in his eyes is the last thing I see.

TRISTAN

I put the chip in my pocket and head downstairs to poke around Martine's office one last time. The gate buzzer sounds, echoing harshly through the entryway. I pause a second before going to the box and pressing the speaker button.

"Who is it?"

There's a pause and some static before a voice comes through.

"I'm looking for a friend. I was hoping you could help me out." The man's British accent is unmistakable.

Fuck me. If it's Townsend, things have gone from concerning to far worse. Because if he's shown up to collect Jay, I've got nothing to give him. And if he knows where we are, I have to wonder who else does.

I don't bother answering or checking through the front windows to make sure it's him. I head right to the bedroom and grab my bag and Isabel's backpack that I know holds her most important things. The rest can be replaced.

The intercom makes some static again. "Red, if it's you, I just want to talk to her, all right? I know she's here."

It's Townsend, all right. If he weren't a trained killer, I might buy the concern in his tone. Chances are high he's itching for a chance to put a bullet in my brain, though.

I go down the hallway to the back door, pausing to check the courtyard through the window. I don't see anyone but have my gun drawn just in case. If he's as close as Jay seems to think they are, it's likely he would have come alone. If he's working with the Company, there's not a chance. I open the door slowly and take another scan to ensure the coast is clear before I step out.

A barely audible *whir* ends with a painful stab just below my collarbone. I curse and slip back into the house, putting the door between me and whoever took a shot at me. Except this doesn't feel right. I bring my hand to the pain, expecting gushing blood and loose flesh, the typical remnants of a bullet wound.

Except it's not a bullet. Not the kind I'm overly familiar with, anyway. I withdraw the dart, its sharp metal tip tinged red. Its contents are empty, already in my bloodstream. Whatever was in it is either meant to kill me or put me to sleep. And I can't do a fucking thing about it now.

Think think think.

I don't have much time. The buzzer goes off again. Townsend. He's not alone. I have no idea how many there are. Maybe more than I can likely fight off this way. Takes a lot to get my adrenaline going, but a gunshot will usually do it. But my next steps seem too slow. I blink a few times. The hallway is already starting to blur. I fumble for my phone and bring up Isabel's number. I try to tap on the keys to tell her to stay away, but they're mixed up. I can't even tell if they're letters or numbers.

I retreat farther into the house. My eyes drift closed for a second. I stumble forward but manage to keep my hand around the gun. They'll be coming. I just need to keep my eyes open long enough to get a shot off.

Isabel.

I won't let them get to her. The thought of her brings me the surge I need to get to the sitting room. I park on a chair in the corner with a clear view of anyone who'll be coming for me. But by the time I hear doors opening and steps, my vision's unreliable.

Something dark passes in front of me, a blur toward the front door. I tighten my grip on the gun, barely. Muscles are weak. Brain's not firing orders the way it should. *Stay awake...*

"Find her." Townsend's voice, angry and accented.

The rush of boots up the stairs and above me.

Isabel.

I remind myself that she's gone. Safe. I have time before she comes back. Time to fix this.

I blink when a man is suddenly standing right in front of me. Two of them. I blink again to be sure. Yes, it's two. I remember the gun. Stare down at it and my unmoving hand, a delayed conversation between my sluggish brain and the instincts that normally come so easily. *Shoot them. Shoot to kill.*

I lift it, but it's ripped out of my grasp before my finger can move the trigger.

"Don't think you'll be needing that, Red," he says with a nasty grimace.

"Townsend."

"How'd you guess?"

"Jay," I murmur.

His shadow, the man behind him with long black hair and black clothes, moves too quickly for me to process. Rope around my arms, binding me to the arms of the chair. Legs too. I can't muster any panic, only lazy acceptance.

I meet Townsend's impatient stare when he pulls up a chair and sits down in front of me.

"What about Jay?"

"She mentioned you." I shake my head, but it only makes everything swim. "The fuck did you give me?"

"Heavy tranquilizer. Figured it was best to leave nothing to chance."

"Not really fair."

He smiles. "Nah, but I don't play fair, mate. Those rules are made for other people. Now that you're comfortable, let's get to the talking part before you pass out on me." He looks at my gun, rolls it around in his grasp almost admiringly, and then raises his eyes back to me. "Where's Jay?"

Through the fog, I recognize that *I don't know* isn't an acceptable answer, and one that's likely to get me shot in the leg. I'd likely do the same if our roles were reversed.

"Someone took her," I say, somehow coherent enough to not drop names unnecessarily. He doesn't need to know about Martine. Not yet.

He lifts an eyebrow. "She was here though?"

I nod. "Left in the middle of the night. I looked everywhere."

He shares a look with his dark-haired friend, who corroborates my account. "All the rooms are clear. No sign of her."

Townsend frowns and looks back to me. "You brought her here?"

I nod again. "To keep her safe."

He grimaces slightly. "See, I don't know if that's really true, because she turned on her tracker. And our agreement was that she'd only ever do that if she was in danger. Real fuckin' danger that only someone like me could get her out of. So now I'm here, and she's fuckin' gone." He tenses his jaw, the muscles there bulging noticeably. "Is she dead?"

I shake my head wordlessly. Martine won't hurt her. Not until she gets what she wants, anyway.

He stands abruptly and kicks the chair so it slides back a foot. Points the gun at me.

I close my eyes, feeling the fatigue take a firm hold. Need to stay awake. Need to get to Isabel. But before I can open them, something hard and cold crashes down on me, turning everything black.

3

ISABEL

Mold permeates the air so strongly I can feel it poisoning my lungs. All I can see are two walls. Some boarded-up windows. The blackened floorboards I'm lying on and the rickety wooden chair in the corner where the man who smothered me sits. His attention is fixed on his phone, which he's holding sideways, both thumbs in action against the screen's surface.

Panic surges as I become more awake. I try to even out my breathing, which is nearly impossible with the rag in my mouth. My brain tries to identify the taste. Like the gamey scent of a person mixed with something…chemical. Altogether it's unpleasant enough that I'm struggling not to gag even though it's nearly impossible to draw air in through the cloth that's tethered to my face.

Something about my awakening must draw the man's attention, because he looks up from his phone and comes toward me. His boots fall heavily on the floor, reminding me of his massive size and weight. He yanks on my arm, drawing me into an upright seated position. I use my heels to push myself away from him, but he yanks me harder.

"Stop it!" he barks.

I begin to tremble but for the moment am frozen into temporary submission. How am I supposed to *not* cower near this man who could break me in a heartbeat? The panic I endured when he blocked my air until I passed out resumes full force. Except now I have even fewer options. Wherever I am is far from public. Far from friends and help.

Tears sting my eyes. This is bad. I've finally gotten myself into a mess I can't get out of. I know it…

The man lowers to his haunches. Night has fallen, but even in the semi-darkness of the room, I notice details I missed before. His slick jaw and what must be hundreds of tiny dashes inked on his forearms. He seems to notice my appraisal and grins.

"You like 'em?"

Our eyes meet. That small connection has my heart threatening to fly out of my chest. He looks down, sweeping his giant palm from his forearm to his bicep, pushing the hem of his sleeve up to reveal even more lines. Desperate to avoid his eyes, I focus on something else. His clean, trimmed nails. His polished boots. Despite the filthy room we're both occupying, the only thing that isn't regulation on him are the tattoos he's petting.

"They call me Bones. And this is my little graveyard, see?" His tone is casual, almost proud. "I get to scratch you into my skin here when we're done, Isabel. You want to pick out your spot? It's getting crowded, but we'll find you a place, I promise."

I don't know why I do it. I look up at him again. Gauge the soullessness of his eyes. The glimmer of zealous malice I've never witnessed in another person before now. Vince Boswell has nothing on this man. And what I see scares me more than the physical body before me—a force I have no hope of conquering. He's not just trying to scare me. He's completely serious. He's going to kill me.

When he starts laughing, I lose control and begin to heave. The taste and smell and fear are too much. Can't breathe. His laughing ceases, and his smile turns into an ugly grimace.

"Goddamnit."

I heave harder, unable to hold back. *Please*, I try to say through the impossible muzzle he's put on me. Finally he rushes to untie it and tears the cloth away just in time for my sickness to spill onto the floor. I empty my stomach and feel no relief. Tears roll down my cheeks as I suck in shaky breaths.

Bones jumps to his feet, cussing as he does. "Look at that fucking mess! Look at it!" He points to it angrily like somehow I'm not totally aware of what I've done.

"I'm sorry," I whisper.

"Shut up!"

I close my eyes, pushing more tears free. This is hell, and he's the devil. He marches away, and I hear a door slam closed after him. Then a car door. His return is marked by the unapologetic sound of his boots up the stairs and through the door. He drops a roll of paper towels, a black plastic bag, and a bottle of cleaning solution onto the floor beside me. I nearly launch myself forward into the puddle of vomit when he comes behind me and unties the binds around my wrists.

"Clean it up," he shouts. "Right now."

I reach for the paper towels with trembling hands. "I'm sorry," I say again, because it's all I can think to say.

Then he's on his knee, grabbing my hair hard and tilting my face up to see his. "I said shut up, and I meant it. If I hear you breathe another word, I'm stuffing that rag down your throat, and next time I'll let you drown on your vomit. Do we understand each other?"

My only answer this time is a few ragged breaths. My tears seem to have locked themselves in the corners of my eyes, where they won't offend him. He releases me without another word, and I don't waste a second before I start cleaning up. In the effort, I recognize that the floors are coated with a thick layer of dirt and mold that comes up with every swipe. I don't dwell on it, though. I stuff the towels into the bag, twist it up tightly, and rest back on my heels once I'm done. I don't want to, but I risk a look up at him, hoping for approval.

He's a few paces away, watching my every move with his arms crossed like some diabolical drill sergeant who takes deep pleasure in the discomfort of his recruits. When he walks toward me, I lower my head like a child awaiting the next strike. He yanks me up by my arm, and I swallow the shriek that wants to burst free. With a few swift motions, he binds my hands in front of me with the rope in his pocket and tugs on it to test his work.

He's a Boy Scout for sure, as there's no hope of me getting out of it. Wordlessly he turns and pushes me toward the back of the house until we step into a closed-in porch. The windows are covered with sheets of plywood, and most of the space is filled with garbage and furniture piled up in the corners. He pulls down a dirty mattress and drops it onto the floor.

"You can sleep here."

I eye it warily, unsure what his plan is. He doesn't look at me like he wants anything more than my silence and obedience, and I pray that's the case. I could never fight him off, and he'd likely kill me if I tried.

I meet his eyes again. Stone cold. His jaw is tight as he approaches. Against every instinct, I hold my ground. I will myself not to scream or cry. He grabs my jaw, squeezing tightly. He pulls his gun from the band of his cargo pants and rests the metal tip against my lips.

"Open."

I'm shaking again, to the point where I can't control it. I close my eyes. Pray…

Please, not like this… Not with this animal…

Bones doesn't wait for me to comply. He pulls my jaw down and inserts the muzzle into my mouth until I can taste the metal against my tongue. It takes everything inside me not to scream. Not to beg for my life.

"Look at me."

I blink my eyes open, making him out through the sheen of my tears.

"Make a sound, and you won't need a gag." His voice gets lower. His eyes darken and glimmer at once. "Not a single. Fucking. Sound."

I can scarcely breathe, let alone acknowledge his threat. But I think we both know I heard it.

TRISTAN

A hard slap jolts me into consciousness. Townsend's hands are on his knees as he bends to see me at eye level. I squeeze my eyes closed at the sharp pain in my head, akin to the kind that graces hangovers I try to avoid. What the fuck happened?

"Wakey wakey." Townsend's upbeat tone isn't helping matters.

"What happened?" My voice is raspy as I look around.

"Tranquilizer dart. Remember?"

I try to put together the foggy pieces of what happened. The tracker I found in Jay's room. The dash out the back. It's all blurry after that. Something I'm used to, just not when it comes to my present. "I guess," I finally mutter.

"I've torn the bloody house apart, and I can't find Jay. Her tracker is pinging right here though, so you need to perk up and start talking, mate."

I remember the microchip in my pocket. Not sure I'll tell him, though. I'm too groggy to work on strategy yet. Best to just keep him talking.

"How do I know you're not here to kill her?"

He laughs but tilts his head like he might entertain the question. He sits on the chair in front of me, and I get the feeling we've been here before. An untimely case of *déjà vu*.

"Jay and I have an arrangement."

"Her and her fail-safes." I'd laugh if it wouldn't hurt to, because Jay's layers are well beyond what I would have imagined her capable of.

He nods knowingly. "Yeah, she's always got something up her sleeve. But I'm her last resort. She helps me, and in return, I drop everything and help her should the need arise."

"She helps you? You're an employee."

His eye twitches—almost imperceptible. "Do you have any idea who I am, Red?" He asks like he's waiting for an invitation to tell me his nuanced version of his life story. Too bad I don't care for that side of it.

"British Armed Forces. Ex-spy. Kicked out of the UK, and Russia's not picking up the phone either." I shrug. "Surprised I didn't see you in Rio."

His expression is conspicuously calm. He doesn't like that I know what I know. "That's some of it. You haven't seen me because I work from home mainly."

"If you're lying low, what's Jay got to do with it?"

He glances over to the black bag that's rolled out flat on the couch—a veritable tool kit for torture and…whatever else, I have no idea. There are at least a dozen pockets with shiny metal tools, vials, and a healthy stash of syringes in the end pocket. He follows my gaze.

"That's my bag of tricks. Going to help us with our chat, I think." He pushes his chair to the side, tips it so he leans over the bag. He drags his fingers over a few of the pockets before stopping on one. He pulls out a clear vial and a syringe. Shifting closer to me, he looks through the tiny bottle. "See, I'm not like you, Red. You couldn't pay me enough to run around the world taking the jobs you do. I guess you could say I'm in semi-retirement."

I'm eyeing the vial with as much interest as he's giving it. I'm not overly keen on getting shot up with whatever it is, but I'm encouraged that his last trick didn't kill me. Then more details from his file start filtering into my brain. Suspected association with the death of other spies and certain prominent military figures. Death by nerve agents. Acid attacks. Training in chemical and biological warfare. Healthy fear of what's in the vial pushes me into a sharper state of consciousness.

"So what do you do? If she's got a file on you, that means you work for the Company."

I tense when he uncaps the syringe and begins slowly drawing the liquid into it. "Jay gets me all the materials I need. Things that are hard to get legally. I cook up a good batch of potion here and there. Float some to her friends in the Company. And that's our arrangement."

"She doesn't have friends in the Company anymore."

He lifts his chin a little but doesn't answer. "Let's just get you talking, shall we?"

I could tell him about her indiscretions—all the intel she's already shared with Crow and me—but even in this bind I'm in, I'm not sure revealing that little tidbit is the right call.

"What is that, exactly?"

"We call it SP-131. An oldie but goodie. Russians started mixing it up in the eighties and found it worked like a charm. Still does, so I've been using the same recipe for a while. Loosens the tongue, and it'll feel like a good therapy session by the time we're through."

He lifts his brows with a smile, like this is good news all around.

I'm not sure what's more unsettling. The loosening of the tongue or the not remembering. Losing more memories is a suffocating thought. So much is still out of reach.

"Listen, I'll tell you what you need to know. You don't need to use that shit."

"I need to know where Jay is," he says, flicking the filled syringe barrel. "And if you haven't told me yet, you're not bound to without a little help. I don't fuckin' trust a word that comes out of your mouth anyway. I'm not wasting any more of my time."

His dark-haired friend joins us and hands Townsend a cell phone. "It's for you."

Townsend takes it and traps it between his ear and shoulder while he ties a rubber tourniquet around my bicep. "Bones, have you got the girl?"

I can hear a man's deep voice on the other end, though it's quickly drowned out by the drum of my heart in my ears. He can't have Isabel. No fucking way.

I glance out the window. Pitch black. A rare car passes by on St. Charles. I have no idea what time it is, but the girls would've been back by now. I whip my stare back to Townsend, who's ended the call. He hands the phone back to his partner.

"Who's the girl?" I ask, even though I already know. Even though saying it out loud reveals there's someone important enough to me to mention.

His knowing sneer turns my blood to ice.

"Your girl, mate. You've got my girl, and now I've got yours."

4

ISABEL

I should sleep. Instead I'm lying on the dirty mattress Bones pulled down from the trash heap for me, listening to every sound. The rare clap of screen doors along the street. Voices that are muffled by the walls between us. Sirens that are too far away to give me hope. We're in a neighborhood, but if I start screaming my head off, I'm not sure anyone would immediately hear me or know where to look. Even then, we may not be in the kind of place where calling the authorities for help is frequently done.

I wouldn't dream of making a peep anyway. The low drone of Bones's snoring rumbles through the first floor, a circumstance that offers the smallest measure of relief. That and the merciful absence of rodent activity in the pile of things beside me. I'm guessing the house was long abandoned by its human and any other inhabitants long ago.

I close my eyes and sigh. I should sleep. Get some rest for when I may need energy. The fearless voice in me tells me to stay alert, though, so I can be ready to fight or run at the first opportunity. My eyes have adjusted, but it's too dark on the boarded-up porch to take up a meaningful search for anything useful. A weapon. A way out other than the padlocked back door. I can't risk fumbling around and waking the giant in the other room.

I think of the brief but truly horrifying encounters I've already experienced with him. I've never been more scared in my life. With all I've seen—all the men who've come after Tristan and me with the single goal of killing us—I've never felt fear the way I have with Bones. There's something vacant in the way he looks at me and the way he speaks, like he's reduced things down to very basic principles. I'm certain I could never reason him into sparing my life. In fact, I'm inclined to believe that he genuinely wants to add my death to the tally on his skin.

I close my eyes as a fresh wave of desperation crashes over me. I allow myself a silent sob into the night but keep my tears locked up tight, not wanting to risk even a sniffle. But my God… What if I die here? Snuffed out and forgotten in this place that's been forgotten by everyone else. No, I can't let it end this way.

Obeying Bones may keep me alive, but if things change, I have to be ready to fight back, no matter how dim my chances of survival may be. He's obviously ex-military with zero patience and no semblance of a conscience. The only way to overcome him would be to catch him off guard.

I steel my nerves and search for resolve. As soon as enough light seeps into the room, I'll search for something to keep hidden for when the right time comes. That's what Tristan would do. He's always ready. Always thinking. More calm and collected than I ever gave him credit for.

I swallow over the knot in my throat. Tristan…

Is he looking for me? How could he possibly find me here?

A car door slams loudly, ramping up all my senses. It's close. Closer than the others I've been straining to hear all night. Then the unmistakable sound of footsteps up the front steps. More than one. A man's muffled voice. Someone new. Then clear as a bell as he enters the house.

"Have a seat." The crash of something or someone hitting the floor.

"Make sure he can't move an inch."

"Got it," Bones answers gruffly.

"Where is she?" Tristan's voice.

I jolt upright and come to my knees, ready to bolt toward the heavenly sound.

"I'm the one asking the questions here, Red. Shut up until I'm ready to deal with you."

Hearing Tristan is a shock of relief, followed by the horrifying realization that he's been taken too.

There's a scuffle I'm blind to decipher. Then I'm no longer alone on the porch. A light switches on, shooting a blinding glare from a single bulb above onto the space. I blink against the harsh rush of visibility.

"Ah, there you are. Isabel Foster."

I rear back when the man crouches beside the mattress. He's tall but lean in stature. Totally different from Bones. Not to mention his accent. His scalp is covered in a short blond fuzz, his face is freckled, and his pale pinkish lips curve up with a smile.

"Who are you?"

"Name's Townsend, love."

I shake my head slightly. "Wh-What do you want from me?"

He doesn't answer. He only looks me over with his unforgiving gray eyes. I can't hold too much appeal in my current state. I'd been dressed for the festival, but I've been suffocated, sick, and tossed around pretty roughly since then. But his interest doesn't appear sexual in nature, thank God.

"You hungry?" he asks.

I frown. Is he serious?

"You deaf?"

"No," I answer sharply.

His eye twitches a little. "I asked you a question. Are you hungry?"

"A little, yeah. Mostly thirsty."

"Bones!" He shouts over his shoulder, causing me to jump. "Go grab us some food. And a bottle of water for the girl."

Bones joins us a few seconds later and tosses an unopened bottle of water onto the mattress beside me. He doesn't pass up the chance to sneer at me, like my mere presence offends him. The shell-shocked part of me is flooded with an irrational fear that I've spoken at all. Hopefully the ban on sound has been lifted with Townsend's arrival.

"What should I get?"

"Use your best fuckin' judgment. How about that?"

Bones hesitates, not seeming to know how to proceed.

Townsend rolls his eyes, but Bones doesn't see it. "How about some sandwiches? And some more waters." He lifts his chin to me. "That sound all right to you?"

I trap my bottom lip between my teeth and answer with the smallest nod I can manage. I don't dare look at Bones until he's disappearing through the door.

Townsend chuckles a little. "He's very literal, that one. Have to spell things out or he gets confused, you know? He's a rules man. Doesn't like ambiguity or coloring outside the lines."

I smile tightly. This is too casual. Is he trying to be the good cop since Bones is clearly a monster?

"He didn't hurt you, did he?"

"I'm fine," I say quietly, not trusting he cares at all.

He glances around, his attention landing on the trash heap. "Conditions could be better, but we do what we can on short notice."

I want to ask him why he's here and why he's taken us, but the fear of misstepping keeps me silent.

"So you're the girl who's thrown everything on its head." He looks me over again, almost in disbelief. "Isabel, I need to ask you something."

I hesitate. "Okay."

"Can you tell me where Jude McKenna is?"

I exhale roughly. Shit. How do I answer that? I look over his shoulder, wishing Tristan were miraculously there to give me a signal— to tell the truth or part of it, or keep my mouth shut until told otherwise.

Townsend seems to sense this. He follows my gaze and returns it back to me. "That's what I was afraid of." His lips thin into a disappointing line before he rises and shuts the door, which doesn't latch and remains partially open.

Fear twists my empty stomach. I've done the wrong thing. And now it's too late to go back.

TRISTAN

The room shifts. Its high ceilings seem to stretch out a little higher when I look up from my seat on the floor. Plumes of black decorate the walls, turning solid and grimy where they meet the baseboard. Little particles of mold are invisibly developing on the periphery. How long until everything is consumed?

Townsend shot me up with his bullshit serum before we left, which made me a little more pliable for him and his goon to stuff me in the vehicle for the ride here. Even with the visions slamming me every few minutes, the drugs didn't disable my ability to map where he was taking us—to this condemned house on a nearly empty block in the lower Ninth Ward. Neighbors are too far away to give a shit what happens here.

The SP-131 coursing through my veins isn't anything like the tranquilizer, though I'm sure remnants of that are still lingering in my system too. This is different. I'm fucked up in a way that doesn't compare to anything I've experienced. Relaxed when I'm supposed to be on high alert. I keep losing my train of thought. Layers are missing.

I start at the soft sound of Isabel's voice. I look around, but she's nowhere. Neither is Townsend, and the guy with the big neck has since left. She's here. He has her. In this awful place.

I like it fine right here with you.

She whispers in my ear. My eyes go wide and my gaze darts around the empty room. It's her voice, disembodied from the Isabel I know. The Isabel I know…

I wince because suddenly I'm not sure I know what that means. The mark at the end of my gun. The woman in my bed at night giving me every last piece of herself. I shake my head.

"No," I mutter to myself. "There's more."

I let my eyes close and rest my head against the wall. Isabel floods the black canvas.

She's in the middle of the four-poster bed covered in cream and lavender silk. Her eyes glimmer, filled with love and lust. I fist my hand in the duvet and yank it off, but there's another one there. Then another. I tear at them, but she's buried under the layers.

I climb up the bed to get to her, but she's suddenly gone. I slide my hand over the warm sheets, bury my face into the pillow, following her scent. Come back to me…

"Stone!"

I lift my head off the desk. I slide out of the chair and go to the front of the room.

The man with dark-rimmed glasses and a rail-thin frame leans back in his chair, dropping his pen onto his cluttered desktop.

"I'm not going to watch you flush your future. You want the grade? You meet with the tutor. Twice a week."

The sunlight glints off his dull gold nameplate, reminding me he holds just enough power over me to keep me listening. Mr. Brucher has been riding my ass since senior year started, and I'm convinced that nothing but working to my potential will satisfy him.

"I can't afford college. I already told you that."

"There are tons of scholarships out there," he says firmly. "Need-based grants too. Take the SATs, and I guarantee you'll score through the roof. You need to bring your grades up, though. Colleges need to know you'll put the work in."

I don't want to flush my future. I also don't want to waste my time. We both know my options are limited.

"The chances of anything panning out for me are pretty small."

He drops his glasses onto his desk and pinches the bridge of his nose. "Stone. Damnit. Just see the tutor."

Sensing weakness, I head for the door. But he pushes up from his desk and follows me out of his classroom.

"Stone. Library. Now," he barks, pointing in the opposite direction I'm walking.

Fuck.

I pivot and follow him down the hallway as slowly as I can manage. One push through the library doors, though, and my feet won't take me any farther.

"Tristan. This is Isabel."

I don't recognize the girl next to him. Little diamonds in her ears. Her hands tucked into her designer jeans. Eyes like a summer storm.

"You're here until four thirty. Got it?"

I don't answer him. I take a few steps closer and drop my book on the table with a thud that makes her jump.

She smiles nervously when Brucher leaves. "Hi."

I give her another once-over. She's definitely not from here.

"Where'd they bring you in from?"

She hesitates. "Alexandria."

Probably a prep-school brat using this time to beef up her résumé for college applications. The irony.

She drums her fingertips on the table, and then points to the book between us. "You're reading Chaucer?"

"Supposed to be."

She smiles a little. "It can take a little effort to get into. Not everyone's favorite."

"Yeah, I don't think I'm going to need to read Middle English ever again, so I'm not sure I need to start now."

Slowly she pulls at the loose-leaf paper that's wedged in the middle of the massive tome the school lent me.

I catch her hand, stopping her. "It's not done."

"I can help," she says quietly. "That's what I'm here for."

"I don't need your help."

Her cheeks flush as she pulls out of my grasp and tucks her soft brown hair behind her ear. "Listen, I don't know why you're being like this."

"Pretty simple. I don't want to be here."

Five minutes ago that would have been true. Now it's a half lie, because being in her presence is prickling my interest, even if I don't care about being brought up to speed on the subject matter at hand.

Only then do I realize we're mere inches apart. This close to her, the little signals that go off when I'm attracted to someone are firing. Too bad I have no intention of following through with this tutoring bullshit.

She looks down at the library carpet under our feet. "Fine. But we're here now. So we should just make the most of it."

"How about we both save some time and you can let my English teacher know I'm all set with the tutoring. I can read and write just fine."

"Then why are you failing English?" She cocks her head, challenge flaring in her eyes.

I'm not stupid. I just don't care. But I care that she's judging me. I'm more than meets the eye. But next to her, maybe I'm not.

"Why do you care?"

"Because I'm your tutor."

"No. You're not."

I take my book, walk around her, and leave the way I came in. I get to my locker, cussing Brucher and this life that never seems to give me a break. Pretending like college is even a possibility is just one more excuse for someone to screw me.

I hear her swift steps. The air moves behind me as she walks past. A surge of attraction slides through me as I watch her move down the hall until she's a silhouette against the afternoon sky pouring in through the double doors.

I grab what I need to finish up my homework at home and slam my locker shut. The walk to the door is a reckoning. If I don't see this through, Brucher's going to be back on me tomorrow about it. I can already hear him. I can bring my grades up on my own, but he's not going to make it easy on me now.

I step outside and head down the street a few feet. Then I see her. She's in the bus stall by herself, a book in her lap.

I slow in front of her. "You bussed in?"

She looks up and nods.

"That's a long ride."

"Kind of a waste, I guess." She looks back down at her book.

I won't let her ignore me, so I take the seat next to her.

"What are you reading?"

She closes the book and stuffs it away in her bag before I can catch the cover. She looks over her shoulder at me. "I didn't come here to talk about that."

She's going to keep on about the tutoring. I survey the sparse traffic up and down the street.

"When's the bus come?"

She looks at her watch. "Fifteen minutes, I think."

"Okay, how about I give you fifteen minutes to convince me why I should waste your time and mine with The Friar's Tale.*"*

A smile plays at her lips. I'm wishing I had an excuse to accidentally touch her again.

"Sometimes we hide our truth between the lines," she says softly. "It's not always about plucking out the obvious answers from the text. Everything Brucher is making you read is more about deciphering what the author isn't saying by looking more deeply at what he does. The truth is hidden in the poetry."

Something darkens her gaze, something a little wise and a little sad. I want to know what it is. I want to know her truth, but if I have any chance of that, I have to go deeper.

"Okay."

She frowns a little. "Okay?"

"Let's do this."

5

ISABEL

"Come on, Red. Let's get this over with." Townsend's voice floats through the door opening.

I hear a shuffle and then an odd groan from Tristan. Something's wrong. With Bones out of the house, I get bold and creep closer to the door. I peek around until I can catch a glimpse of the two men. Tristan's propped against the wall, his long legs stretched out. His chin rests against his chest as if he's asleep.

Then Townsend slaps him, jarring him awake.

"Where's Isabel?" His words are raspy and slow.

"She's fine, all right?" Townsend says almost reassuringly.

Tristan's eyes are glassy. He looks drunk. He couldn't be, though. Townsend's done something with him. Anxiety swirls through me.

Townsend's crouched beside him. "Where's Jay?"

Tristan frowns. "She left her tracker at the house."

The other man laughs. "Yeah? I figured that one out."

"It's in my pocket. Found it after."

Townsend's smile fades. He fishes into Tristan's pocket and retrieves something so small I can't see it well from this vantage. A tracker? Was someone tracking Jay this whole time? If so, why wouldn't they have followed her to Crow first? Why now, when she was safe at Halo?

"You said someone took her. Was it you?"

"No. This bitch, Martine."

Townsend can't seem to hide his intrigue. "Tell me about Martine."

"She's a friend of… I don't know. She takes care of people, I guess. I don't trust her, though."

"And where would she have taken Jay?"

"I don't know. She didn't fight it. I watched the tapes."

Townsend traps his lower lip between his teeth and rises abruptly. He paces a tight circle around the floor. I duck back behind the door so he doesn't notice my eavesdropping.

"They were supposed to keep her safe. I promised I'd keep her safe," Tristan mumbles. "It's my fault."

"Who's 'they'?"

"Halo. We were going to keep her off the radar. The Company'll kill her."

Hesitantly, I peek around again.

Townsend bends toward Tristan and shouts angrily. "Why would you care so fucking much, Red? You started all this shit. You should have killed the girl. Now everything is fucked, thanks to you."

"Jay wanted out too."

Townsend pauses. "Excuse me?"

There's a long silence. I scarcely breathe. Jay wanted out of the Company? Did she tell that to Tristan last night when they were alone together? Even if she did, I don't trust that she'd tell him the truth. She's too cunning. If she left Halo willingly with Martine, she had her own motivations, and we have no way of knowing what they were.

God, if she'd just waited a little longer, maybe all of this could have been prevented. Townsend could have taken her, and we could have gone our own ways. But maybe it could never be that simple.

"Who could possibly want this life?" Tristan finally says.

"Are you trying to tell me Jay let herself get kidnapped so you could hide her away and make a better life for her?" Townsend makes the prospect sound as ridiculous as it is.

"I don't know her game."

"Fuck me," Townsend mutters, his aggravation apparent. "You'd better hope I find this Martine woman, or you're a dead man. Where'd she take her? Do you have any idea?"

"Could be anywhere. Tons of properties. You can check the files. That's what I was doing when you showed up."

I shift back on the mattress when Townsend pivots toward me. The door swings open again, and his figure passes over the threshold. His countenance is less friendly. He's got a gun in his hand, and I have the strong sense his patience has been tested.

He looks down at me. "Who's Martine?"

I swallow hard and jolt back farther when he lifts the gun at me.

"Now is the time to talk, love, or I'll finish the job Red should have and we'll be one step closer to fixing this fuckin' mess he's made."

I suck in a shaky breath. "Martine Benoit. I don't know her very well. She owns the house."

"Why take Jay there?"

"They took me in when I needed a safe place to stay. We were hoping they'd keep Jay too."

"How did you find out about it?"

My lip trembles. He flinches and lunges toward me so he's on one knee and the muzzle of the gun is pressed to my forehead.

"My mom," I say in a shaky voice. "She's friends with my mom. It wasn't safe for me in DC anymore. The Company killed my friend, and my mom sent me to Martine's to start over."

He stares at me, his eyes a little wild, baring his teeth. If this is coming from concern for Jay, I have to find it in me to relate.

"I swear to you, we brought Jay to Halo to protect her. Martine would never hurt her. She's not the killing type. She took her away from the house to get information from her about the Company."

He seems to relax some. "She'll never get her to talk."

Probably not. Jay's too smart. She'll only give Martine what she needs to.

He gets up, looking less fierce but still agitated. This time when he leaves, he slams the door securely shut and I hear the lock turn. Panic flies through me. I crawl to the door, hesitant to test it but unable to hold back. Sure enough, when I try to turn the knob, it doesn't budge. Shit. That means I can't get to Tristan and he can't get to me. Not in his current state.

I press my ear to the door and listen, dread swimming in my veins at what I may hear. *Please don't hurt him…*

I hear boots on the floor, like pacing. Then Townsend's voice.

"Find out what you can about Martine Benoit and report back. She might be close. Check records. Bribe whoever you need to. Fuckin' find her. We're running out of time."

Then nothing for a long time but more pacing. Then the pacing stops, and I feel like I can't breathe. I press my palms to the door, feeling helpless. Tristan is in there at the mercy of Townsend. Tristan wouldn't approve of me getting brave right now, but he's also not in his right mind, and one of us needs to be thinking about how to keep us alive.

Dawn is peeking through the edges of a couple of the boarded-up windows, and the lightbulb above is casting plenty of light on the porch now. I move as quietly as I can toward the pile. Most of what I see is trash I'd rather not touch. Toys, window screens, insulation. I'm not going to be able to defend myself with plastic toys, so I carefully push through it as far as I can without disturbing the pile.

Finding nothing, I try not to cry out of pure frustration. I look up at the furniture stacked nearly to the ceiling. A rotten lounger and a wooden chair with graying wood that matches the ones inside the otherwise empty house. One spindle hangs loose. I stand to see it's split lengthwise, leaving one end fairly sharp. Hell, it's better than nothing.

I lean in and pull it loose from the leg without much trouble, except it's far too long to hide in my clothes. But I can't split it without making noise I don't want to make.

Hearing the faint sound of laughter, I freeze. I hurry to tuck the spindle under the edge of the mattress and wait to identify the noise. It's not coming from inside. No, it's from outside, and it's not that far away.

Young voices.

All the windows are boarded up. I can't see anything outside these four walls. So I turn off the light and look around to identify all the places where the early morning light comes through the rotting walls. Opposite the pile of all the trash is a sliver of light between the floorboard and the wood siding. I go to it soundlessly and tug very slowly on the board, a more challenging task with my wrists bound together. But with a little effort I manage to free a length of siding. I have to almost lie on the floor to see out.

A little girl is playing in the empty lot behind the house. It's overgrown with grass, but I can see other houses just beyond. She's close enough that I could get her attention if I yelled. But I can't make a sound. I start to tremble with the possibility of getting us out of here, away from these mad men. Then we'll run. We'll run and hide, and they'll never find us. I don't care what we have to do. God, I'll never run toward trouble again if we get out of this alive. With this resolution in my heart, I loosen another board. It makes a slight squeak when I wrench it off the last nail.

I glance back at the door, my heart pounding wildly.

I wait. I try to breathe. I pray they didn't hear me.

TRISTAN

I open my eyes halfway. Head is throbbing. Mouth is dry. It takes a minute for the room to stop moving. Townsend is on the chair in the corner, arms crossed, head back. His mouth hangs open as he snores silently.

I need to get out of here. I try to move, but my restraints don't let me. Tight ropes around my wrists and ankles. No hope of getting free yet.

Isabel.

She's safe, all right…

Townsend's freckled face launches into mine. I almost knock

myself over trying to get away from it. I blink hard and look back to the chair. He's still there, unmoving save the occasional swallow. Jesus Christ. Whatever he's given me has me tripping hard. I just need to come down from it. I can't stop these visions. Everything's blending together. Reality and flashes of memory and the nightmares I'm already too familiar with. Just need it to stop.

I bring my hands up to rub my eyes, but when I do, a swirl of colors assaults me.

"This will only hurt a little." Townsend's voice is calm in my ear.

I look up. The house is gone, replaced by four metallic walls. An industrial light illuminating all of me and some of his face. I'm under a white sheet folded at my waist. My body is a patchwork of bandages and bruises.

"What happened?"

Townsend rolls up by my side on a doctor's stool. "You got in a pretty bad scrape. On the upside, you fared better than just about everyone else. Good thing too. It's going to save your life."

My head is too foggy to make sense of what he's saying. I don't know this place. Where was I last? I'm not supposed to be here...

I look around again, hoping I'll catch on to something that will give me a clue. The room is bare besides the two of us and Townsend's black bag laid out over a rolling metal tray. The light glints on the vials and metal tools inside.

Only then do I notice my arms locked down tight beside me with bed straps. Why are they holding me down? Why is Townsend here? He's flicking the barrel of the syringe with his nail. Then he guides it expertly into a pulsing blue vein in the crook of my arm.

A flash of panic. He's not a doctor. I don't want any more of this shit...

"What are you doing?"

He doesn't look up as he withdraws the needle of the emptied syringe from my arm and holds the entry spot firmly with a patch of gauze. Finally he meets my eyes with a smile that makes my stomach roil.

"Going to make this complicated situation a little simpler, mate."

A door slams. My eyes fly open. The guy with the big neck has returned, a bulging plastic bag in each hand. He looks down at Townsend, who's blinked awake.

"You going to stand there forever, Bones?"

"There's no table."

Townsend rubs his neck and stands stiffly. "Improvise, mate. Eat your fill, and bring the rest back to the girl." He motions for him to give him one of the bags and looks over at me. "You must be getting thirsty by now."

I am. I'm bone dry. Not hungry but more thirsty than I can ever remember being. My vision is fuzzy around the edges. How long can this high last?

Townsend takes a water out of the bag and throws it at me. I catch it to my chest, where it lands with a thud.

Isabel's mischievous smirk taunts me as she saunters the last few steps across the café. I unscrew the cap and take a swig of the cool water she just tossed at me.

Goddamn, she's a vision. I'm hooked on her. Totally obsessed.

Judging by the way she's been tempting me with almost-touches all afternoon, she's got to know it. She slides into the coffee shop booth beside me, sips her hot cocoa, and starts flipping through the pages of the term paper topics Brucher handed me earlier today.

I couldn't care less. Not with Isabel's leg pressed against mine. Not with the possibility of us hanging at the end of every exchange. Every wordless look that means this is going somewhere.

I drape my arm over her shoulders and pretend to look down at the paper, but all I'm doing is worshiping her and letting my mind drift. Spending two evenings a week with Isabel has mixed results. I can't concentrate worth a damn when we're together, but when we're not, I work harder. Keeps Brucher happy, and it keeps up appearances so she can go on taking the hour-and-a-half journey into the city.

"Which one do you want to do?"

I press my nose against her hair, breathing in her vanilla shampoo. "I don't care. You pick something."

"I think you should probably have a say in it."

I drag the back of my hand down her arm. So soft. What I wouldn't give to take my lips over every inch of her skin. I've tasted her mouth, but God, I want so much more.

"I thought you were going to write it for me?"

She makes a little sound of amusement. "I'm not writing this for you. I have my own papers to write." I'd almost believe her, except for the way she tilts her head ever so slightly, giving me better access to her neck, where I can't help but kiss her.

Her eyes close, and I know she's paying about as much attention to the term paper possibilities as I am.

"You're sure?" I mutter.

She nudges me away with a coy smile. "You're not paying attention."

"I only want to pay attention to you."

"Well, that's not going to get this paper done. We should figure it out so I can help you outline it."

I sigh and force myself to focus on the paper. Blah blah blah. I really don't care. "What if we worked out a trade?"

"A trade?"

"You can write my term paper, and…"

She looks over at me, her eyebrow lifted. "And what?"

I lick along my bottom lip, all my thoughts pivoting toward her once more. "And I'll kiss you all over your body while you do it."

Blood rushes to her cheeks, turning them a dusty pink. "That sounds like it could be a little distracting."

"That's what you do to me. Even when you're not here, I can't stop thinking about you."

"Tristan!" Townsend's on his haunches, pointing to the water bottle. "Drink, or you're going to dehydrate on me. You're not looking right."

"Isabel," I mutter.

He stares at me, amusement glittering his eyes. "Isabel, Isabel. It's the only word you know, Red. That girl's going to be the death of you. Mark my words."

6

ISABEL

Bones is back. I can tell by the mix of voices behind the door and the vibration of his heavy steps through the house. The little girl outside is too far away, and the risk is too great. I stack the boards back up along the wall and hope I get another chance later.

I go back to the mattress and wait. A few seconds later, the lock jiggles and Bones barrels through the door. I press back against the wall, seal my lips closed, and stare down at his boots. If it's routine he wants, he'll get it from me. He drops a packaged sandwich onto the mattress.

"Eat," he says before closing the door behind him.

It doesn't latch this time. A blessing and a curse.

The lock gives me an extra couple of seconds to react before someone comes in. But at least I can reach Tristan if I need to, and I can see some of what they're doing. I curve my fingers under the mattress until the tips reach the spindle. If one of them leaves again, I could try something. Townsend's nothing like the other man. He's not thin, but he's not a physical killing machine. I could hurt him given a good opening.

I think about Vince and how I hesitated. Not this time. If I'm lucky enough to get a gun in my hands...

The voice in my head, the one who's bent on getting us out of here, isn't a voice I should recognize. But it's mine. I'm scared to death, but I'm ready to fight for Tristan when he can't fight for us.

A quick peek around the door, and I spot Tristan lying on the floor. I grip the wooden edge of the door tightly. I focus on him, study him until I'm sure I can see his chest moving. Bones is in the chair on his phone again. Townsend isn't in the room. I can't risk pissing Bones off again, so I close the door as quietly as I can and creep back to the loosened boards.

I take them down, slowly, carefully, when I wish I could rip the whole damn wall down and scream like the caged animal I'm turning into. But I don't. I take my time and pray I see the girl when I lie flat to the floor to look outside again. She's there, but closer. My heart leaps. Excitement and fear. She can help me, but she's just a child. Someone I can't reason with as easily as an adult.

She's got dark-brown hair pulled into a high ponytail. She's marching through the grass, swatting the high blades with a stick. Daylight's broken. The hum of cars and life in the daytime give me hope. This place is alive.

"*Los pollitos dicen*
Pío pío pío
Cuando tienen hambre
Y cuando tienen frío."

Her young voice dances through the field. Her little body lurches forward with long steps that mark each stanza of the song. Something in Spanish about little chicks telling their momma they're hungry before bed. The girl can't be more than four or five, which would make sense why she's here playing and not getting ready for school.

I just need to get her attention. I glance back at the door, barely cracked. Not enough of a sound barrier for me to call out to her. Lying down, I thread my bound arms through the opening in the wall. Once I'm as far out as possible, I snap my fingers. Twice. Quickly. I pull my arms back and look through the hole.

She's stopped and is staring at the house. I can see her little brows wrinkled in confusion. I freeze and strain to hear movement in the house. Nothing. Quickly I shove my arms out again and wave as wildly as I can. *Please see me. Please come closer. And for the love of God, please stay quiet.*

I pull my arms back and look through. She looks around and back to the house before taking a few hesitant steps closer. *Yes.* My chest is heavy with the effort not to scream. Not to cry. She takes slow steps toward the house until I can see her better. My heart is flying. I'm scared to death she'll scream or make a racket and get me killed.

It feels like an eternity by the time she's close enough to the house that I could whisper and have her hear me. I bring my face to the hole and smile, hoping not to scare the living hell out of her.

Her brown eyes are wide. I bring my finger to my lips and hush as softly as I dare. Then I crook my finger to motion her closer. She doesn't move. *Please, little girl. Please, I promise I won't you hurt you.*

Too bad she can't read my mind. She holds her place, too scared to go farther. I lift up on my shoulder and glance around. There's a dirty matchbox car in the corner. I grab it, try to clean it with my shirt, and push my arms through the hole again, offering the crappy thing to her in my desperate attempt to bring her closer.

Seconds tick by. Then the warmth of her little hand snatching away the toy. I pull my arms back slowly and look through. She's close. Close enough.

I smile, and she smiles too.

"Can you whisper?"

She shakes her head. She can, but I don't think she understands me.

"*Yo soy Isabel. ¿Como te llamas?*"

"Mariana," she says softly.

Heavy, hot tears burn in my eyes, but I suck them back.

"*Necesito ayuda, Mariana.*"

"*¿Esta es tu casa?*"

"*No. Un hombre malo me llevó. ¿Puedes llamar la policía?*"

Her eyes go wide, and she shakes her head fervently. She looks around as if someone's suddenly out to get her. She's going to run away, I know it.

"*Mariana, está bien. Está bien.*"

But she's backing away and then runs out of sight. Back home.

I sit up, trying not to let the hopelessness pull me under as I place the boards carefully back and crawl to the mattress, where all I can do is wait.

Mariana.

That she shares the name of my dead sister feels like an omen— an auspicious one or not, I don't yet know. I close my eyes and try to envision the little girl running to her house and telling her parents about the house where the bad man is keeping me. Maybe they'll call the police. Maybe they won't. Maybe Mariana will have just learned to play in a safer yard. One where murderers don't lurk.

Tears fall down my cheeks, but I don't make a sound.

TRISTAN

I do my best to keep my eyes open while Townsend paces, but I keep slipping in and out of consciousness. Every time his phone goes off, he steps outside. It feels like we're waiting, but I'm not sure why. I manage to push myself into a seated position again.

"What are we waiting for?"

Bones lifts his eyes to mine, not answering. He drops his focus back to his phone.

He's no help. Maybe I shouldn't press the issue until this drug is out of my system. Then again, maybe a hit of adrenaline is what I need to pull me out of it. I can't get reckless with Isabel so vulnerable, though. Townsend comes around the corner.

Bones looks up at him. "When are we taking him in?"

I catch the briefest hint of hesitation in Townsend's expression, which he quickly masks. "Soon, mate. Dunny's still looking for Jay."

"What about the girl?"

"I'm taking care of it," he snaps. "Play your fuckin' game, and I'll tell you when I need you."

The veins in Bones's neck pump up a little, but a moment later, he's wired into his phone again. His thumbs fly feverishly over the screen. How many hours have passed? If they're biding time before turning me in to the Company, what are they going to do with Isabel?

"Where's Isabel?"

Townsend looks like he's ready to snap. "For the love of Christ, will you throw him in the back with her? If I have to hear her fuckin' name out of your mouth one more time…"

Bones jumps to his feet and grabs my bound hands, dragging me unceremoniously across the filthy floor all the way to the back. He kicks the door open and shoves me over the threshold until I'm in another room.

He leaves, shuts the door, and locks it. Isabel is curled into a ball on a mattress a few feet away. My first instinct is to shimmy closer and wake her, make sure she's okay. Promise her everything will be. Once I can shake this fog and get my head straight. But I sit there a while just looking. Breathing. Trying not to completely freak out about the visions that have been plaguing me. Visions of us. Of the Isabel I used to know. They could be hallucinations, but they feel too real. Like the way they felt too real when I kissed her for the first time in Rio a month ago. The way I knew how she felt before I ever touched her.

Whatever is in Townsend's tried-and-true serum is pulling down memories I never asked for. But despite our dire circumstances, a part of me is glad to have them.

I move closer in a few awkward slides. When I reach her, the mattress shifts a little, revealing a sliver of rough wood peeking out. I pull it free. A splintered chair spindle. A weapon I'm glad to see. I shove it back under the edge as Isabel stirs.

She pushes herself up, blinking away sleep, but soon there's nothing soft or relaxed about her expression. Her eyes glisten with emotion.

"Tristan."

She lurches her body toward me, touching my face like she has to make sure I'm real. Finally she lifts her bound arms over my head so our chests collide. I can feel her heart beating through her thin shirt. Silent sobs rack her delicate frame, and I curse my inability to hold her. I fold my fingers into the band of her jeans and caress her soft skin.

"I'm going to get us out of here," I whisper. "I promise. My head's just really messed up right now."

She pulls back. Her eyes narrow with concern. "What did they do to you? I saw you lying on the floor. I was so scared."

"I'm okay. I wasn't going to put up a fight until I knew where they'd taken you. Townsend gave me some stuff to loosen me up so I'd tell him what I knew about Jay. He shot me with a tranquilizer before that. I'm just trying to pull out of it." I shake my head a little, not sure how to explain the visions or if this is even the time.

"I'm so sorry." Tears spill from her eyes. "I tried to fight him off, but he was too strong. I never had a chance."

I brush my lips across hers, hush her, and tug her a little closer. I can't help but imagine her trying to face off with Bones. It's a miracle she's alive and in one piece. "I had no idea they were tracking Jay or I would have never let you leave. Trust me, it's not a mistake I'll be making again. Are you all right? Are you hurt?"

"I'm okay. Just tired…scared." Her gaze darts to the other side of the porch and back to me. "I talked to someone outside. A little girl. I told her to call the police, but I'm not sure if she will."

I tense a little. I'd rather avoid a run-in with the cops, but I could use just about anything as a diversion right now.

Her face falls as she seems to sense my hesitation. "Was that a mistake?"

"No, it's okay. You did the right thing." I don't want to tell her we can use all the help we can get, because she's already at a breaking point, scared for her life and mine. Rightly so. I smile a little. "I found your shank. Remind me never to get into a prison brawl with you."

Another tear rolls free when she smiles. I'm not sure if my heart's ever hurt so much, seeing her this way. Dirty and terrified, clinging to hope. This…this is every reason for pushing her away. Leaving her all those years ago may have been the least selfish thing I've ever done, because even now, even with our lives hanging in the balance, I'm not sure I could let her go again.

"I don't know what to do, Tristan." She lifts her arms away. When she rests her hands in mine, the contact is like a shockwave.

Little pulses of recognition take my thoughts in a dozen different directions. The past. Now.

"Don't get brave, Isabel. Not yet. I can't…" I lie back and press the heels of my hands to my forehead.

"Tristan."

Her hands are on me again. Then her lips. "Tell me what I can do."

"It's okay. I just…" I sigh, not knowing how to finish, and let my body melt into the mattress.

We climb the concrete stairs to the house. My mom is working a double, which means we'll be alone until Isabel has to go back. Her parents have gotten used to her staying late, though I don't think they like it, judging by the calls and texts she gets as the afternoons wear on.

I've yet to meet them, but I get the feeling they're not always happy about the time she spends with me. She says they're compulsively overprotective. Letting her take the trip to Baltimore twice a week is a huge concession for them, but one she fights for even harder now.

It's been three months. My grades are up, but that's no excuse to stop seeing each other. The year will go by fast, and we haven't talked about where we want this to go yet. A part of me is afraid to ask. No doubt this connection we have is a wrench in her plans. I don't think she took the tutoring gig to fall for a kid on the wrong side of the city.

Still, she's here. Following me through the door. Looking around the house with more curiosity than concern. For the moment, I'm relieved I've never seen her place so I don't have to compare it to here. This is home. It's my truth. A place with four walls, a roof, a decent landlord, and rent we can afford.

I slice my fingers through my hair nervously, waiting for her to say something. She walks into the kitchen, brushing her hand across the Formica countertop as she goes. Then her lips curve into a smile.

"Is that you?" She points to the school photo curling under the magnet that holds it to the fridge.

"Third grade. Way before things got awkward."

She laughs and looks with rapt interest at the rest of the little photos and mementos my mom has collected here.

"You're so cute."

Even if all we do is kiss and hold each other, I can't wait a minute more to touch her. So I take her hand.

"Come on."

We go to my room, where I ignore another pang of insecurity.

"It's nothing special," I say.

I'm a cocktail of feelings right now. Raw and exposed here but eager to impress her, to make her feel things that scare both of us.

She walks to the window and turns her back to its unimpressive view a moment later. Her expression is calm, but my heart takes up residence in my throat. I manage an uneasy smile.

"Sorry," I mutter quickly.

"Why are you sorry?"

I shrug. "Your place is probably a lot nicer."

She comes to me, presses her hands to my chest, and gazes up at me. "I like it fine right here with you."

7

ISABEL

Tristan's sleep is long and fitful, like he's being held under against his will. I touch him but not enough to rouse him. Just enough that maybe in his dreams he'll know I'm here. I try to focus on the positive. At least we're alive. But Tristan is my rock. Seeing him this way, knocked down by whatever Townsend gave him, is heartbreaking and frightening. How can I protect him? How will we ever get free?

A faint rapping interrupts my incessant worrying. Quickly I crawl to the other side of the porch. I lift away one of the boards below the window, then the other. I lie down and bring my face close to the opening. I smile when I see the little girl again.

"Mariana."

She smiles too. "*Traje esto para ti.*" She threads a tiny pair of scissors through the opening.

I take her gift, flooded with relief and gratitude that she came back...to help. "*Gracias.*" I take a deep breath, measuring my next words. I don't want to scare her again. "Does your mother have a telephone?" I ask in Spanish.

"*Sí.*"

"Can she call a friend for me?"

Her eyes brighten, and she nods. Thank God.

I sit up, the scissors in hand, and look around for anything to write on. There's rotten wood in abundance, so I grab a small piece and scratch letters into it with the tip of the scissors.

NOAM NAMIR

Will it be enough? I wish I had a phone number, but all I can do is hope Mariana's mom will take up the search and somehow get through to Noam. I scratch one last word into the wood, hoping to convey my despair.

HELP

I pass it through the opening. Mariana takes it and stares down at it with a little frown.

"Mariana," I whisper.

She lifts her gaze.

"Be careful. The bad man will hurt me if he hears you."

"Okay," she says in a hushed voice.

I look over my shoulder. Not trusting Townsend and Bones to stay away long, I turn and wave a silent goodbye to her through the opening before rising and putting the boards back.

I crawl back to Tristan and rest my hand on his arm. He's burning hot. I contemplate the little scissors I've tucked into my front pocket. I could cut through the rope, but as soon as they found out, I don't know what they'd do. Especially Bones. Such an infraction could be an instant death sentence.

I investigate Tristan's ties as he sleeps. He's bound heavily with thick knots around his hands and ankles. If I can free him, I can get us closer to breaking out when we need to.

I spend the next several minutes partially severing the sides of the rope hidden against his skin. With a little force, he could probably snap them free.

I'm ready to start doing the same on my own when the doorknob jiggles. I stuff the scissors into my pocket and wait for the door to swing open.

Townsend walks through. I glare at him, holding my place beside Tristan. Townsend's face breaks into a crooked grin.

"You his little guard dog now?"

Hell yeah, I am. It takes everything in me not to lunge at him and scratch his evil eyes out of his skull.

"What do you want?"

"Not you." He nods to Tristan. "A few people have their sights on him, though. You're important enough to him that it's made this an interesting game." He pauses a moment, his grin fading. "Game's over now, though."

My blood runs cold. "What?"

"The people calling the shots aren't the patient type. They want their man back."

He reaches for me, and I dig my nails into Tristan's arm. He groans and flinches but doesn't wake up as Townsend rips me away. Bones is waiting in the empty room.

"Bring him out." Townsend jerks his thumb behind him toward the porch.

Bones snaps into action, passing us on our way into the large empty room.

"Bad news is your little red-haired friend doesn't know where Martine took Jay either. So I'm done fuckin' around with you."

Skye.

"No," I sob.

"Afraid so." He releases me and shoves me toward a chair. "Sit."

No. I'm not going to sit here politely so he can kill me. I hold my ground.

"All right, then. Don't sit. Doesn't matter."

Bones drags Tristan in. He's awake now but not putting up much of a fight. By choice or circumstance, I'm not sure. Our gazes lock. I hope he can read the terror that's ripping through me, because I don't think we have a lot of time.

Townsend nods to Bones. "Hold her. Go easy, though. I don't want her too banged up."

Tristan's expression becomes rigid. "Townsend, what's your plan?"

Townsend crouches and unrolls a black bag. "Taking care of some unfinished business."

Bones comes toward me. My adrenaline flies. There's no time. Do I fight if I know I can't win?

"Isabel, don't."

Tristan's voice distracts me long enough to foil any efforts I may have made. Evading Bones is pointless. He wrestles me into a bind in a matter of seconds. He holds me by the arms in a viselike grip so he's behind me and I'm facing Townsend.

My chest heaves with panicked breaths.

Tristan pushes himself to sit upright. "Killing her isn't going to magically bring Jay out of the woodwork. I already told you what I know."

Townsend keeps poking around his bag. "Unfortunately that's true. Totally separate matter. Boss wants her dead, and the issue's a bit overdue. Don't worry. We'll make it pretty." He takes out a clear, thin vial and a syringe. "Isabel Foster disappeared in Rio after getting mixed up with the wrong people. That dead body you planted was a mistake. Wrong girl. See, Isabel made it back to the States after all." He starts filling the vial. "Sad story when another one of America's youth loses the battle with drugs."

New fire heats Tristan's eyes. "Are you working for the Company, or do you want Jay for yourself? You can't have it both ways."

Bones strengthens his hold on me, as if I have any chance of breaking free. Townsend doesn't answer right away. He's still messing around with his bag. Pulling out a couple more vials, like he's getting ready to mix up something special.

"I can, actually. It stands to reason that if I could find Jay, I could find you, which was a circumstance they took into consideration once she went missing. So we struck a deal."

"What's the deal?"

"Jay's immunity for you," he says simply.

Tristan snarls. "That's a bullshit trade, and you know it."

Townsend cocks his head. "I'm the only one who can bring you in with a clean slate."

"What the fuck does that mean?"

Townsend chuckles softly and starts drawing liquid into a syringe from the different bottles. "Never tried this twice." He looks over at Tristan, lifts his eyebrow. "You really don't remember me, do you?"

TRISTAN

Maybe the drugs are suddenly making me feel ill. But when Townsend fixes his stare on me, something about his patronizing smirk and the knowing in his eyes threatens to turn me inside out. The vision I had of him at my bedside shooting me up comes back to me full force. Then I know it was real. It's all real.

He chuckles again. "Don't look so surprised, mate. Getting shot up in a war zone doesn't wipe your memory unless you get it in the head. Jay sold it to you pretty well, though. I'll give her that."

The pendulum of my heart swings heavily in my chest. Dissociative fugue. That's what Jay had called it. I'd read up on it plenty since. It made sense with everything I'd been through. "It was from the trauma. That's why I can't remember."

He nods a little. "The trauma helps. Makes a clear marker in your brain so you know what you want to block out. Then this little cocktail does the rest. Clean slate." He pauses a beat. "And we're going to help you in the trauma department soon. Watching your precious Isabel take her last breath ought to do it, I think."

He glances over to me, as if asking my opinion on the matter.

I grimace. "Over my dead body."

He grins before returning to his medley of bottles. "That shouldn't be necessary. The Company wants you alive. As soon as we take care of those pesky memories of yours, they can do what they want with you."

I'm seething. Yes. Of all the things I'm feeling in this moment, anger rises to the top. Pure, red rage.

I clench my teeth. "And Jay?"

Townsend stands and walks toward Isabel casually. Every cell in my body lurches toward her, but I'm about as helpless as she is.

"I have a feeling Jay will show up," he says. "I'll be ready when she does. But I can't wait around here, or the Company will change the game again. Besides, Bones here wants to get paid. Don't you, mate?"

Bones smiles and looks at me—the bounty.

"Little higher," Townsend mutters, tapping on Bones's hand so he'll move it higher up her arm.

She rears back against his massive chest and kicks her legs. Townsend jumps back, holding the syringe away.

"Now, now, no point fighting it."

Her eyes are wild. "Fuck you." She keeps fighting. Kicking and screaming when Bones repositions her. He shoves her against the wall, ramming her face against it with her bound arms awkwardly crammed to her side. Tears cascade down her cheeks as she fights to no avail.

Townsend comes close again and carefully unties the rope around her wrists, allowing Bones to take up the task of restraining them. Everything is happening quickly. They don't have a gun to her head, but they may as well.

Townsend hums softly and runs his thumb along the crook of her arm. "No coming back from this, love. Going to be the best high of your life."

"Townsend!" I shout his name and yank against the rope that's holding me hostage. Time is running out. To negotiate. To survive. And even though my head is still swimming, I'm certain this isn't a vision. This is real life playing out. My worst nightmare unfolding in front of me. "I could have killed Jay, but I didn't. I showed her mercy. If you care about her, that has to count for something. Do whatever you want with me, but Isabel's already dead on paper. You don't need to do this."

"Mercy's not a word in my vocabulary. You should have done your job, Red." He presses the needle against her skin.

"Break free, Tristan," Isabel cries. "Break free!"

Townsend pauses to chuckle. "The eternal optimist, this one."

I look down. The frayed ends of partially severed rope scrape against my wrists when I move. Jesus Christ, she cut the rope. She must have done it when I was passed out.

I twist my arms violently with every ounce of strength I possess. Once, twice. On the third wrenching try, it gives with a silent snap. I glance up. His thumb is on the plunger. *No, no, no.* I need more time. Anything. Begging will just inspire him to do it faster so he can watch me suffer.

"Did Jay tell you I fucked her?"

Townsend freezes. The muscles in his jaw tighten. It gives me a second more to tear the ropes free from around my ankles. I barely catch a breath before I get to my feet and lunge for him. Before he can make a full turn toward me, I take him by the back of his shirt and swing him hard against the other wall. His head hits with a thud before he falls to the floor.

Bones leaves Isabel to barrel toward me. But before he can reach me, Isabel's face appears over his shoulder. She lassos her arms around him. Something glimmers in her hand. She raises it and slices it down into the root of his neck. His shocked grunts melt into the puncturing sound.

The feral noise that comes from her matches the violent strikes she makes. Fast and hard. Despite the way she's coming at him, he manages to grab her by the hair and tear her off his back.

She lands with a crash. He stands there, wide-eyed and panting, heavy streams of blood pumping from his wounds, seeping into his clothes and onto the dirty floor. He looks between Isabel and me, as if he's deciding who he wants to kill first. I don't give him a chance to think it over. I motion him toward me and back up at once, creating as much distance between us as possible. And delaying the inevitable. If Isabel didn't hit his jugular vein, he'll be as lucky as I once was. Either way, he's bleeding out fast.

He stumbles toward me and reaches around his waist for his gun. I pitch forward then and slug him hard in the nose. Again and again until I'm sure I've broken knuckles and stunned him to the point of retreat. He drops to his knees. Then to his hands. Slowly they slide on the blood and grime until he's flat on the floor.

I grab for his gun moments before Isabel's scream ricochets through the room. I look up.

Townsend's got his arm around her neck. The syringe is in his hand. His teeth are bared, and his eyes are wild. Isabel kicks and flails until he brings the needle closer, as if he's going to stab her with it.

"Enough!" The word leaves his throat like gravel.

I lift the gun and aim it at him, waiting to get a clear shot. This isn't the showdown he planned. I've never been so relieved in my life to see the tables turn. But he's blocking himself too well with her body. Hurting her would be a death sentence for him. Then again, maybe he believed my taunt—that I've been sleeping with Jay, the woman he's come to save. I don't know if they're lovers, but God knows what's going on in his head right now. Or what he's threatening to shoot into the girl I love.

"What's in the syringe, Townsend?"

He's breathing hard. Worried. "Pure white heroin, mate. More than enough to get the job done."

I'm not relieved, but it could be worse.

"It could take hours," I say evenly.

"Or minutes. She's got no tolerance for it."

I curl my finger over the trigger. "Do it, Townsend. I fucking dare you. I can walk out the front door and get Narcan in her as soon as I put a bullet in your brain."

Isabel makes a frightened sound that dies in her throat when I take a step closer.

The shrill sound of a phone rings through the air and stops me. Again and again it rings.

"Reach into my pocket, love, and answer that for me, will you? Put it on speaker," he says.

With shaky hands, she does as he asks.

"What is it, Dunny?"

"I think I found Jay." The voice on the other end has to belong to the dark-haired one. The one I haven't seen since they took me here.

The silence is broken only by the sounds of our breathing.

"Where is she?" Townsend asks.

"She might be holed up at a local church. The red-haired bitch finally talked. I don't know what we're going to be walking in on, though."

Townsend locks his gaze to mine. "What do you think, Red?"

"I think you should let her go right now before I shoot you."

He smirks a little. "You want your girl. I want mine."

I cock my head. "Is mercy a word in your vocabulary now?"

I should shoot him and go find Jay myself. But with the needle positioned right at Isabel's neck, I'm questioning my threat. I can't let her overdose, even if I can react and find help to reverse it before it slows down her breathing to nothing.

Something else holds me back too. If what he said was true… If he's the reason I can't remember anything before the mission that went so horribly wrong, then I need to know why and how. If I ever have a chance of getting my memories back, he may be the only one who can help.

"Towns, what's going on? Do I need to come out there?" Dunny's voice crackles through the phone.

"I'm on my way. Watch the clock. If you don't hear from me in ten minutes, shoot the girl."

"Got it."

Dunny ends the call before anything more can be said. The phone hangs loosely from Isabel's bloody hand, fresh fear in her eyes. Townsend pushes her forward, away from him. He tosses the syringe to the floor and walks toward the black bag like a free man. I track him with the gun.

"No," I say firmly. "The bag stays with me."

8

ISABEL

I'm vibrating. Adrenaline and fear race over my nerve endings. The old me might have collapsed under the intensity of it all. But somehow I'm holding on to it. Managing it. Wearing it like a second skin. Like the blood drying on my hands, it's become a kind of armor.

Noam used to tell me to act first, think later. The liquid rage pumping through me now sharpens my focus and makes me realize what I'm capable of when I'm running on instincts alone. Everything's been reduced to one simple thing. Stay alive. At all costs.

Townsend and Tristan are in a staring match over the black bag. Bones is a silent, motionless mass on the floor.

He's gone.

I killed him.

I killed a man.

I killed a man who would have killed us.

I should be in shock or attaching a mountain of regret to the violent act. I can't really process it right now. When I lunged after his massive frame, all I could think about was how much I hated him. How badly I wanted to stay alive and protect Tristan. I didn't hesitate. I didn't take a second to consider the potentially fatal consequences for Bones or let it stop me from doing what I had to do.

The front door swings open with a rush of daylight and fresh air. Noam's figure appears. His slick tan scalp and muscled frame are a welcome sight. Zeda's beside him. They look around, taking in the mess we've made. No one moves.

"I got your message." Noam meets my eyes.

The full force of his worried look creates a fine crack in my new armor. Mariana's message got to him…by some miracle.

"Clock is ticking, mate. Time for me to go," Townsend says, interrupting the moment.

I look back to him, sealing up the crack with the new hatred I've adopted for him. He stole Tristan's memories… Memories he'll never get back. If Townsend's buddy didn't have Skye, I'd shoot Townsend myself. The supercharged energy skittering through me convinces me I could do it, the same way I went after Bones.

I walk toward Townsend, stopping an arm's length away. My breathing is hard. I hate him. More than I did moments ago. But the dynamic's changed.

I hand him his phone wordlessly. "Where is she?"

He takes it and puts it in his pocket. "Back at the house. She came looking for you a couple hours ago."

"Shit," Zeda mutters from behind me.

He glances between Tristan and me. "I'll call Dunny on my way. He'll leave her at the house when I give him the go-ahead. Then she's all yours."

Tristan goes to the bag, rolls it up, and stuffs it under his arm. "I'll make sure it goes down that way. Give me the keys. I'll drive."

Townsend hesitates a moment before dropping them into Tristan's hand.

Tristan looks at me. "You go with them."

I tense. "Tristan, you're still—"

"I'm fine," he says, his tone sharp. "I'll be right behind you."

But I know he won't be. He's going to get Jay. He's going to the church to find her.

He breaks our stare and shoves Townsend past us, through the door. I hurry behind him, knowing all the while I can't argue with him when he's like this.

I squint in the sunlight. The neighborhood is quiet. Two more condemned houses sit across the street with red Xs spray painted on the vinyl siding. The lots on either side of the house are empty. No one would have heard my screams. No one but little Mariana swatting grass in the backyard…

Townsend gets into the passenger side of the SUV.

Noam puts his hand on my shoulder and looks me over. "What the hell is going on? What happened to you?"

"I'm fine," I say, but I'm fixed on Tristan.

He's already rounding the vehicle. We lock eyes for a brief moment. He shakes his head. There's no stopping him. No point in even trying.

The tires squeal against the road as they pull away, and then they're gone.

I turn back. "We have to hurry."

Noam and Zeda don't ask questions until we're piled into Noam's vehicle.

He throws it into gear, and we lurch forward. "Isabel. Want to clue me in here? Zeda told me about Jay needing a place to stay at Halo."

Noam has a lot of catching up to do, but he's come this far to save me.

"Tristan's a hitman."

"Sorry, a hitman?" His eyes go wide before returning to the road.

"He was hired to kill me but decided not to pull the trigger at the last minute. So now the people he worked for are after both of us. Townsend is one of them, but he's here for Jay. It's a long story. She used to work for the Company too, but now that she's with us, she needed a safe place where they couldn't find her. She and Townsend have some kind of personal connection, so he basically nabbed everyone he could get his hands on who might know where she is, including Skye."

Zeda's reflection meets mine in the rearview mirror. "We split up after you disappeared. I made her promise not to go back there without me."

"Well, they've got her now. And she's telling them Martine has Jay at the church."

Noam and Zeda share a quick look.

"What is it?"

"I just don't think the reverend wants to get involved with this is all," Noam says.

"Isn't he part of this? Isn't he with Halo?"

"He helped Martine with a few things before," Zeda says. "He never came right out and criticized her, but the relationship cooled at some point along the way. Skye said he wanted to keep his focus on the congregation and not complicate it with Halo business anymore. It's all niceties on the outside, but that's Martine trying to keep him close. She hates losing connections."

I frown and whip my gaze over my shoulder. "Did you have any idea they might be there this whole time?"

She throws her hands up. "The church is like five blocks away. If Martine thought Halo wasn't safe, I figured she would have taken her a lot farther away. Especially considering who we're dealing with here."

I curse under my breath and straighten in my seat. "Nothing quite like hiding in plain sight."

Noam glances over at me. "If that was Townsend, who was the guy on the floor?"

I close my eyes a moment, collecting my armor against the deluge of emotion waiting to crash down on me the minute I let it. "Someone in the Company who was here to bring Tristan back in for the price on his head. Bones… That's what he called himself, anyway." I ball my fists against the seat, flooded with satisfaction that I won't be joining the graveyard of tattoos on his arms.

"Are you hurt?"

I do a mental scan. My adrenaline's waned enough that I notice several thrumming pains along my right side where I landed after Bones threw me. I push my fingers into my hair and massage my scalp, which is sore where he yanked me off him.

I exhale a shaky breath, coming down from the high a little more. Jesus Christ. What possessed me to jump on him? What was I thinking?

I wasn't thinking. I was surviving. He could have killed me in a matter of seconds. It was nothing short of a miracle that he hadn't already...thanks to Townsend's calculating patience.

"I'm fine," I mutter quietly and rub my dirty hands onto my jeans, which does nothing to improve their appearance.

We pull onto the highway, and I distract myself trying to look for the SUV Tristan left in. He must be driving like a maniac, because there's no sight of him. I glance at the speedometer. We're only going fifteen over the limit.

"Does this go any faster?"

Noam smirks. "Yeah."

TRISTAN

The adrenaline rush must have worked, because I'm more alert than I've been since Townsend drugged me up. We're flying down the highway, eating up the distance between Skye and hopefully Jay.

"How's this going down?" Townsend finally says.

I switch lanes and zip past a car that's holding up the passing lane. I've got no interest in outlining a plan for Townsend to twist for his own benefit.

"How about we enjoy the ride and you enlighten me instead. Tell me what you gave me three years ago. Everything before that's a blur."

"That's the way it's supposed to work," he mutters.

"And what, do you have like an underground lab where you figure out how to fuck with people's heads?"

I glance at him, but he's staring at the road, his expression grim. "I can't take credit for all the tricks in my bag. But yeah, sometimes I cook a few things up myself."

"What is it?" I ask with more force, determined to get some answers before we leave the vehicle and the game changes.

"It's called Elysium Dream." A long moment passes before he continues. "It's a strong antipsychotic combined with a bunch of other shit. Originally designed as a one-two punch to combat PTSD and depression. Now it's a twist on a throwaway drug that didn't make it through trials." He blows out a sigh. "I don't honestly know if it would have worked twice on you without melting your fuckin' brain. Don't suppose the Company really cared either way, though."

I glance at him again briefly. "Why bother giving it to me to begin with? I was barely alive when they took me in."

"Because they wanted you. I figure you were a good soldier, right? Had qualities that probably caught someone's eye at some point along the way. They didn't want to waste them, so they turned you into the kind of person who could do the work they needed done."

"Seems like a lot of effort. For what they pay us, you could convince a lot of people to do what we do."

"Don't underestimate yourself. The rest of us?" He points to himself. "We start out messed up and they train us to be even worse. You just went the other way. It was worth a shot at least."

He's painting me like I was a model soldier. Someone like Brennan. A patriot. But I wasn't. I was messed up and running away from my life.

"I wasn't perfect by any stretch. I know that much."

"No, but you had a conscience, and that just won't do." He looks out his window, hiding most of his face. "All having a past does is feed you inconvenient emotions. Fear. Compassion. All the little things in life that teach a normal person how to make normal, ethical choices. Be glad we wiped it away in one fell swoop and you didn't have to watch your humanity get stripped away one hit at a time."

I clench my teeth. I do remember my doubts. A natural hesitation occurred before I committed myself to the task of taking lives for pay. But it wasn't much. Not enough to stop me from going through with it.

The sick feeling I had before returns because I realize I have no idea who I am or who I was. They stripped me of things I'll never get back. Even if the memories are flowing in now, I've changed. The memories are a start, though.

"I get visions," I say quickly, acutely aware of the limited time I have. "Flashbacks. The serum you gave me brought them on like never before."

"That's probably normal. Nothing's a hundred percent."

We get off the highway. We're getting closer to Jay. There could be more blood. Maybe his…

"Can you reverse it?"

We share a quick glance. He frowns. "Never thought of it."

He probably doesn't understand why I'd want to. Sounds like not having a conscience or a past is a desirable circumstance, the way he talks about it.

"For the record, I didn't sleep with Jay."

He's quiet for a long time. "I know."

"She's important to you."

The corner of his lips lift. "I haven't lied to you yet. What's the point?"

True enough. He's been painfully honest. Makes me want to keep him around as much as I want to end him. I can't think that way right now, though.

"If you care so much about Jay, then you've got to know the Company's going to want her dead. No matter what deal you struck up with them."

"I'm not daft. I know who I'm up against here. But you snatched her, so I didn't figure it'd be a hardship sending you back in, you know?"

I hold my tongue, choosing not to dime out Crow, who was integral to Jay's kidnapping. And worse. I remind myself to be far away when Townsend finds out what Jay endured at the hands of Crow's goons.

"I didn't hurt her. I was after information."

He chuckles. "She's a wealth of information, isn't she?"

"Unfortunately for her." I glance at the clock. "Time to make that call. We're getting close."

He sighs and pulls up the number. "You're not stopping for the girl, are you?"

I don't answer him. "Just make the call."

He mutters a curse under his breath and brings it to his ear. I hear Dunny's muffled greeting.

"I'll meet you at the church in five minutes. Leave the girl at the house."

Townsend hangs up before Dunny can say anything more. "What do you want, Red? Isabel's safe now. You should get out of town with her and not waste time."

"And I'm supposed to let you take Jay when she's the only one who knows how to bring them down?"

He looks at me, silence stretching between us. "That's your plan? You think you can take them on yourself?"

"Not without help."

"You're more fucked in the head than I thought. If you want to stay alive and you want to keep Isabel alive, then your best bet is to disappear."

"There's no running from them," I say quietly, wishing it weren't true. "Not forever, anyway. They'll be after you too. Then what?"

He laughs a little. "I'm good at disappearing."

"With Jay?"

"Given the chance, absolutely. I came here with no other aim."

"And your associate?"

He frowns a little. "If you go into that church with me, Red, it's going to get real complicated real fast."

"He wants the payoff for bringing me in."

"He certainly doesn't care what happens to Jay. How do you think I enlisted their help?"

I already knew why Dunny and Bones were in this. Townsend's earlier hesitations gave him away. The second Dunny sees me with Townsend, he'll know he's out of a payday and likely a job. Of course Townsend is anything but predictable. And I have no idea where Jay stands in all of this. I still don't know why she ran off with Martine.

Maybe Townsend's right. Maybe I should drop him at the curb and go back to the house, collect Isabel, and get as far away from this place as I can.

But letting Jay slip through my fingers means I'll never get the intel to end this. And I suspect Townsend knows more about why my memory was wiped than he's letting on. He's more than the Company's puppet, especially if Jay's placed her confidence in him.

We pass the mansion on St. Charles. All I can see is a bright ceiling light from the library shining through the windows as we speed by. Isabel will be there soon, and hopefully Skye is safe, as promised. A knot of worry lodges in my stomach. Whatever happens at the church has to happen fast. I doubt after everything Isabel has been through that she'd follow me there, but I'm quickly learning to stop making assumptions when it comes to her. This way of life is peeling back her inhibitions, not the least of which is the ability to take a life when her own is threatened.

I turn onto the street that will take us to the church. Townsend drums his fingers on the armrest as I park down the street in front of Noam's studio. We wait there in tense silence.

"I could end this now, you know," I say.

Townsend's blank expression doesn't change. "You want something."

"Jay's cooperation."

He lifts his chin toward the church. "If she's in there, you could get that on your own."

"I want you to figure out how to undo whatever you did to me." I lift up the bag that's been tucked beside my seat.

He glances at it and then to me, his lips a thin line. "I can't promise that. I'm not in the business of putting people back together, mate. Not my specialty."

"Maybe not, but you know enough to try. That's more than anyone else can do."

He rubs his forehead vigorously. "Yes. I can try. If the SP-131 showed results, I can play with the dosage. Do some research. I don't know. *Fuck*. Yes. I'll fuckin' try, all right?" He waves his hand toward the church. "Can we go in there and get her now? Before Dunny does something stupid and gets her killed?"

"Speaking of Dunny… What are we going to do about him?"

He sighs again with a resigned look. "I actually liked him."

I withdraw Bones's gun and release the magazine, checking to ensure it's full. "I hope you came here with more firepower."

He jerks his thumb behind him. "It's in the back."

"Let's get this over with, then."

9

ISABEL

We find Skye tied to a chair in the library with a rag cinched around her mouth. Her eyes are red from crying and her face is bruised, but otherwise she seems okay. Zeda rushes to unbind her while Noam stalks around the house, his gun ready. The house is torn apart. Every drawer and cabinet is open and emptied onto the floor. Most of the furniture is turned over and ripped open, almost as if they'd resorted to mindless destruction when they realized they couldn't find who they were looking for.

Once she's loose, Skye lets out a quiet cry, which she covers with her hand. Zeda kneels beside her and pulls her into her arms.

"I told you not to go. Goddamnit, Skye," she whispers. "I would have come with you."

She hiccups over a sob. "I know. It was stupid. I'm sorry."

"Are you hurt?"

"I'm okay. He just scared the hell out of me." She draws in a shaky breath. "Honestly, I think I've been through worse."

Zeda shakes her head and tightens her arms around her friend. I want to comfort Skye too, but I've been through my own hell. I don't know if I'm the person to calm her down right now. Also, I need to figure out a plan, because Tristan's already two steps ahead of me.

I go deeper into the house and find Noam lingering inside Martine's office, which appears to be the most wrecked. Paperwork is strewn everywhere. Cabinets are flung open, revealing feeds from several surveillance cameras set up around the house on a large computer monitor. He's staring at them with an almost mesmerized look.

"Noam."

He spins. "Everything okay?"

"Tristan's not coming here. I'm pretty sure he went right to the church."

He tucks his gun into the band of his pants. "And?"

"And he's going there to get Jay."

"That doesn't mean you need to follow him."

"This isn't a joke," I snap. "People's lives are in danger. They almost killed us."

He lifts his eyebrows and looks me over the same way he did before. "Isabel. You've been through a lot. I mean, look at you."

I clench my fists. "You can come with me, or you can stay. It's your choice, but I'm not staying here while Tristan's on his own. No one he's with has his back."

"You just told me he's a hitman. Am I supposed to be more concerned for his well-being than yours?"

"They shot him with a tranquilizer less than twenty-four hours ago, and then Townsend gave him something else that was supposed to get him to spill his guts and confess where Jay was. He's been slipping in and out of consciousness for hours. He thinks he's fine now, but if he goes down, they're going to kill him. I'm not taking that risk."

"If it's as dangerous as you think it is, he's not going to want you there."

This I know. Doesn't matter. This fight isn't over.

"Fine, I'll go alone." I walk away, intending to slip out the back door.

"Yeah right, Izzy. I don't think so." He grabs my arm, halting my retreat. "Can you wait a damn minute?"

I pivot and level a hard stare at him.

"Noam, listen to me. I've been kidnapped. Tied up. Hit. Threatened. I almost got shot up with a lethal dose of heroin. Then I stabbed someone to death. I don't even have a minute to wash away the evidence of what I've done, let alone process it. This is hands down the worst day of my life, but it is *not* over. You have thirty seconds to help me or I'm leaving, whether you think it's a good idea or not."

A flash of pain passes behind his dark eyes. "Isabel. Jesus, I'm sorry. It's just that with everything you've been through, I'm worried about you running back into this. Why don't you let Tristan do what he does and stay put? You're running on pure adrenaline right now."

I tug my arm out of his grasp.

"You taught me to act first, think later. It's kept me alive more than once."

"Okay, but that's not a way to go through every second of your life."

"My life is measured in seconds," I snap. "Surviving is measured in seconds. Tristan could need me, and the seconds I'm spending here convincing you could cost him his life."

He stills and searches my gaze. "Just remember who you're ready to make sacrifices for. Do you really know this guy as well as you think you do?"

I try to tamp down the spike of anger his words inspire. "You don't know me. You don't know him either. Hell, you don't even know Martine or what she might be capable of. She's not a saint, okay? Jay has something she wants, and she'll stop at nothing to get it."

He draws his brows together. "I know her better than you think."

There's something there, a quiet understanding that Martine is not who she proclaims herself to be. I'm compelled to peel it back and find out more, but there's no time for that.

"I have to go," I press. "Are you coming with me or not?"

More precious time bleeds away.

"This way." He walks past me and heads to the front of the house.

The girls have moved to the couch, and Zeda is cleaning up Skye's bloody nose with a damp cloth.

"I'm taking Isabel to the church," Noam says. "If Tristan hasn't shown up here by now, he's probably already there."

Zeda stands. "I'll go with you."

He shakes his head. "No. You should stay with Skye. In fact, you should get her out of here as soon as possible. Come back for your things later. It's not safe here anymore."

The way Zeda looks at him is too familiar. I've seen it before in my own reflection—affection and deep-seated fear with a touch of knowing better than to talk someone out of a path they've set their mind to.

TRISTAN

Sunset basks Cambronne Street in an amber glow. Nightfall would be better, but for now, the neighborhood is quiet. We turn the corner and climb the steps to the church—the same ones I found Isabel on after she fled DC for New Orleans. I don't think about the things we talked about or the changed man I confessed I was becoming that day, because I have no idea what's waiting for me on the other side of the doors. I could become the worst kind of human in a matter of minutes. A man she might wish she never met.

The front doors of the church are unlocked. Townsend goes in first, me behind him. At first, all seems normal. The faint scent of incense hits my nostrils. The silence is heavy with that eerie kind of heaviness spiritual places seem to carry. A figure of Jesus hovers above the stage in the back. One glimpse at the focal point has me uneasy, like my clothes are too tight. Like a hundred sets of eyes are on me, even though we're alone. I've only ever believed in human beings passing judgment on each other, never in the fairytale god in the clouds who looks more like an easygoing guy than the kind who would threaten me with fire and brimstone if he were to show up in person.

"Help... Help me."

A strangled voice seems to come from the figure's direction. The hair stands up on my arms.

Townsend glances at me only a second before rushing up the center aisle, gun in hand. I follow.

What I couldn't see before is quickly revealed. A dark-skinned man dressed in all black is lying on the floor, holding his side. The red carpet beneath him is stained a deeper shade.

"Who are you?" I ask.

"I'm Reverend Stephens." He closes his eyes with a painful wince. "Please don't hurt me. I beg you."

"We're not going to hurt you. Where's Martine?"

We don't have time to help innocent bystanders right now, not that Townsend would ever consider it. As much as the reverend probably does need an ambulance, I can't stop us here.

Townsend's hands tighten around his gun, but he wisely refrains from pointing it at the man.

The reverend shivers, closes his eyes, and opens them once more. "She's here. I should never have let her stay. This isn't our fight."

Before I can press him for more, a shrill sound carries from farther back.

"Let's go," I say, urging Townsend toward the sound.

He goes around the stage, through a hallway that leads to another wing of the large brick building. We pass classrooms and slow when more sounds echo down the hall. Something like desks being dragged. The clang of things crashing to the floor. Townsend pauses just outside the doorway. He peers through the sliver of a gap between the door and the jamb.

Turning back, he closes his eyes and silently curses.

"You aren't here," he says almost soundlessly.

I nod. I have no idea what's going on in there, but chances are good it's better if all parties don't know I'm here. At least for now.

He whips around, gun raised, and steps quickly into the room.

"Killian." Jay's voice is weak and watery, but I recognize it.

And the desperate way she says Townsend's name tells me he's not a threat to her, which was something I hadn't ruled out. If he was her last resort all this time, why did she take out her tracker?

I shimmy closer until I get a view into the room.

Martine's body and most of her face is obscured except for the arm holding a gun to Jay's head. They're standing behind a large metal teacher's desk that's set in front of several others in disarray. There's a travel bag a few paces away. She must have been trying to move her again.

Townsend's joined Dunny in the standoff. They don't have a clear shot, but Martine's cornered. There's only one way out of the classroom. This can't end well.

"Let her go." Townsend utters the demand through gritted teeth.

"Then what? Let you kill me? I don't think so." Martine's voice is surprisingly even.

"We came for her. Not you."

Martine laughs. "Oh, I know who you came for."

"Then you know we're not going to leave without her. Hand her off, and we'll forget this ever happened."

"I'm afraid that's not going to be enough."

Tense silence. Her voice breaks it.

"Do you have Tristan?"

"No. He slipped past us," Townsend lies.

"And Isabel?"

He shakes his head.

Opportunity glints in her cool eyes. "I can help you find her. And when I do, I know how to use her to lure him out. She's the only one he cares about, and she'll do anything to be with him. You find one, you'll have your hands around both of them."

My whole body goes rigid. Bitch. Martine's not just spouting nonsense to buy a way out of this standoff. No. She'd use Isabel in a heartbeat. And she'd sell me down the river just as fast. I have no doubt about it.

"Why don't you let Jay go and we can talk more about it?"

"I'm not letting her go until I talk to someone with authority. I want to talk to Soloman," she says firmly.

Jesus. Dunny shoots a pointed look to Townsend. Townsend's shoulders are an impenetrable block. If they weren't aware Jay was talking about the Company, revealing critical details about the organization that feeds them all, they know now. Dunny's finger curves over his trigger. He doesn't work for Townsend. He works for the Company. And he could be seconds away from making a bad decision.

"What do you know about Soloman?" Townsend asks.

He's trying to keep her talking, but I'm less worried about the gun in her hand than the information now flying out of her mouth.

"I know he's the only one who can invite someone to the most important table in the world."

Townsend's jaw clenches and unclenches a few times. "Yeah? What's that got to do with the price of tea in China?"

Martine's cheeks are red, her natural flush mixing with the heavy makeup she wears. But she looks worn down now, like she's clinging to the cool demeanor she puts off. She presses the gun tighter against Jay's temple.

"I want a seat. I've got the money. The information. The power. And most importantly, I have her. And I'm not handing her over until I get what I want."

I don't wait for more of the negotiations to play out. I slip away soundlessly. Down the hall and out a side door. I circle the building, carefully peeking in windows until I get to the right one. Nothing's changed on the inside. Townsend and Dunny are arrowed at Martine. She's smiling. I can't hear them, but somehow I can feel her condescending confidence even from here.

She thought she was so smart, taking Jay to use her as a bargaining chip. As soulless as I'm sure Soloman and his band of influencers are, I'm sure they wouldn't roll out the red carpet to someone trying to extort them. No one likes to be twisted that way. Especially people who are used to power. Real power. Martine toys with people's lives when they're desperate and quick to bend to her demands. But she's too greedy to make the distinction. The Company would eat her for breakfast. Too bad they'll never get the chance.

I don't have the clearest shot, but it's a better angle than the others have, even if I'm farther away and have a pane of glass between us.

I lift the gun, squint one eye closed, and take aim. Townsend's lips are moving. Martine's smile gets wider. A vision of Vince Boswell striking Isabel so hard she bounced off the bed flashes briefly across my mind.

I take an even breath and take stock in the soft hammer of my heart. Like the life force I'm about to steal away for the hundredth time.

Jay closes her eyes, almost as if she can feel it coming. And when I exhale—I'm not sure why I do it—but I send up a prayer that my aim is true.

10

ISABEL

My hand is curved around the door handle when a gunshot pierces the dusky air. Then another. So loud I jump and my heart lodges somewhere in my stomach.

I look at Noam. He covers my hand, yanks the door open, and barrels in ahead of me. We run up the aisle of the church. The reverend is a few feet from the pulpit. His hands are bloody, covering a wound in his gut. His skin is ashen. I rush to him and cover his hands with mine.

"Reverend."

He winces. "It's not safe here. Call the police."

Noam disappears into the back. Damnit. I should follow him, but I can't leave the reverend here like this. I unbutton his jacket slowly and examine the wound. A single shot, but it's gushing. He's losing too much blood.

A siren blares faintly in the distance. It's getting closer. Someone must have called the police at the sound of the gunshots. We're running out of time.

The front door swings open. Zeda rushes through it and runs to us.

She pauses only a second before grabbing one of the silky cloth runners off a table and dropping to her knees. She folds it into a ball and presses it against the reverend's wound.

"What are you doing here?"

She looks around. "Same thing as you. Making sure no one does anything completely stupid."

"Where's Skye?"

"She's fine."

Noam appears again. He stops short when he sees Zeda. I recognize the flare of anger he quickly masks.

"Isabel, we have to go. Zeda can take care of him until the cops get here."

I stand. "Where's Tristan?"

He doesn't answer me but kneels by the reverend. He touches his face, his pinched features betraying his concern. "Hang on, Reverend. Ambulance is coming. I hear them. When the police come, you only saw the man who shot you, okay? No one else."

They share a look I don't understand. They have history. Some unspoken code. The reverend frowns but then nods. "All right."

Noam doesn't ask me again. He grabs my arm and drags me toward the back, down a long hallway, until we're slamming through another exit that deposits us into an almost empty parking lot. A big white van with the church's name and logo painted on the side is parked close. He guides me toward it.

"Where are we going?"

"We have to get you out of here before the police come."

"Where's Tristan?"

He slides open the side door. Tristan's there. He hauls me into the van and holds me so close against his chest, I struggle to take in my next breath. The door slams shut behind me. I hear Noam shut himself into the front, and a second later, the van is in motion. He takes tight turns and stops hard before speeding forward. I don't care, because I'm cocooned in Tristan's arms, which I'm convinced is all I'll ever want for the rest of my life.

"I'm sorry," he whispers against my ear.

I almost don't hear it. I do, but it doesn't make sense. He's said it before, but I don't care why. I can't imagine a single thing he could be sorry for that I would care about.

Somehow it makes me smile. An unexpected bubble of laughter erupts in my chest. He pulls back and looks at me. His eyes are sad and a little bewildered.

"Whatever you're sorry for, I don't care. You're alive. I'm alive."

The last word gets caught in my throat. I'm alive. Against all odds. And if we're safe…finally safe…that means my armor's chipping away so fast, I may not be able to stop it. My throat burns and tightens. I may be seconds from falling apart, but I can't bring myself to care about that either.

He palms my cheek. "Martine's gone."

Something stills inside me. Gone?

"Your man's a good shot." A raspy voice with a British accent that's sure to haunt my dreams jolts me backward.

I twist to look behind us. The tint of the windows and nightfall almost obscure his face, but Townsend's there in the back row with Jay firmly beside him. Her head is pressed against his chest, his arm holding her there. Her hair hides her face.

"What happened?"

"She tried using Jay to barter for a seat with the Company," Tristan says.

My eyes widen. "Are you serious?"

His somber expression doesn't change. "Do you doubt it?"

I really don't know what to think. I was sent into her home by my own mother when I needed a safe place. I remember the ambition in her voice when she talked about Jay, though. Of course, Tristan had his reservations all along.

"What about Dunny?"

"He couldn't make it," Townsend answers flatly.

I don't ask him to elaborate. What matters is he's no longer a threat, no matter who made sure of it.

I relax against Tristan's side. The weight of everything that's come to pass seems to fill the long stretch of silence. It's dark and bloody and best left unspoken. At least for now.

A few minutes later, Noam pulls up to a building that looks like a small warehouse. He punches a code into his phone, and a large door opens in the side. He pulls in and it shuts behind us, shrouding us in more darkness.

We file out as a handful of fluorescent lights blink on fully, illuminating the largely empty space.

"Welcome to my place," he says, dropping the keys onto a lone round table. Everything—the table, the kitchenette, the few random chairs and couch—seem far too small or too minimal for the massive square footage around it. He points to the metal staircase. "There's a bedroom upstairs. Pullout couch down here. I'm going to make some calls. Make yourselves at home."

"I appreciate the offer, mate, but you don't need to put us up." Townsend's arm is still around Jay, but she's more alert now, taking in the surroundings.

Tristan takes a couple of steps from me toward them. "You and I need to talk."

Noam walks toward me. "Zeda's got some extra clothes in the bureau upstairs if you want to get cleaned up and change."

"Thanks."

He rubs his hand up and down my arm once. "I'll go grab them."

Townsend and Tristan leave through a separate door that takes them outside while Jay wanders over to the couch. She sits down, not making a sound. Part of me wants to go to her. She seems shell-shocked, but maybe it's relief that this is finally over. Either way, my concern for her wins out. I follow her to the couch and take a seat next to her.

"Are you okay?"

She looks at me with a weak smile. "I'm fine."

I doubt she is, but sometimes it's nice to be asked. I'm sure she'd rather have someone else comforting her, which would make two of us. After everything I've been through today, somehow I'm able to accept

Tristan's absence yet again.

"Why did you leave?"

She drops her gaze to her hands and picks at her cuticle, not answering.

"Tristan found the tracker in your bathroom," I say.

"I flushed it. Thought it would have found its way far from the house. I wasn't trying to lead him to you."

"But why? Didn't you want him to find you?"

"Of course I did. I turned it on as soon as Crow took me, even though I knew Killian wasn't close enough to get to me in time. Then we were on the road. I thought it would have been enough time for him to catch up. He took too long. I got scared that his alliances had changed. The Company can turn anyone. I've seen them do it over and over again. I guess I convinced myself they'd turned him too, and if he could find me, they'd kill me."

"So you went with Martine."

She nods. "She and Tristan were jockeying for my confidence. It was making me uneasy. They obviously have never been on the same team, and I didn't want to be caught between them and wind up dead. So I told her I didn't feel safe. She offered to take me someplace else for a while. I thought it might give me some time to come up with a plan. I didn't buy her sweet old lady act, but I honestly wouldn't have guessed she was capable of wanting to join the ranks of the Company. I thought I could outsmart her, but all I did was severely underestimate her."

"Tristan killed her?"

She looks up at me with those severe blue eyes. "She had a gun to my head, and Tristan had the best angle."

I'm quiet after that.

I find Noam's shower and wash the horrors of the day off with hard scrubs that leave my skin red and raw. As I do, I reach for the familiar sting of loss and regret knowing Martine's dead and the muddled cocktail of emotions that comes with loving a man who kills without ever feeling those things. Except the sting is dull at best. All I can muster is tolerable discomfort.

My feelings for Tristan haven't changed. Any doubts I had about being with him, knowing what I know, dissolved somewhere on our travels. Inside the chaos our life has become, I've learned how to love all of him. All his flaws. All his darkness.

TRISTAN

Locusts chirp in the vegetation along the street. Townsend paces the empty sidewalk, back and forth, while I lean against Noam's building. He's puffing on a cigarette. If I smoked, I'd probably want one or ten right now too.

"You were quick on the draw back there."

His lip quirks up. "Dunny?"

I nod.

"Not my weapon of choice, but I get by."

About three seconds after Martine dropped, Townsend turned on Dunny. Further delay would have been dangerous. Dunny would have been asking questions about how he was going to get paid without the goods—me. We didn't have time for that mess. We barely got out of there ahead of the police or any other witnesses noticing us. Last thing I need is to be on a most-wanted poster.

"With your travel companions out of the picture, I have to ask, who else knows you came here?" I ask.

"I never gave them our target location. Bones and Dunny didn't even know until we showed up to stake out the house. Unless they fed it back to the Company when I wasn't paying attention—which I don't see why they would and risk messing up their payday—you probably have a few days before they're on your scent. The police will find records on Dunny eventually, once they figure out who he is. Double homicide will hit the news circuit. That'll tip the Company off. Then you'll have someone else here trying to pull the same thing." He stamps the cigarette butt into the sidewalk. "Which means we should split up sooner rather than later."

"And I'm supposed to let you both just walk away?"

He stares up at the night sky without answering. I roll the little glass bottle around in my pocket and trace the masking tape label on the bottle with my thumb. SP-131. Asking Townsend to cook up something else for me carries its own risks. He could give me anything. Kill me. Melt my brain like another dose of Elysium Dream would have. But whatever's in the bottle I swiped from his black bag before we went into the church is a concoction I already know.

I pull it out and hold it up. "How much of this can I take?"

He drops his gaze, squints, and then relaxes with recognition. "I gave you a low dose because you already had the tranquilizer in your system. I needed you lucid to answer questions, not pass out on me. You could easily double it or more."

A vision of him plunging several units of the clear liquid into my vein flashes in my brain. It's barely out of my system. I can't believe I'm considering pumping more in. But the possibility of getting my memories back is no less intoxicating than when Isabel recognized me that day in Rio.

Sometimes you can't know what you truly want until you get a taste of it. The nightmares and visions that hit me at random times were like flinging one piece of a puzzle at me at a time. This is more. I feel like under the right circumstances, maybe I could put it all together. Enough pieces of the puzzle could start to reveal the big picture, and this veil over my past could be lifted for good.

I put the vial back in my pocket and catch Townsend staring at me.

"I wouldn't make any big plans if that's what you're thinking of doing, Red. It could take you out for a couple days."

"Got it."

The door slams. We both turn. Jay walks toward us, her arms folded over her chest.

"Where's Isabel?" I ask.

"In the shower."

"You should get some rest."

She shrugs. "We can't stay here." A moment passes. "What do you want from me, Tristan?"

"You know what I want."

She tilts her head with a soft sigh. "I can download every detail from every job for you and give you a thorough rundown of everyone in the Company. It's not going to bring them down."

"Then what will?"

She purses her lips, like she's calculating exactly what to say. Always calculating…

"Right now you only have one enemy in the Company. Kristopher Boswell and his children. The Company is leveraging its collective resources to hunt you—*us*—down, but it's not personal. You have to remember that members aren't bound to each other by honor, but only to the laws they've established among themselves for the benefit of the whole. They have as many enemies between them as they have friends. Everything is about strategy and measuring gains and losses."

"Your point?"

"My point is that you should be concentrating on Boswell and Soloman. Reverse engineering every hit is only going to piss everyone off. And I mean *everyone*."

"So give me another option. You want to end this too, right?"

She hesitates. I can see her mind working.

"We have to. We have no other choice. I never thought I'd say it, but we're in this together."

"Are we now?" Townsend's sarcasm is both playful and begrudging, like I'm the last person he wanted to team up with.

She rolls her eyes. "Your plan didn't work. And neither will yours, Tristan. They don't have you or me in their custody. They're down two more men, and now they have a fourth target to add to their list."

"So I take care of Boswell," I say. "That's easy enough, even though they'll be expecting it."

"They will be. But this is what you do. These kinds of people know how to pull strings and play puppet master. That's what they're good at. They don't know how to work their televisions, let alone protect themselves from someone like you."

Townsend chuckles.

"But Soloman's the key. Even with Boswell gone, he'll be under pressure to fix this to prove it won't ever happen again. The members are in this for power and influence. He's in it for money, and he gets plenty of it from them. If you can take him out, the Company will be in a panic. Without leadership, without knowing the extent of their exposure once Soloman isn't there to hold it all together, they'll disassemble."

I roll the vial around in my pocket absently, absorbing everything she's said.

"You're certain that would do it."

She lifts her shoulders a little. "I'm not sure of anything anymore, but it's our best shot."

"I guess I need to get a meeting with Soloman, then."

She nods. "He travels alone. He expects his clients to also. No bodyguards. No assistants."

"You'd think in his line of work, he'd be a little paranoid about traveling without protection."

"Everything is a gentlemen's agreement. A handshake commitment between two amenable parties. No witnesses. He's more worried about indiscretions than he is about someone killing him in a meeting."

"That's about to change."

A long moment passes. She looks to Townsend and then down at the dirty sidewalk. An unspoken question lingers between us.

"I want to help you, Tristan. I *will* help you."

"But you want me to let you go."

She releases a tired sigh. "Splitting up is safer for everyone. You know that as well as I do."

True enough. I don't trust Townsend. I'd be looking over my shoulder at every turn. That and he'd be waiting for any opportunity to disappear with Jay. Trying to hold them here is impractical, and as much as Jay knows, only so much of it will be useful to me now. Plus, Townsend can keep her safe, a relief unto itself.

"Where will you go?"

"I have a place," Townsend says. "It's remote. They'll have an easier time finding Jimmy Hoffa."

"I think Noam might be heading back soon to get Zeda. He can probably give you a ride to the car if the coast is clear."

Jay shifts the weight on her feet a couple of times. "You can reach me through the chat. It's protected. They never had access to it."

"Okay. That'd be good."

Fine drops of water drip from the sky.

Not quite knowing how to say goodbye but eager for this day to be over, I push off the building and head toward the door.

"Tristan," she says, stopping me.

I look back.

"Be careful."

I answer with a short nod and turn my back to them both. Inside I see Noam, who agrees to drive them back to the church. The reverend is stable, but Zeda's still with the police. It's going to be a long night for both of them.

I climb the metal staircase to the room upstairs. When I enter it, Isabel is arranged messily on the bed, her chest moving softly. The sight of her, safe and unburdened of her worry in sleep, is like a freight train through me. My heart aches in my chest when I realize all over again I could have lost her. Townsend—the bastard who came here to rescue Jay and turn my brain into an empty wasteland—could have killed her right in front of me.

My throat constricts, and my breaths come hard and unevenly. Somehow she saved us both...

Raindrops ping loudly on the metal roof now.

Suddenly I'm more exhausted than I ever thought possible. I undress, fall into bed beside her, and give in to sleep.

11

TRISTAN

It's perfect weather for mourning. I'm sitting at the little breakfast table. We used to eat here whenever we could catch a meal together between her work schedule and mine. Rain drizzles down the windowpane, making the view out the front window even more miserable. Death in the springtime, when the earth is just starting to come back to life, seems so wrong.

I see Isabel's faint reflection in the glass as she comes up behind me. She kneads my shoulders through my dress shirt. It feels good, breaks through the numbness that's been building up since Mom died. Funerals are supposed to give you closure, but I don't feel any different. The parade of her coworkers, people from our neighborhood, and a few teachers from school through the funeral home didn't usher in another stage of grief. I just feel raw.

I close my eyes and sigh heavily. I reach up and take Isabel's hand in one of mine, caress up and down her forearm. At least she's here. The best thing to help me get through the worst thing. She walks around me and sits on my lap. We've been connected all day. A hundred little touches that reminded me she was with me every minute.

She touches my cheek. "You doing okay?"

People have been asking me the same thing all day. But this is different. The way she's looking at me, with more love than pity in her eyes, makes me think she could actually bring me through this if I let her. I close my eyes and swallow hard. I fight it. I push it all down. All the pain. All the love she makes me feel. The grief is tearing me apart on the inside, but somehow her arms around me feel like the safest place I've ever known.

"It's going to be all right, Tristan," she whispers. "We're going to get through this."

The gentle slide of her fingertips along my nape—every touch—is searing. An invitation to show her how bad it hurts.

I hide my tears against her chest until there's no stopping this rush of emotion. I've gone from raw to bleeding. A fragile shell collapsing in on itself. I draw in a ragged breath, exhale a painful sob. The cradle of her embrace is all I know as the past week comes crashing down on me in a sudden deluge. She answers with gentle touches and soothing words. I'm right here. Everything's going to be okay. I love you so much.

I cry until I'm empty. The worst of the pain recedes to the dark corners of my heart, making room for something else. Hope. Desire. Isabel.

I don't know how long we stay that way, holding each other like one of us might disappear if we dare let go. I just want to touch her everywhere, soak up every inch of her warmth and energy. The past is death and loss and pain. She's here, light and alive. The only thing in my world that really matters now.

When I think I've pieced myself back together enough, I look into her stormy eyes.

"I want you to stay."

Her lips part a little. "I'll stay for as long as you need me."

"What about your parents?"

"They'll understand. They know I want to be here for you right now. Nothing else matters."

She threads her fingers through my hair absently. I close my eyes at the sensation. Every touch makes me crave more. It seems crazy, but I never want to be apart from her. I think I could hold her this way and revel in her for the rest of my life.

I touch her face. Trace her lips, darker now from the makeup she wore today.

I lean in to kiss her. Softly at first. A re-exploration of something we know well by now. The comfort of silken lips and velvet tongues. The promise of more…of all the places we haven't gone yet.

I take the kiss deeper and slide my palm up her thigh, pushing her black dress up with it. Need to get closer. Need to feel her go breathless. And when she does and we break apart, heat and hesitation swim in her pretty hazel eyes. I go farther, easing my hand between her thighs. Farther and farther until the only thing stopping me is the barrier of her panties. I can feel her heat through them.

We're barely breathing. This isn't how it usually is. Our touches are always careful. Cautious. Measured. I never want to push her. I always let her show me how far she wants to go. But I feel so desperate now. Desperate to overwhelm this agony that's still clinging to the edges of my heart. With her…

Her eyes flutter closed. The little puffs of air from her uneven breaths tingle my lips. She makes the smallest sound of protest when I push the fabric over, push inside, and stroke along her slick inner walls with my fingers. I try not to think too hard about how badly I want to claim this part of her in other ways. With our bodies pressed together like this, there's no hiding how this is affecting me, though.

I brush my lips over hers, the barest graze. "Isabel…"

Give me more, *I silently beg.* Give me everything…

She slips her hand from my neck down to the second button on my shirt, like she wants to tug it free. Being this close, this deep, this everything, I'm ten seconds from dragging her to my bedroom and ripping her clothes off. I need to know where this is going before I go too far and ruin everything.

"I need you," *I utter through my teeth, preparing myself for the possibility of stopping this. Letting her go seems impossible. In this moment, I'm certain I've never needed anything more in my life.*

The little flare of her anxiety melts into something else. Hints of arousal. The anxious shift of her thighs. Soft whimpers tumbling from her lips.

It's not a green light, but I can't bring myself to slow this down yet.

I scoop her into my arms and carry her to my room. I kick the door open and step into the darkness. The moody sky casts a blue hue on the walls and my unmade bed. I lower her to her feet but keep her tight against me. Somehow in the few seconds that have passed, I've reined in my desire a few notches.

Then she circles her arms around my neck, lifts to her toes, and brings our mouths together again, like we're two magnets no force can keep apart. I feel her teeth, her tongue, and the unmistakable intent behind the kiss. It's deep and passionate and threatens the patience I'm trying like hell to cling to.

I drag my hands up her sides, find the zipper in the back of her dress, and pull it down until it falls into a pile at her feet. I break the kiss long enough to admire her body and obsess over the lacy black undergarments covering the rest of her.

A sharp surge of desire I'm helpless to subdue rushes over me. I nudge her back so she falls down onto the bed. She stares up at me, her cheeks flushed, her chest moving under quick breaths. She's perfection. My whole life.

We're eighteen, and we think we know everything. Maybe we know nothing. But the way she makes me feel is real. When she's in the room, suddenly I'm safe and loved and the most important person in her world. No way can I reason my way out of being with her now, even if I wanted to.

And I don't. I'm aching to get inside her. To fuse our bodies together until I forget anything exists outside the perfect way she feels. I unbutton my shirt and toss it away.

Following her onto the bed, I settle between her thighs. There's so little between us. It's heady and intimate and right.

She skims her hands down my torso and rolls her hips. My breath leaves me in a rush of relief and longing for more. I brush my lips over hers, the barest graze. "Are you sure you want this?"

Her eyes sparkle in the dim light. "I want this."

Thank God. I pray she doesn't change her mind. We've waited long enough. Passed up dozens of chances waiting for the perfect time…the moment when it all felt right.

"I'll go slow," I promise. "I don't want to hurt you."

Ever. In any way.

But she's a virgin, and I can't take that first stab of pain away, no matter how much I wish I could.

She caresses her palms down my chest, resting over my heart. "I don't care about the pain. If it hurts, it won't be forever. And it'll be with you."

ISABEL

I'm sitting on the edge of the bed when Tristan's sharp intake of breath breaks my silent staring contest with the wall. I release my legs from my chest and turn toward him. His breathing picks up and then evens out. He sits up and puts his head in his hands a moment before looking up. Our eyes meet in the dark.

"Are you okay?"

I nod and lie. "I'm okay."

I'm not sure how long I slept before the specter of Bones's face propelled me into a heart-thumping state of perpetual alertness. I've been staring at the wall ever since, waiting for the nightmare to recede. I tried to replace it with something else. Something happier and sunnier. But thoughts of my carefree past only remind me of what I've lost. A walk or some tea would be a nice distraction, but being in the same room as an unconscious Tristan is better.

Selfishly, I'm glad he's awake now so I can soak up more of him. He motions me toward him. I crawl up the bed and settle between his thighs. He leans against the wall and I against his chest. He's warm, like a heated blanket around my torso.

"What was the dream?"

He doesn't answer. Instead his lips drift to my shoulder, his hands to the apex of my thighs. I'm bare under the oversize T-shirt, a circumstance I'm grateful for when his fingertips graze me slowly.

My breath leaves me. "Oh."

When I shift against him, I can feel his erection, which I'm guessing his dream inspired. I snake my hand behind to circle his hot flesh. He sucks in another sharp breath and plunges his fingers into me at once. I moan and arch against him.

"Are you sure you want this?"

His voice is gravel against my skin. Something about the way he says it makes me shiver.

"I want this."

He tightens his arm around my torso, holding me there in an unexpected embrace.

"Do you know I love you? That no matter what happened, I always did? I need you to believe it, because then I can live with myself. If you believe it, it'll be real."

I cover his arm with mine, returning the message without words. I need him. I love him. Always want to be with him. That's never changed over time and distance and this dark turn our lives have taken.

"I believe it." My voice breaks when I say it.

"I just lost sight of the thread between us. It was never broken. I promise you."

I can't utter another word without breaking down. I don't want to hurt. I want to love. I want to lose myself in him. Banish the hurt and the pain.

He seems to know, because he slowly loosens his grasp, shifts us so we're both lying down, and spoons his hard body behind me. He trails his fingertips down my arm, sending goosebumps racing over my skin. His soft lips follow. Endless minutes are spent in this silent worship. Our limbs tangle. The slide of his skin over mine is the sweetest torment. This is what heaven is like… The perfect place where love and longing promise paradise.

When I turn my head to taste his lips, he eases into me. Slowly, and then deeply, with such intention that I'm rendered breathless. When he thrusts again, he breathes life back into me with his words. "I love you."

I sift my fingers into his hair, and he lowers his lips to my neck. He licks and sucks my skin while we move together like we're one body, feel everything together like one heart. And when we come, we share the rush. We chase it and swallow it. An explosion of sensation unlike anything I've ever felt. The release is so strong, it feels bigger than our bodies. A force field of pleasure. Paradise.

He stays inside me, and the euphoria hums between us for what feels like forever. Sleep tugs at me, but I'm unwilling to let go of the moment to the uncertainty of my dreams. When he finally moves, he rolls me to face him. He touches my face, traces my lips.

"I remember you."

"You mean, in your dream?" I can't hide the hope lacing my tone.

"Yeah, but it's more than that. I remember *us*. Not everything, but it's coming back. My mom's funeral. You stayed."

My heart launches into a sprint. Suddenly my own mind is flooded with memories from that day. From the awful task of burying his mother to enduring the small stream of mourners who offered their condolences. He'd broken down in my arms that night in an embrace that ended in his bed. Our first time would be seared in my brain for as long as I lived. He'd been so careful with me. Soothing me through the pain. Then finally giving in to his passion until we were both spent and more in love than we ever thought possible.

I push up to my elbow and look down at him. "You remember that night?"

"Whatever Townsend gave me broke new memories loose. The drug must still be in my system. I don't know if the flashbacks will last, but I've never experienced anything like it. It's like…" He licks his lips and exhales softly. "It's like everything always felt out of reach. So thin and foggy that I could hardly be sure if the flashbacks were real. Even if I got little glimpses, it was like water through my fingers. And now… now I've got a hold on something."

I don't know how to express what this news is doing to me. Tristan having his memories back would be the best gift anyone could ever give me. But what if it doesn't last…

He seems to read my mind. "I took the vial from his bag."

"And?"

"And I think I want more."

THE RED LEDGER

part 6

1

ISABEL

Perdido Key, Florida

A cloak of misty gray fog hovers at the water's edge, hiding the horizon of endless sea. Uneven wooden pickets pierce the dunes on either side of the narrow path that leads from the cottage to the beach. I brace my hands on the deck's rail and think about venturing down to the water to explore. The fog is comforting for the anonymity it offers, but eerie too. Though I haven't had the luxury lately of being able to see more than a few steps ahead anyway.

After a morning of goodbyes and loose planning, Tristan and I pulled away from New Orleans with the aim to find a quiet place to hide away for a while. I'm eager to put distance between us and what happened. Martine's death. Bones's murder. Facing my own death and the revelations around Tristan's memories. It all seems like an awful nightmare I can't shake.

I close my eyes and concentrate on the waves rolling in. Little by little, the rhythm works against the panic that's stitched itself into even my resting thoughts. I'm tired. I should go inside and catch some sleep, but I don't trust my dreams. Tristan's fatigue took hold moments after we arrived. I'm certain whatever drugs Townsend gave him to even the fight is the cause.

A week here may not be enough to restore what's been lost.

Maybe it's the events of the past couple of days or the years of desiring a real life with Tristan that does it... Either way, I feed a little fantasy that the beach house isn't just a pit stop on the journey, but that it's ours. Mentally I pick new colors for the little bedrooms and spruce up the outdated beach-inspired furnishings. I make a plan to fix the sticky slider that opens to the deck. I take in a deep breath of ocean air and imagine what it might be like to have coffee out here in the mornings, just the two of us.

I pretend this is home.

That quickly, I recognize how foolish my thoughts are. Reality is a painful strike against the fleeting moment of relief.

I open my eyes, leave the deck, and take the sandy path to the water. The salty mist cools my skin as I walk. When the chilly waves crash over my feet, I absorb the discomfort and let myself sink in place. Looking around, I can see more than before. The waves breaking in the distance. A low-flying pelican. Behind me, the beach house with its fern-colored siding is barely visible.

Situated on a remote stretch of the Gulf, the house sits high on stilts that elevate it above the sand, almost defiantly ready for the storms that batter these shores.

I walk back a few steps and plunk onto the sand. I drop my head in my hands and wait for the crippling wave of emotion that's now long overdue. I prepare myself to give in to it and savor the relief of having cried my heart out. But my eyes don't sting. Everything hurts, but that telltale prickling doesn't show up. The tears don't come.

Maybe tears can't heal these new wounds.

"You okay?"

I draw my hands away and claw them into the sand as I jolt back. A few feet away stands a young man. The first thing I notice is his hair—

light blond and matted into long, messy dreads that frame his face and his deep-set brown eyes. Every inch of his skin is burned a dark golden from hours, maybe days, in the sun.

He shifts on his feet, resituating the straps of his large pack over his shoulders. "Sorry. Didn't mean to sneak up on you. This fog is crazy, huh?"

"Yeah." I exhale a shaky sigh. "Is it like this a lot?"

"Don't know, really. I'm just passing through."

"Where are you headed?"

He shifts the weight of the pack again before easing it off his back and onto the sand. "Heading to the Keys. You mind?" He gestures to the sandy spot between me and the pack.

I hesitate a little because I'm still shell-shocked from recent events. But nothing about this guy is setting off alarms. Plus this is hardly a private beach. If I don't like his company, I can walk a few yards to the house and wait for him to pass through.

"Go ahead."

He drops down as I answer, reclines onto his back with a relieved grunt, and tucks his hands behind his head. He lifts an eyebrow and tilts his head toward me. "Bad day?"

"Something like that."

"I hear ya. I've been going pretty hard the past few days. Weather's coming in, and I was hoping to make it over the bay before it caught up to me."

"Are you close?"

"I think so."

"Do you have a map?"

"Yeah, I check it every once in a while. I don't mind taking my time, though. Should be fine either way. Plenty of piers between here and there I can camp under if the water doesn't get too rough."

He closes his eyes with a sigh, and I get the sense he doesn't really care if I'm here or not, which is an odd relief. The comfortable silence with a complete stranger is a pleasant distraction from my own troubling thoughts. After a few minutes, he pops up on his elbow, his gaze suddenly bright.

"Hey, do you happen to know what day it is?"

I smile a little at his obviously lax attitude toward time and circumstances and pull my phone from my pocket. "March thirtieth."

He grins with a relaxed bob of his head. "Cool."

I'm ready to put the phone away when it hits me. "Oh, wow."

"What?"

I laugh softly. "I just realized something." I shake my head a little and stand. "Sorry, I have to go."

He looks up at me, not moving. "Nice to meet you. I hope your day gets better."

"Thanks. I think it will. I hope you beat the weather."

"No worries. I'm Caleb, by the way," he says, waving me off.

"I'm Isabel."

TRISTAN

"Tristan." Her moan breaks free like a forbidden thing.

Everything about what we're doing is forbidden and likely to get us in a world of trouble if her parents catch us. Too bad I don't care.

Not when Isabel's falling apart under me. Her eyes slip closed. Her body grips me everywhere. I'm consumed by her pleasure. I've never witnessed anything more breathtaking than the expression on her face when I make her come. I've never felt anything this intense. Then again, I've never been this in love.

The persistent spring wind drags branches across her bedroom window, their rustling mingling with her quiet whimpers. Nothing but the two of us drowning in each other. I sweep my lips across hers and swallow the sound of my name on her lips, over and over…

"Tristan. Tristan, wake up."

I blink awake. Isabel's sitting at my side, her hand resting gently on my shoulder. I take a few uneven breaths and slowly separate the erotic dream from the real-life Isabel who seems oblivious to it all. I look around the room and remember where we are—our little hideaway on the beach.

"Is everything all right?"

Her smile answers for her. I rub my eye with the heel of my hand.

"What? Why are you smiling like that?"

Her tongue peeks between her teeth and her eyes glitter.

Between the vivid dream and this burst of happiness in her, she's irresistible. I pull her down onto me and drag my hands up her sides.

"You woke me up from a really nice dream. You'd better explain yourself."

She giggles. I cherish the sound and the delicate softness of her body. And now I'm preoccupied with eliciting more of those sounds and worshiping all her perfect curves. I roll my hips against hers, unable to resist the pleasurable friction between us.

She nips at her bottom lip. "You've been having a lot of those dreams."

I roll us so I'm above her. "How can you blame me? I think some of my best memories might have been forged with you under me."

The line of her body bends slightly, molding our torsos together a little more. "That might be true."

I bend to kiss her, slowly and deeply, intent on merging reality with the dream and making new memories of her crying out my name. But even as I start to lose myself in her taste and her scent and her heavenly body, I recognize she came in here and woke me up for something else.

"Why did you wake me up? Did something happen?"

Her lips twitch a little. "Do you have any idea what day it is?"

I frown. "No. Does it matter?"

She smiles again. "It's your birthday."

I still and take that in. I haven't celebrated a birthday since I became Tristan Red. But Isabel seems so overjoyed with this news, I try to muster some enthusiasm for her sake.

"Thanks for remembering," I say, though it sounds flat out loud.

Isabel doesn't seem to notice.

"I woke you up because I didn't want you to sleep the whole day away. We should do something."

I try even harder to get on board with her excitement. "It's not a big deal. It's just another day."

She widens her eyes and smacks her palm against my bare chest. "It *is* a big deal. And we're going to do something."

I shift against her and dip down to nibble at her collarbone. "I thought we *were* doing something."

"We have all day for that."

"Oh good," I hum and go lower to suck her nipples through her shirt until they pebble for me.

She inhales sharply and pushes at my shoulders at once. "Tristan, I'm serious. I want to do something special."

I sigh and reluctantly entertain her request. "Okay. Like what?"

"We could go out to dinner. There must be some nice places along the water here."

I glance out the bedroom door to the foggy shore. "Not much of a view. Plus I don't really want to have dinner with a bunch of random people when I'd rather just be with you."

She keeps tugging on her lower lip, which does nothing for my resolve.

"What's your favorite food?"

I lift my eyebrows. "I'm not picky. I'll eat pretty much anything."

"What if I cook for you? We need to get groceries for the house anyway. I'll whip up something special for dinner. And it'll just be us." She threads her fingers into my hair. "It'll be normal."

The promise of commemorating my birthday or spending a night in with her doesn't sway me. The last wish on her lips does, though, because she needs something normal more than I need anything. I recognize the dimming in her eyes. The wordless sadness that got heavier the farther we drove away from New Orleans and everything that happened there. Things we still haven't talked about…

I trail my fingertip down the bridge of her nose and kiss her softly. "That sounds perfect."

I really want to keep her trapped here beneath me so I can make love to her for hours, but somehow I know that as amazing as that would be, she needs this more. And the more I think about a home-cooked meal, the hungrier I realize I am.

So I let her shimmy away. She tosses my shirt at me with a smirk. "Come on, sleepyhead. Let's get domestic."

2

ISABEL

I scramble around the kitchen and do my best with the cheap appliances and sparse kitchenware available in the rental.

"Can I help?"

I turn around, and Tristan is standing between the kitchen and the largely empty living room. The fans whirring from the vaulted ceiling make shadows on his face. He's barefoot and holding a glass of white wine in his hand. The vision is totally foreign and one hundred percent welcome. I save the snapshot in my head for when I need a reminder of what I want.

"No, I've got this. Go drink your wine and relax, birthday boy."

He twists his lips and watches me take the baked fish out of the oven.

I shoot him a glare. "Seriously. Go away. You're making me nervous."

"All right," he mutters and walks onto the deck.

This crappy kitchen is stressing me out, but I'm determined to make Tristan a special birthday dinner. About fifteen minutes later, I've managed to plate up some decent-looking seafood tacos and a fresh side salad. Hopefully they taste okay. Presentation is half the battle, so I take stock in that, pour myself a glass of wine, and join Tristan outside with our plates. We settle at the little table, positioning both our chairs next to each other so they face the sunset and a much clearer view of the ocean. I can't help but smile. Even if the food is awful, everything else feels too close to perfect.

Tristan holds my gaze a moment before leaning in to kiss me. "Thank you."

My heart does something explosive at the intimacy of it all. Then he distracts me by lifting his glass to mine.

"To our first date," he says.

I laugh. "I guess I'll never forget our anniversary now."

"Which means I'll never forget my birthday again."

We both laugh and drink our wine like we do this all the time. It feels surreal and wonderful.

We're starving, so we dive right in.

"Wow, this is awesome," he says with his mouth full.

I take a bite and am relieved the meal is not only edible but tasty. "Not bad. I guess I managed to remember a few things my mom taught me in the kitchen."

"This is probably the nicest thing anyone's ever done for me." He hesitates a minute, finishing another bite. "Except maybe cut my ropes with tiny scissors."

The corner of his mouth lifts. I'm glad he's too focused on his food to meet my eyes, because the injection of reality throws me off balance. I swallow down a big gulp of wine and am grateful when the conversation shifts to the horizon, the wanderer I met on the beach earlier, and wondering whether he made it over the bridge. Easier topics. Convenient snippets that fit into the fantasy I'm clinging to now like a desperate belief in Santa and magic.

Tristan clears the plates and comes back with the bottle, refreshing our glasses. The sky changes colors, from pink and orange to a deep purple that almost matches the water. He takes my hand and holds it firmly in his.

"You can talk to me about what happened, you know."

I tense my jaw and look at him, silently begging him not to go down this road. I already tried crying it out. It didn't work. *I'm fine. I'm going to be fine…*

"I know it's probably eating away at you. Maybe you think this is normal stuff for me. I just want you to know, I've been in some pretty awful situations, but that was probably the worst thing I've ever experienced. At least that I can remember."

"I don't really want to talk about it." I take a deep breath and refocus on the dying sunset. It's bland now. All its magic has been eaten up by the impending nightfall. Just like our perfect birthday dinner. Poof.

"Isabel…"

I pull my hand from his, walk to the other side of the deck, and stare at the rolling waves.

I hear his chair push back and then his quiet steps toward me. I feel his heat. A gentle sweep of his hand down my back. I close my eyes when he wraps his arms around me from behind.

"You were incredibly brave. I hate that you had to be, but it's over now. You're allowed to let yourself feel things."

"Regret? Disgust? Pure horror? No thanks. I'm bottling it all up just fine. It's not like we have time to put me on a therapy couch to deal with it properly anyway."

"Maybe we don't, but no one's trying to hurt us now. You can bring the walls down and talk to me."

I don't know what to say. Maybe bottling it all up is a huge mistake and I'm setting myself up for a massive breakdown. But the harder this armor around me gets, the more I appreciate it.

"There's nothing wrong with being stronger," I finally say, the words themselves lacking the strength I'm hoping to convey.

He turns me slowly in his arms and tilts my chin up for me to look at him. "You were strong before. I'm different from who I was before I met you, but I don't have the capacity to feel things the way you do. I think it's something that got stripped away with my memory. I don't know how to explain it except I recognize that you should be more upset than you're letting on, but if I were in your shoes, I'd probably react the same way. That's not necessarily normal or healthy."

I sigh. "Just… Don't worry about me, okay? I'm fine. I promise."

His gaze travels over me, his doubt and concern quietly existing in the silence. "Sorry," he says softly. "I didn't mean to ruin dinner. Everything was perfect."

"It's fine. I have to learn to appreciate the good moments when we have them. Seems like clinging to hope that they'll last forever is a setup for disappointment."

"That sounds awful when you say it like that."

"Well, we can't stay here forever, can we?"

His mouth forms a rigid line, like he doesn't want to let the disappointing truth pass through. Doesn't matter. I know this peace can't last.

"We don't have to think about that right now," he says.

"Why wait? Why bring me here and make me want something better only to rip it away when we have to move on in a few days? Why tear off my armor when it's the only thing that kept me alive? Maybe I don't want to be vulnerable ever again, knowing there's someone who's capable of killing me at the next turn."

"We can stay here as long as you want. As long as it's safe… But you're right, there's work to be done."

I cross my arms over my chest tightly. "Work?"

The line between his brows deepens. "Let's not do this right now."

Inside I'm jumping at the invitation to ignore reality. But knowing Tristan has a plan forming makes me curious about what it is. Not because I'm ready to jump into it but because I want to prepare myself. Nothing could have prepared me for Bones and the things that happened in that awful house.

"I'd rather know what we're heading into than pretend this can last."

"How about we agree to save the world tomorrow." He eases his palm over my cheek and leans in so our faces are close. "You wanted today to be special for me, right?"

I relax my shoulders. "Of course."

"Then give me tonight. Let me make love to you. Let me take my time with you. We'll figure out the rest in the morning."

Before I can muster any sort of argument, his lips cover mine in a tender, possessive kiss. He cradles my face in his hands, angling us so he can go deeper and take more. The fervent exploration of mouths robs me of any dissenting thoughts and draws our bodies closer. The world outside our moment quickly starts to blur.

Maybe reaching for our happily ever after is a waste. When he touches me and holds me like I'm precious, everything shifts. I close my eyes and wonder if this is all that matters. The here and now. The gift of his touch. A night that belongs to us. Waking up to a new day in his arms and not losing a minute of it hoping for more.

TRISTAN

I pour myself a large cup of black coffee, slip soundlessly out the back door to the deck, and dial Gabriel's number. Early morning brings high tide up the beach, but the waves are lazy and quiet in the distance. I'm both tired and recharged. Once Isabel gave in to me last night, I made good on my promise. Night bled into morning before we finally succumbed to sleep, but I wouldn't trade a minute of the satisfaction. I'll sleep when I'm dead.

After a few rings, her grandfather's accented voice greets me. "Hello?"

"Gabriel, it's Tristan."

A brief pause. "Tristan." He releases a heavy sigh, like he's been unburdened suddenly. "Where are you?"

I pause. "A few hours away."

"Is Isabel okay?"

"She's fine. A little shaken, obviously, but I think she'll be all right. I'm guessing you heard what happened."

"I can't believe it. I can't believe she's really gone." He's quiet a moment. "The funeral is next week. Reverend Stephens will be out of the hospital by then and will give the service. It gives everyone time to travel too. Martine was very connected. Her death will come as a shock to a lot of people."

I hesitate because I'm not sure how broken up he is over this or if he has any idea I'm the one who ended her life. I'm not exactly proud of it, but it's what needed to be done. The fact that I killed her won't keep me up at night. At least not the way I know Bones's ghost is haunting Isabel's dreams. I don't want Isabel building a wall around her heart, but I hope she can come to terms with what happened sooner rather than later.

"If you're going to stay in New Orleans, you should be extremely careful," I say.

"I have to stay. Lucia will be here tomorrow to help take care of affairs. The house was destroyed. There's a lot to be done."

"What will happen to Halo?"

"That remains to be seen. This obviously changes things. Martine held the reins for a long time, and I never argued. I didn't thrive on the power play the way she did. I used our resources sparingly, only when necessary. She amassed so much wealth…"

His voice drifts off, as if he can't understand what would motivate her to such greed.

"I know. I went through her files. Millions. Plenty of real estate too. What will happen to all of it?"

"The ministry's assets were placed in a charitable trust. In the event of Martine's death, Lucia and I become the trustees."

"That's quite an inheritance."

"Some of the money is tied up in the cause. There are channels to distribute the rest. The complexity of this net she built means Halo has to go on, and the trust will continue to support it. But the mission… These things can change. They must."

I start to pace the deck, sensing there's more. Gabriel didn't love the direction Martine was taking Halo, but that doesn't mean he's closing down the operation now that she's gone. The circumstance of her death could mean a whole new direction for the organization.

"Tristan, I have to ask you something. With everything that's come to pass, have you made a decision about the Company? Will you go after them yourself?"

He doesn't realize I made that decision before we'd ever met. I'm not sure if mine is the answer he wants to hear, but seeing as he holds no authority over me, I figure the truth is best.

"I don't trust anyone else to the task. This needs to end."

"How do you plan to do it?"

"Jay's become an ally. I plan to pull this weed out by the roots. She'll help me do it."

At least I think she will. We'll see if she answers when I come calling for more intel.

"And Isabel?"

Will I keep her out of harm's way? Will I take care of her? This is what he wants to know. He doesn't realize how willful, brave, and determined she can be, though.

"We're in this together," I say at the risk of ratcheting up his worry. "I can assure you nothing is more important than keeping her safe. Always."

He sighs. It's a worried, tired sound. "I'm glad you called, then."

I slow my pacing.

"When Lucia gave Isabel her new identity, she set her up with a bank account. We funded it thinking she would be staying with Martine for quite some time. Things have changed, and if you really intend to go after them, money shouldn't be a consideration. I'm going to move funds around and make a transfer into her account once the bank opens. If it helps, or if it can buy her freedom from these people, it'll be worth whatever Martine did to get it."

"Lucia's agreed to this?"

"She will. Please tell Isabel."

"I will."

We hang up, and I finish my coffee, which has grown cold.

I'd never been money hungry. Of course I needed to survive, but having access to that kind of money brings new possibilities. Fewer limitations.

The door slides open, and when I turn, Isabel walks through. She's wearing one of my black T-shirts and holding a ripe peach we bought at the local supermarket yesterday, an endeavor that was more enjoyable than I ever thought it could be. Next to the horrors we've seen, being able to pick out produce together was more than pleasant—it was a glimpse into what a normal life could look like for us. A life where we weren't running, where we could work and run errands and spend every night the way we spent last night.

"Morning, Red." She smirks before taking a bite.

I lick my bottom lip and look her over while last night plays like a fast reel in my mind.

"Isabel."

She walks up to me and kisses my cheek. I turn and take her mouth. Peaches and Isabel's sweet taste. When we pull away, her smile returns and her eyes glitter with affection.

"I think I like when you call me that," I mutter.

She laughs and takes another bite. I'm not sure why, but it feels like an evolution. Like acceptance. Like I'm the one who's reclaimed her heart. Tristan Red. Not the man I used to be, who still seems like a stranger most of the time.

"Who were you talking to?"

I redirect my thoughts to the conversation with her grandfather and the fortuitous turn of events at Halo's helm.

"Gabriel. He gave me his number when we talked before. I promised I'd keep him updated so he knows you're safe."

She stills. "Is that all?"

"He and your mother are going to be assuming responsibility for Halo's assets. They're significant. Martine had her fingers in a lot of pots. She couldn't buy her way into the Company, but maybe it'll be enough to help us take them down."

Her eyebrows shoot up. "Us?"

"Keep an eye on your bank account."

3

ISABEL

Of all the things that drove the big choices in my life, money never ranked highly among them. Thanks to my father's high-ranking government job, I always had everything I needed and most of what I wanted. My parents wanted me to be successful in whatever I did and could afford to put me on that path, but I always cared more about being happy over being rich. No amount of money could have brought back the happiness I'd once tasted with Tristan. That much I knew.

Still, I'm not immune to the shock of seeing my inflated bank balance when the transfer hits a few hours after Tristan told me to expect it. Martine's humble mission didn't match her bank account, it would seem.

I put my hand over my mouth. "My God, Tristan, what are we going to do with this much money?"

He rolls over on the blanket we've laid out on the sand, slides his aviators down his nose half an inch, and peers at my phone screen. He arches a dark eyebrow before rolling to his back and replacing his sunglasses over his eyes.

"Tristan!"

He grins. "What do you want me to say? Don't spend it all in one place."

I let out a short laugh. "I can't think of a single thing I could buy with this much money. Maybe a private island."

"You never know. We may need one after this is all said and done."

I blink a few times. Recount the zeros. Try to wrap my head around the amount. This is insane. Hell, wouldn't this be enough for us to disappear forever?

"You're sure we can't just move somewhere and live on this for the rest of our lives?"

"If I thought it'd be that easy, we'd be there already."

I sulk a little.

Being here in Perdido Key feels like we're on the edge of the world, but I know better. Danger could be closer than we know. The Company has caught us off guard before. Even if weeks or months go by here without incident, that's not enough to rest easy.

I put the phone down and take in Tristan's reclined figure. His chest is bare and marred with scars I wish I could erase forever. The instinct to run and hide suddenly morphs into something else—the instinct to right all the wrongs, take back what was so cruelly ripped away, and build the life we deserve.

"You said we'd figure out how to save the world this morning. It's almost noon."

He rolls to his side and props his head on his hand. "Are you in a rush?"

"Clearly, I am."

He pushes his sunglasses into his hair. "Why are you pushing the pace?"

"Why aren't *you*?"

"Because you need some time to recover after what happened."

"Okay, but while we're here, they're not going to lose interest. They'll never be *less* motivated to destroy us until we stop them. Once they find out about Martine and Dunny, they'll be regrouping and coming up with a new plan of action, right? Maybe that's when we should be putting ours into motion. Like Jay said, she didn't expect us to maneuver with Boswell so quickly. It caught them off guard. They may be deadly and soulless, but they're still an organization. They're bigger and have more moving parts. We can always be more agile."

He swings his gaze over the pretty aquamarine water and then back to me. "We need to get a meeting with Soloman. Take him out." He hesitates a minute. "Then we need to set our sights on Kristopher Boswell. Probably Vince and his sister too."

I tense, not only because of what I went through with Vince Boswell but because of the relationship I had with Kolt not that long ago. Kolt may have fallen for me, but he also betrayed me every minute he pretended to be someone he wasn't. If his mother and uncle were instrumental in putting the hit on my life, then those two people are between us and our freedom. Still, I'm grateful they're second on the list so I don't have to dwell on it too much right away.

"How do we get a meeting with Soloman?"

Tristan purses his lips a little. "Crow has a connection, but the last time I relied on him to carry out a plan, it was catastrophic. Also, if Jay's willing to help, I can't have Crow involved. Once Townsend finds out what happened to her, he's more likely to outright kill Crow than let a plan unfold with him in it."

"That's true. So we go to Jay first?"

He nods. "I'll message her."

"You really think she'll help?"

"I have a feeling she will. We're in the same boat now. She wants Soloman out of the picture as much as we do. Her life depends on it too."

He may be right, but I'm too impatient to wait to find out. I grab my things and make my way up the path to the house.

"Where are you going?" he calls after me.

I hurry up the stairs and into the house, find Tristan's laptop, and bring it to the wicker dining room table.

Tristan bursts through the door just as I key in his password.

"What the hell do you think you're doing?"

"Taking initiative."

He rolls his eyes and pulls up a chair. I'm opening the chat terminal as he turns the laptop toward him, putting an end to my hijacking of the machine. "Anyone ever tell you you're impulsive?"

I just smile and rest my chin on his shoulder as he types into the chat.

> RED: I have a client for Soloman. How does he
> get a meeting?

"You have a client? You can't mean you."

"No. Mateus," he says.

"Mateus? He'd come all the way from Brazil—"

"He'll do whatever I ask him to do. And he's probably not in Brazil anymore. He could be anywhere."

> JAY: What's his industry?

Tristan rests his fingers lightly on the keys, not depressing any of them. He's calculating, so I don't distract him even though I'm definitely more eager than Jay for the answer. His history with Mateus was never fully explained to me. All I know is he has a debt to Tristan, a multi-million-dollar condo in New York City, and access to private jets and pilots on standby. And he may be one of the only people Tristan trusts.

> RED: Imports and exports.

> JAY: Don't bullshit me. If he's introduced
> through the wrong people, the plan will fail.

The corner of his lip lifts, but he hesitates a moment before responding.

> RED: Textiles. Brazil with global reach. Money is
> no object.

A few minutes pass as we watch the screen and wait for her to respond. I sit back and cross my arms. "So are you going to tell me what happened between you two?"

TRISTAN

A burst of visions flicker across my mind. The red glow of the neon signs that lit up Mateus's face the night we met. The busy bar that muffled our introductions and the conversations that followed. The hand-drawn map he gave me with an offer I could have easily refused.

Isabel links our fingers together, drawing my focus back to her thoughtful gaze. I think back to when I all but dragged her into Mateus's home a month ago with no explanation. He'd known then that Isabel was important, even if I couldn't fully grasp it myself.

There's no reason not to tell her about our history except that no one ever knew what I did for Mateus or why. It happened before the accountability that came with the assignments Company Eleven fed me for years after.

"I met Mateus a long time ago. Before I'd accepted any jobs from Jay. She'd been pressuring me to get started for a few months, but I kept putting her off. I told her I was still healing and figuring out my way around Rio, which was half true. I used to hang out at this bar called Banana Jack, close to where I lived at the time. It was nothing special, but I ate half my meals there. I didn't go to socialize, but the small talk helped me learn the language. Plus it got me out of my own head, which at the time wasn't a great place to be. Anyway, that's where I met him."

"I thought he lived in Petrópolis."

"Sometimes he's there if he's not traveling or working. He came to Rio for business pretty often. He owned a condo on the strip, which ended up being mine when everything was said and done. You saw it."

Her eyes widen. "The penthouse? How can he afford all these places?"

"He owns one of the largest textile companies in Brazil. He owns everything from the cotton plantations in Mato Grosso do Sul to the garment-making operations in Petrópolis. It's a billion-dollar industry, and he's got a nice piece of the pie."

"So how'd he get mixed up with you?"

I laugh. An argument could be made the other way around, but for the most part, I was the sinner and he was the saint in the friendship. If nothing else, his optimism about Isabel's return to my life was evidence of that.

"We got to talking one night over burgers and a few beers. He later admitted the meeting wasn't by chance. He noticed me a couple nights before. I guess he could smell the former military on me and figured I might be someone who could help him."

"And you did."

"He offered me a job. Said he'd pay me ten thousand dollars just to try. If I failed, I'd be lucky to escape with my life. A few had already tried and failed. Some didn't make it out. If I succeeded, he said he'd pay me a lot more. I figured the ten grand would set me up for a while, maybe help me put Jay off a little longer. But I also didn't want to make a target of myself by expecting this huge payout if I succeeded, so I told him he could owe me a favor instead."

"What was the job?"

"Karina."

She searches my eyes. "Karina?"

Isabel knew her as Mateus's lover and the woman who kept their house in order. She wouldn't have recognized the Karina I found in the slums years ago.

"Mateus lost his parents young, so he moved to Rio to find work. He became best friends with Karina's much older brother. They did everything together until Mateus got out of the favela and made his own way. Obviously he did well for himself. His friend took a different path and got mixed up in the middle of a nasty gang war that ended up killing him. Mateus was so wrapped up in building his empire, he never thought about Karina or what might have happened to her until they crossed paths again. She was still a young girl in his mind."

I glance at the screen. Jay still hasn't written back, so I continue.

"Part of Mateus's company runs out of Rocinha. He was on his way there to check some things out with his team when he saw her. She didn't recognize him, probably because her boyfriend was beating the shit out of her, but when Mateus went to intervene, his people held him back. The guy she was with was a lieutenant with Comando Vermelho, and it would have caused problems. Mateus couldn't let it go. Not until he got her out of there."

"She couldn't just leave?"

"He tried to reach out to her through other people. Told her he'd set her up someplace safe, but once her boyfriend found out what Mateus was trying to do, he made it impossible for her to leave. He made sure she was protected at all times. And it's not like you can just walk into the favela and knock on the door anyway. So Mateus started hiring people to try to sneak her out. It's like a maze in there, so he had to hire locals who knew the layout. I was the first one who didn't. I'd never gone to Rocinha before that night."

I hadn't forgotten the dark journey through the labyrinth of alleyways that trapped the stifling summer heat. Or the blinding flashes of gunfire as I ascended the two-story concrete apartment in Rocinha in search of a woman I'd never met. Or the look in her eyes when I asked her who she was, armed only with Mateus's physical description of her. She wouldn't budge until I told her Mateus had sent me.

"You must be her hero," Isabel says softly.

I look into her eyes, searching for some recognition of that feeling of being someone's hero. I come up short, because even though saving Karina solidified my relationship with Mateus, ultimately I considered it another job. The first of many.

"It was the only time I took a job saving someone's life instead of ending it." I push my fingers through my hair and fist at the roots, causing an uncomfortable sting.

That night in Rocinha set the rest of my life in motion.

"I killed five people that night to get to her. I got her out of there without a scratch on her, went back home, and slept like a rock. I woke up the next morning with a message from Jay about a hit in São Paulo she wanted me to take. Twenty grand. I told her to send me the details." I exhale, briefly reliving that hit too. "So, no, I'm not a hero. But I did manage to do at least two things right." I look up, hating the sadness painted across Isabel's features. "Her and you."

4

ISABEL

I sit there in stunned silence, searching for the right words. I don't think Tristan feels remorse—at least not like other people do. But he recognizes when something isn't right. Like he said last night, reacting the way he reacts isn't normal, but it's who he is. The choices he's made are hard to think about and even harder to accept. Like death…like regret…if you dive too deep into the feelings, you'll drown in them.

So I don't. We can't turn back the clock. It's a matter of acceptance and forward motion now. That, and I decided a long time ago to just love him.

I reach up and touch his cheek. He captures it and turns to kiss my palm sweetly.

"I wish I could be more for you," he whispers.

My heart hurts when he says it because it reminds me of another time. Whenever he used to apologize for the inequity between our lives, I would dig my heels in with the same kind of defensive determination that steadies me now. No matter what he ever said, he was always enough.

"You're everything to me. Nothing's changed."

He looks down and toys with our laced fingers. He doesn't believe me. He never used to. "Everything's changed."

"This is us, Tristan. This is who we are. We've been through hell. We're a little broken now, and…and that's okay." I swallow over the knot in my throat, thinking of the journey ahead of us and who we'll become on it. "Just because this isn't the life we expected doesn't mean this isn't the path we're meant to be on. Maybe we were chosen for this because we're strong enough for it."

He looks up with the same silvery-blue eyes that took me under the second I saw them. He smiles a little, but it's tense and lacks the hope I'm clinging to.

The laptop chimes when a new message from Jay comes in, snagging our attention.

JAY: Javier Medina. Have your client find a mutual connection and set up a meeting. The hit should be personal. Nothing too high profile or there may be conflicts. If they accept, Soloman will reach out.

RED: Who's Medina?

JAY: He's the man to know if you want anything coming in or going out of the Port of Miami.
He works under the director and makes things happen under the radar. Don't underestimate him.

RED: Thanks.

Tristan closes the laptop and drags his thumb across his lip a few times. "I need to call Mateus. See where they overlap."

"You're sure he'll do this?"

"Positive."

"You realize that if they accept Mateus's request, the clock is ticking on someone's life. Someone he'll have to name."

He doesn't make eye contact when he rises and begins pacing. "Yeah, I know."

"Who could he choose? I mean, I'm sure he has enemies, but he's not someone who would do something like that in the first place. Right?"

Tristan paces more but doesn't answer me. The thought of picking a name out of the air to place on the Company's hit list makes me uneasy. The only people I'd wish that fate on are already in the Company, which does us no good. Then again, I've lived a sheltered life. Mateus hasn't. He may have kind eyes and the heart of a savior, but he can't have linked himself with Tristan ignorant of what he does or what he's capable of. Which means Mateus may not be far away in terms of moral code.

Tristan's brow is furrowed. "I need to think. I'm going to take a walk. I'll be back in a few." He finally glances up like he's just realized I'm in the same room. "Don't go anywhere without me, okay?"

"I'll be right here."

When he goes outside, I watch him walk down the beach until he's a tiny speck on the sand. I go back to his computer and reread the chat with Jay. I wonder if Mateus might already know Medina or how he'll go about getting a meeting. Tristan's account of Mateus's history is news but not surprising. He's wealthy and suave, of course, but there's something gritty and authentic about him too.

I pull up a browser to search for Javier Medina. I navigate to his photo on the port's website. He's young, mid-thirties with a pleasant smile. Under it all, he's the man who can lead us to Soloman. As long as Mateus can pull it off.

I click around a while longer and finally move on and open my email. I don't know why I do. Perhaps out of habit or boredom. To the rest of the world, I'm a dead woman, so there's no reason for anyone to message me unless it's someone in the very small circle of those who know I'm alive. Someone like Kolt Mirchoff.

His name stands out from the surrounding junk-mail senders. The subject line: *Please read*.

I blink twice. Notice the gradual uptick of my heart. Withdraw my hand from the keypad as I decide whether or not to read the message. What could he possibly have to say? Somehow I already know he'll try to change my mind about what he's done and how I should feel about it. I hover over the trackpad and finally click the message, revealing its full content.

Isabel,

I know you probably hate me by now. There's a lot you don't know. There's so much I want to tell you so you can understand what really happened, but I'll probably never get that chance. I can only hope you read this, and once you do, you can decide for yourself.

I didn't come to Rio to hurt you. My life was a mess, and when the opportunity came up to teach at the school, I took it. My uncle told me to get to know you and ask about your family. That was it. He didn't tell me why, and I didn't take him that seriously because all I cared about was getting away from my life for a while and he was the one making it happen.

He didn't tell me to sleep with you. He didn't tell me to fall in love with you. But I did. That was real, and I promise you, if I could take it all back and know you'd be safe right now, I would. I was ignorant and self-centered, which is probably exactly what you'd expect from a guy like me. It's probably why you always held something back when it came to us. I didn't know what I had until you were gone. Now I'm more fucked up than when I left school. I don't think I can go back. I need to make this right, but I can't unless you let me.

They don't think I know what's going on, but I do now. I'm listening when they don't think anyone is. I'll help you. I don't care what I have to do.

Please, Isabel, find me so we can talk.

I love you,

Kolt

I shove up from the table and walk to the windows that face the beach. Tristan is nowhere to be seen, and for once I'm grateful. The mere mention of Kolt makes him bristle and question how I feel about him. This is so much worse. It's a plea. One that sounds genuine and heartbreaking, and even though my heart belongs to Tristan, the place where I held my affection for Kolt is taking a serious hit.

But what if this is nothing more than lies? What if he knew his family wanted me dead and he forced himself into my life, using their sick game as an excuse to get me into bed? If that were true, then who knows what else he's capable of? Penning a letter to draw me out would be the least of it.

Somehow I can't bring myself to believe that, though. I can still remember the look on his face when I saw him at my parents' house and the way he held me like he might never get a chance to again. That and every other time with him just seemed like Kolt being Kolt. Not some diabolical mastermind. His family and his money got him into Harvard, not his intellect, I'm sure of it. I could run rings around him with my Portuguese and nearly any other topic. He didn't want to hurt me… He didn't want to, but he did.

Damn it.

I go back to the table and reread the email, feeling no better when I do. What if he really wants to help? I check the date on the email. It was sent after that night with Vince in the hotel room when he promised to call off the hit.

I look over my shoulder again. No Tristan.

I hit the reply button and type with trembling hands.

Make me believe you.

TRISTAN

I walk briskly down the shore, turning back once the groups of tourists become denser as I near the condo-lined strip of the beach. I prefer our quiet place. When the search for Soloman takes us away, I'll be sorry to leave.

Isabel could use more time, but the truth is, I could too. The simplicity of the life I had before—kill, survive, recover—is long past. I have Isabel to consider now. I have *us* to consider. The unit we've become, the future I'm fighting for, and the memories and emotions I didn't have before all come into play, making our next steps more complicated.

I take my phone out and dial Mateus. It rings twice before he picks up.

"*Alô.*"

"It's Tristan."

"Tristan… I was wondering when I would hear from you again. How is Isabel?"

"I'm fine, thanks. Isabel is too."

He chuckles softly. "I'm glad to hear it. What's going on?"

I walk for a few seconds. Somehow asking for what I need carries an odd kind of weight. One that feels heavier for all the time I've held it.

"I need that favor now."

The request is met with silence, then, "Whatever you want, Tristan."

"After this, we're square. But I need this, and I need you to see it through no matter what happens."

"Of course. Do you have the details?"

"I need you to get a meeting with Javier Medina. He works for the Port of Miami. I get the impression he makes special arrangements for incoming and outgoing that would be too risky for the director to handle himself."

"It's hardly a midnight voyage into the favela. I think I can manage it."

He doesn't know what he's getting into yet, so he can hardly agree, but I'll let him.

"Where are you?"

"Traveling abroad with Karina. We took an extended vacation after our little evacuation from Petrópolis. But I can be in Miami in twenty-four hours."

"Leave Karina. I don't want her getting mixed up in this."

Another pause. "Call me at this number tomorrow, and we'll meet. I usually stay at a suite at the Fontainebleau. I'll have my assistant reach out to Medina to set something up in the meantime."

"Thanks."

"What name will you be traveling under?"

I spin the wheel on my aliases and pick one. "Ethan Gallo."

"Very good. I'll see you in Miami."

I hang up as the beach house comes back into view. The sun is bearing down, singeing my shoulders and chest. The heat is welcome. So is the burn forming. Something about it reminds me I'm alive. Human.

A part of me hoped this would be a good place to experiment with how much SP-131 my system could handle, but the rest of my memories will have to wait. I doubt they'd serve me in any plan to take Soloman down anyway. Isabel was right. The faster we move, the better our chances of taking the advantage. And we need every advantage we can get.

When I reach the path to the house, Isabel is sitting on the deck, her legs curled up to her chest. She looks pensive, almost troubled.

"Did you talk to Mateus?"

I hesitate. "I talked to him. He's going to work on getting a meeting with Medina as soon as possible."

"What does that mean for us?"

I walk in front of her and lean forward so my hands rest on the arms of her chair. "That means we're blowing this sleepy little town and I'm taking you to Miami."

Her expression is unreadable, as if she's figuring out how she feels about that. Even though she was pushing the pace before, I knew she was hoping to stay longer.

"We can always come back," I offer gently.

She shakes her head and looks past me. "No point going backward." The way she says it is both matter-of-fact and resigned.

"How about I take you dancing when we get there?"

"I doubt we'll have time for that. And anyway, you don't dance."

"No, but I love watching you dance. So let's plan on that."

She sighs, but I can tell I've added at least a little shimmer to the move.

"Fine."

"We'll leave early tomorrow. I have a few things I want to do here before we go anyway."

"Like what?"

"Come on." I reach for her hand and tug her upright.

As soon as she's on her feet, I lead her back onto the beach. She digs her heels into the sand with a squeal when she realizes I'm heading right into the water.

"Tristan, no!"

"What? Look, all those people down there are going in." I point to the busy end of the beach where a few brave tourists are floating in the shallow water.

"They're probably from the North Pole, where the water is never warm. This is way too cold."

I release her hand and wade in past my knees. I suck in a breath and turn with a forced smile. "Come on. Come in with me."

She crosses her arms over her chest and shakes her head. "You're crazy. That water is frigid."

I laugh and sink in a little lower, schooling my features to appear unaffected. But she's right. It's fucking cold.

"It's a perfect spring day for this. It's refreshing, and it'll be fun, and I love you."

Her expression softens a little, and I can almost feel her melting. I reach out my hand in invitation. She uncrosses her arms.

"Don't pull me in."

"I won't. I promise."

She waits another full thirty seconds before shucking her little shorts and T-shirt covering her black bikini. I bite my lip and forget the temperature of the water as she walks toward me slowly and takes my hand.

I back up a couple of steps until she grabs the band of my trunks, keeping me in place until she's right in front of me. The waves push the water up past our hips, but she doesn't skip a beat. She slides her hand up my chest and kisses me. I groan a little, pull her closer, and skim my palms over her goose-pebbled skin. The water's cold, but she's warm and soft. And perfect. And mine.

"I love you too," she murmurs against my lips. "And I'd follow you anywhere."

5

ISABEL

We sleep later than we mean to and hit weekend traffic heading east. What they call Three-Mile Bridge feels twice as long as we stop and go over the choppy bay waters for several minutes before finally crossing over into the next beach town. As we pass by shops and restaurants and parks, I think about Caleb the wanderer and the weather that had him worried, which must have gone north or south of us, because it's been sunny skies since that spooky fog the other morning.

Just as I start to wonder how far he's gotten since then, I swear I see him.

"Tristan, stop."

"What?"

"Just pull over. Quick."

The traffic is still going slow enough that he pulls to the side of the road without putting too much distance between us. I open the car door and get out.

"Isabel, what the hell?"

"I'll be right back. I see Caleb."

At least I think he's the one sleeping in front of one of the beach-apparel stores, with his pack tucked behind him. When I finally reach him, I pause a few feet away and study his sleeping figure on the sidewalk. His head is propped up with a rolled blanket, and his mouth hangs open a little. For someone sleeping on the ground, he looks content.

"Caleb?" I crouch down and touch his shoulder. "Caleb?"

He snaps his mouth shut and opens his eyes at once. He blinks a few times before his lips curl into a sleepy smile. "Oh, hey."

"I saw you when I was driving by. I just wanted to make sure you were okay."

He stretches a little and pulls himself upright. "Yeah, I'm good. Just taking a snooze."

"I thought you'd be way past the bridge by now."

"Oh, right. Weather went north, so it was smooth sailing. I decided to hang out here and chill for a while."

I glance back to the car, where Tristan's parked. He's leaning against the side, arms crossed, with a tight expression on his face. I drive him crazy, but I think he's learning to live with it. I return my focus to Caleb.

"You said you were headed to the Keys, right?"

He nods and scratches his head. "That's the plan."

"I'm actually on my way to Miami right now. Do you want a ride?"

I point toward the parked car.

He follows my gaze and stares at Tristan. "I'm good. But thanks. That's really cool of you to offer."

"Are you sure? It'll take you a lot longer to walk there."

He sighs and leans back against the stucco building, stretching again as he does. "That's all right. I'm not in a rush. I'll miss a lot of things if I hitch a ride. This way is better for me."

He smiles, and I can't help but smile too. I can't imagine walking the length of Florida but find it in me to respect his decision. Hell, maybe he's onto something.

I reach into my back pocket and pull out a wad of cash I withdrew from the ATM. "Here, will you take this at least?"

He waves it away. "No, Isabel. Keep your money. I don't need that."

"I think you do. You'll use it, won't you? Maybe get a room for a night or two? A nice meal?"

His shoulders fall a little, and I don't see the same resistance as he had to the free ride.

"I mean, yeah. I'd use it. But I don't want to take your money."

Resolved, I push it into his hand. "I just had a windfall, so it's your lucky day. Take care of yourself, okay?"

He takes my hand before I pull it away and gives it a little squeeze. "You too."

Ten hours, three pit stops, and a power nap later, we pull into the circular drive at the Fontainebleau entrance and take our place among the Lamborghinis and Mercedes waiting for valet service. Royal palms and sleek yachts line the creek that separate us from the interior strip of Miami Beach's barrier island, all set against the puffy pink sunset. Inside, the slick white marble floors and music thrumming from the poolside club just past the lobby are bold reminders we're not in quiet Perdido Key anymore.

At the front desk, Tristan requests a room and waits for the receptionist to key in his alias. She smiles politely. "It looks like you already have a reservation with us, Mr. Gallo."

He stiffens. "I didn't make a reservation."

"Mr. da Silva made arrangements with us this morning. You'll be staying in the Sorrento Penthouse Suite. I believe it will more than meet your satisfaction." She motions for a uniformed man nearby and hands him our keys. "Our bellman will escort you."

Tristan sighs heavily but doesn't argue as the man leads us to the elevators that bring us to the top floor. Once inside, he deposits our modest bags in the most opulent bedroom of the five we see during our jaw-dropping tour of the ten-thousand-square-foot luxury suite.

Tristan tips the man while I wander outside to the private rooftop pool and try to figure out how I'm going to lift my jaw off the stone patio.

"You look like you might be in shock," he says, joining me.

"This is insane."

"I think Mateus might be trying to impress you."

"Nonsense."

We both turn at the sound of Mateus's warm voice.

He steps through the wide doors wearing a knowing smile and head-to-toe white linen suit. "This is my home away from home. Plenty of room for my friends too."

He extends his hand to Tristan, who takes it and gets pulled into a manly hug.

"Good to see you, *meu amigo*."

Tristan pulls away with a short nod, as if he doesn't want to wholly acknowledge Mateus's sudden show of affection.

Mateus shifts his attention to me, taking my hand and bringing it to his lips the same way he did the first time we met outside his house in Petrópolis. "Isabel." His gaze is as warm as his greeting, but there's tension underneath.

Tristan and I both look up when there's motion inside. Mateus waves another man onto the patio.

"Tristan, Isabel, this is Ford. He'll be on hand should we need his services."

Ford is roughly twice the width of Mateus and at least two feet taller, dressed all in black clothing that contrasts with his golden skin and neatly trimmed blond hair. He nods to both of us, surveys the outdoor space briefly, and retreats into the penthouse wordlessly.

If he's here to watch our back, he won't exactly blend in, but after facing off with a man like Bones, I have no qualms about having a hulk-sized bodyguard shadowing us.

Mateus turns back to us. "He'll be staying in the penthouse with us. I hope you don't mind. He comes highly recommended, and I figured we could use the extra support."

"Hopefully we won't need it," Tristan says.

Mateus glances between us, his gaze landing finally on Tristan. "On that note, we have matters to discuss."

"We do."

There's a brief silence, and I get the strong sense Mateus wants time with Tristan, so I take my cue.

TRISTAN

"I'll be honest. I wasn't sure I would be seeing you again," Mateus says. The air is like warm silk blowing through the rooftop deck as we both take seats by the pool. "Don't misunderstand me," he continues. "I've always trusted your abilities. Ever since Karina, I knew never to underestimate you. But I consider you a friend, and friends worry."

The natural response would be to tell him not to waste his time worrying over me. But his friendship—the one I almost destroyed at the end of a gun—is something I'm more willing to accept now than before. I suspect it has a lot to do with Isabel and the door she blasted open inside me. I don't have a lot of familiar people in my life, but Mateus is one of them. My trust issues aside, his face is a welcome sight. That, and I have a good feeling he'll be key in pushing this plan through.

"Thank you for coming on short notice," I finally say, sidestepping everything else.

"I'm glad I can help." He takes in a deep breath, exhaling slowly. "She's changed, hasn't she? Isabel."

I nod. In so many ways…

"What happened?"

I shrug. "Everything." So much, it's hard to know how to put it all into words. The evolution of us. The things she's seen. The life of flight and danger we're facing every day.

He silently implores me with his steady stare. "I came all this way for you and only you. You must tell me the whole story."

I steeple my fingers under my chin and travel back in time, all the way to the night I deposited Karina on his doorstep, dirty and afraid. Even then he only knew half the story. I always held the truth back, and the longer we knew each other, the less I shared. Our friendship was held up on what I'd done for him and little else. But here he is, ready to make good on his promise after all this time.

For the next hour or so, I fill in the blanks about the Company and details about my past that have come to light. I tell him about Jay and Soloman and the Boswells. I recount Isabel's traumas, from Brienne's murder to Isabel's faked death and the recent estrangement with her parents. I tell him about Bones and, even though that wound is still raw, how Isabel *has* changed well beyond her looks. She's stronger, braver, and colder than she was when Mateus first met her. And while she's folded herself into this life of mine, I'm starting to figure out how to fit into hers too.

When I finish, the only sounds between us come from the busy street and the poolside club pumping music down below.

After a long time, Mateus leans forward and rests his arms on his knees. "This is bigger than a meeting. This is a war. You realize that."

"If we can take out Soloman, I'm hoping we can avoid the war."

He shakes his head, and I brace myself, half expecting him to backtrack now that he knows the extent of our dilemma. A smart man would cut a check and walk the other way.

"I don't know," he says, his voice troubled. "Men like him are a cancer. You think you can cut them out, but the cancer is still there. It keeps growing because other people feed the pieces he left behind. To think you can kill him and hope to be rid of this Company is too simple. You should prepare yourself for what may come next."

"I always do. I take nothing for granted. And I'm not stopping with Soloman. The Boswell family started all of this, at least when it comes to Isabel. They're next on the list. And it may not end there either."

"So what do you want me to do? How do I help?"

I exhale some tension I'd been holding. "Take the meeting with Medina. Let him know you want an introduction to Soloman for a job. And when Soloman is in sight, we take him out."

He purses his lips slightly. "The target?"

I shrug. "That's your call."

His face splits with a smile. "And you think I must have a list of expendables."

"I thought you might."

He sighs and leans back again. "Why do they need a name?"

I lift my brows. "It's not a job without a name."

"It isn't a job until Soloman accepts it. If I wait until the meeting with him, I could say any name or no name if the plan is to kill him a moment later."

"If Medina accepts that, it could work."

"I can be persuasive. To mark someone for death is no small thing, and even if my intentions were true, I wouldn't utter a name without assurances. I don't know Medina, but I know Soloman is the man who can make it happen, so it stands to reason I would want to wait until I establish some trust with him first."

Hopefully it works out that way.

"How do you plan to kill him?" he asks.

"Depends on where we meet. He's likely to recognize Isabel and me by now. We've been causing enough problems for him lately. Our faces will be on his radar. But we'll be close enough to have eyes on the situation. I'm not letting him out of my sight alive, that's for sure. We may never get another chance like this one."

He's quiet a moment. "Would you like me to do it?"

The possibility had already occurred to me. "Would you?"

He nods silently.

"He's known to want to meet in public. Whatever we do will be in plain sight."

Mateus smiles. "You're the expert in that, aren't you?"

"There are a dozen ways to end him, but I'd like to do this without implicating you."

"I'd like that too."

6

ISABEL

My arms slice through the water, one after the other. My legs propel me forward for what may be the hundredth lap of the day. The total silence of submersion hasn't gotten old, as the waiting game to hear from Javier Medina drags on another day. When I surface at the other end, Tristan and Mateus are standing at the edge. Tristan's holding a plastic bag in his hand.

I walk up the steps and squeeze the excess water from my hair. "What's up?"

"We have a meeting with Medina," Tristan says, handing me a towel.

"When?"

"We thought he'd wait until Monday, but he wants to have drinks tonight."

"Okay. So why are you looking at me like that?"

Tristan's mouth twitches. "Mateus had an idea."

Mateus looks as breezy as he always does, hands nestled in his pockets. "I'd like this meeting to be brief. I would also like to avoid certain...topics. All around, it would be better to achieve those things with a ready diversion."

"What topics?"

"Specifically? Our target."

I nod, relieved we're not going to be sending anyone to their grave tonight who doesn't deserve it. Then there's the other matter. "Let me guess. You want me to be the ready diversion."

"Not really," Tristan mutters, which earns a partial smile from Mateus.

"Medina may be less likely to press me for details with an audience. And if he does, you can give me a reason to cut things short."

A little flash of intrigue courses through me. I don't know why, except maybe being a part of the action gives me a measure of control over my destiny and, with that, something to ease my fears. If this is going to be my life, I can't live it on the sidelines.

"I'm in."

The muscles in Tristan's jaw tense before he lifts the bag toward me. "Thought you might consider changing your look. Just in case."

I open the bag to find a few boxes of hair dye. There's a joke about blondes having more fun forming in my brain, but then I remember I haven't been having the most fun as a blonde.

"Works for me."

A few hours later, my blond bob has been transformed into a deep brown that's less youthful but markedly more dramatic, accentuating my natural features. I snag a little black dress and some heels from my suitcase when Tristan joins me in the bedroom.

His body is taut as a bow, his strides dominant and ready. "I can't believe I'm letting you do this. This must be the definition of insanity."

I bend to slip my heel on, steadying myself on the bureau. "I think we both know it could be a lot worse."

"Mateus can manage this on his own."

"I'm sure he can, but why risk it? Obviously I can play the arm-candy part. Then at least one of us has eyes on the situation." I slip the other heel on. "Where will you be?"

"Close."

I turn and go into the bathroom to straighten my dress and check my makeup. Tristan comes behind me, his heated stare burning into my reflection. He rests his hands on my hips and draws our bodies close.

"You're beautiful."

Warmth curls through me, an instant reaction I might never be immune to when it comes to him.

He kisses my bare shoulder without breaking eye contact. "I want you to be careful."

"I will. I promise."

He slides his hands down the side of my dress, catching the hem and pulling it up slowly.

"Tristan," I protest because we don't have time for this.

He hushes me. Withdrawing his touch, he reaches into his pocket and retrieves a wide black strap that he secures carefully around my right thigh. The material is thin but firm enough to sheath the blade of the short, flat knife he eases into it.

I trace the handle of it with my fingertip, memorizing its size and arrangement. The polished metal shines under the vanity lights. "You think I'll need this?"

He covers my hand with his. "No, but I want you to use it if you have to." He drags his gaze over my reflection, pulls our bodies close again, and then pushes my dress up until my backside is totally exposed. Looking down between us, he traps his bottom lip firmly between his teeth and caresses my bare skin. "This shouldn't turn me on so much."

The heat in his eyes matches the flames under my skin everywhere he touches me. The pure force of him existing in the same room does things to my insides. But the danger we're dancing with every day adds a new dimension to everything we do now. The colors of the world around us are more vibrant. The air is sweeter. Every fuck is more intense.

Against every instinct, I reach for the hem and glide it down slowly as I turn to face him. "Maybe I'll model it for you later. Without the dress…or anything else."

A rush of air leaves his lips. "You may be more dangerous than I've ever given you credit for." He leans in, taking my mouth with the perfect firmness of his. "Dirty little saint," he whispers, his need like gravel inside the words.

"I'm hardly a saint, Tristan."

Not now. Not ever. Not after the things I've done.

"You are. Don't ever doubt it." He touches my cheek gently and kisses me deeper.

I'm about to lose my willpower when he pulls away, slowly and painstakingly. His eyes on me draw everything out and feed our connection. Those silver-blue orbs unravel me and hold me together in the same moment.

"I'm serious, Isabel. Be careful. It's a busy bar, but that's not a reason to let your guard down. You have no idea what this guy is capable of."

"I'll keep both eyes open. Trust me. I let my guard down before, and it almost got me killed. I haven't nearly forgotten."

He takes a step back, as tense as he was before. "Are you ready?"

"I'm ready."

"Then let's do this," he says, taking my hand.

Ford drives Mateus and me down the strip to another equally ritzy hotel. Tristan left well before us. I have no idea where he'll be, but I trust I'll feel his presence somehow. Hopefully everything goes as planned and he can stay in the shadows until it's all over.

Mateus and I settle into a leather booth at the hotel bar and order drinks while we wait for Medina to show. We're side by side, only a few inches apart, which is all part of the act. He looks different tonight, more professional than usual, dressed in dark-navy pants and a crisp white shirt that's unbuttoned casually at the top. The bar is busy but not overwhelming, which makes me wonder where Tristan is hiding. Crowds are easier, but they can also be more dangerous. My thoughts drift to the festival on Freret and how the chaos of those streets probably hid my abduction well for Bones. Never again…

"Are you nervous?" Mateus asks, distracting me from reliving all of it.

I force a smile and cross one leg over the other. The motion draws my body a little closer to his and reminds me of the weapon hidden under my dress.

"I'm okay."

He rests his arm along the top edge of the booth and drums his fingers on the leather a few inches from my shoulder. "Tristan worries about you. I do too. I don't want to make you uncomfortable."

I lean my head back on his arm, relaxing into the act of being more intimate with Mateus than I ever would be otherwise. "I know what's at stake. And you don't make me uncomfortable."

He smiles. "Good."

"Thank you for doing this."

"No thanks needed. I owe Tristan a debt."

"I know. He told me about what happened with Karina."

He's thoughtful a moment. "I'm forever grateful. He did what many others failed to do. He has a gift. He's been wasting it on this path."

There's a tinge of judgment to his tone. Not that I would defend the heinous things Tristan's done, but I'm ready to defend the man who did them.

"He wasn't entirely on this path until he accepted your offer."

Mateus frowns, confusion crinkling the edges of his eyes.

"He told me he didn't know what he was capable of before that night. The things he had to do in order to bring her out… Everything changed for him after."

Mateus holds my stare before lifting his drink to his lips. He takes a healthy swallow, hiding the displeasure this news has given him.

All this time, he must have thought this is who Tristan already was. A trained killer. Someone he could use but couldn't save.

I trace the rim of the glass with my fingertip, certain I've said too much.

"Mr. da Silva?"

I look up as a man is hovering near our table. I blink quickly and straighten. Mateus and I don't look like lovers this way, scowling into our drinks. Oh well. Lovers' quarrel.

Mateus rises and takes the man's outstretched hand. "You must be Javier. Thank you for meeting on such short notice."

"Of course." Javier's attention lowers to me. "And this is?"

Mateus waves his hand toward me. "This is Jazmín."

TRISTAN

I've been pretending to read the *New York Times* in the lobby lounge for the better part of an hour, which gives me the barest glimpse into the hotel bar and a clear vantage to track Medina's walk from the entrance to the table where Isabel and Mateus are cozied up together, a circumstance that irritates the shit out of me.

I console myself with thoughts of peeling her knife strap off with my teeth later.

"This joint is too fancy for the likes of you."

I look toward the sound. Townsend is walking my way, out of place here in his cargo pants and cotton T-shirt. He's got a cigarette tucked behind his ear and a nasty smile on his mouth.

"What are you doing here?"

He lifts his chin toward the bar. "Jay said you were meeting up with Medina. I got into town and started tracking him yesterday. Figured I'd find you somewhere along the way. Who's your man?"

I exhale a frustrated sigh. "A friend. Do you mind if we catch up later?"

"You think she can't handle herself? She can be a vicious little thing. I've seen it for myself. I wouldn't worry about her, mate."

I lock my jaw at his mocking tone. If he's trying to start trouble with me, this isn't the time nor the place.

"I thought the plan was to split up," I say through gritted teeth.

"And we did. Now that Jay's all tucked in, I'm back. Let's step out for a few, shall we?"

His timing could not be worse. Medina just showed up, and I'm not ready to give up my post until he's gone again.

"Let's not."

"I insist." Townsend's eyes darken. "You don't want me making a scene, do you?"

I flare my nostrils and shoot one last glance toward the bar. They're all smiles and cozy as ever. I curse to myself and whip the newspaper onto the coffee table before I rise.

"You have three minutes. *Three.*"

Townsend doesn't acknowledge this, but he follows me around the bar to the back entrance of the hotel, which may still give me a view inside. I push through the doors and find the path to the pools void of other patrons. When I turn, the choice words I've been saving for him are swiftly cut off when he slams his fist into my cheek. The contact makes a dull crack. Knuckles on bone.

I raise my fist before the zing of the impact has a chance to fade, but a couple paces away, Townsend's no longer on the offensive. His hands are balled at his sides, his mouth is curled into a hateful sneer, but he doesn't come at me again. It's enough to make me hesitate and think before I satisfy my instinct to pummel him to dust.

"What the fuck was that for?"

"*That* was for Jay."

A fraction of the fight leaves my body as his meaning sinks in. Jay. Crow. The barn in New Jersey where it all went down. I vowed to be far away when Townsend found out the truth, but I hadn't expected him to show up again to settle the score.

"I didn't know that was going to happen, okay?"

"I know. Because if you did, you'd be fuckin' dead!" He emphasizes the last word, a bit of spit flying with the force of it. The veins in his neck bulge, and I get the sense he's restraining himself. The important thing is that he *is* restraining himself and not giving me an excuse to beat the shit out of him—or worse.

I work my jaw and rub the place where he made contact. I could argue in my defense, but the truth is, Jay wouldn't have been taken advantage of had I not lured her out for Crow. And if the tables were turned and Isabel had gone through something like that, it wouldn't matter if Townsend had been complicit or not. He'd be dead if he had any part in it.

For that reason, I allow my anger to simmer.

"Are we through?" I keep my voice as even as possible, void of any challenge that will draw this into more dangerous territory.

"Where's Crow?"

"His family is in New Jers—"

"I fuckin' know that already. I want to know where he is *now*." He pitches forward a step.

I hold my ground and brace myself for another physical attack. "How would I know?"

"Well, you're partners, aren't you?"

"About as much as you and Dunny were. He wants to take the Company down. That's all we have in common."

"Why would he want to do that? They weren't after him."

"He's greedy. Figures he can pocket more with blackmail than carrying out assignments."

He shakes his head stiffly. "He better enjoy it while he can, because I'm going to fuckin' kill him."

I could try to reason with him, but the look in his eyes tells me it's pointless. He's out for blood, one way or the other.

"Do what you want. Not that it matters to you, but I already took care of the guy who touched her. If he lived through it, I'd be surprised."

His jaw bulges as he gnashes his teeth. "She told me. It's the only reason you don't have a hole in your head. Now you're going to help me find Crow so I can put a hole in his."

Fuck. I don't have time for this. All I can do is play along so I can get back to the situation inside.

"Fine. But until Soloman's taken care of, I can't help you. So can we take up this conversation at a more appropriate time and venue? Because I don't have eyes on Isabel right now, and that's a problem."

His seething cools a little. "I'm not letting you out of my sight until I get what I want."

I suppress a frustrated groan. "If you fuck this up for me, you're going to really wish you didn't. Believe it." I point to the door. "I'm going back in there to pretend to read my paper. I want you far away from me."

7

ISABEL

Javier Medina has an energetic air about him. His vivid blue eyes dance around as if he's taking in every detail of our surroundings. His eager smile and shoulder-length brown hair pulled into a neat ponytail at his nape are disarming features too. Dressed in a pale-blue collared shirt and dark slacks, he looks like he just got out from a day at the office, but I doubt that's the case. Instantly I like him and am drawn to his charisma and good looks even though my rational mind is reminding me he can't be trusted.

The waiter brings his beer, and now that introductions have been made, the intention behind our meeting hangs like a heavy fog over the table. I catch myself holding my breath but try my best to curb any outward show of anxiety.

"So," Medina says, resting his hands on his knees. "What brings you to Miami, Mr. da Silva? Your assistant was a little vague."

"I'm here often for business. And sometimes pleasure too. This visit is a little of both."

A grin plays at his lips. I take the hint and twine our fingers together as I angle my body toward him like he's my king. In my periphery, I catch the other man sizing me up, but I pretend not to notice.

"This is the perfect city for both." He clears his throat. "I'll be honest… I read up about you a little. I assume with your business, you're interested in discussing port matters."

Mateus tilts his head. "Not exactly." He absently strokes his thumb over mine. "This is a particularly…*sensitive* matter."

Medina folds his hands together and leans in. "You have my utmost discretion."

"Thank you." A brief pause. "I'm interested in arranging a meeting with an associate of yours. He goes by the name of Soloman."

It takes all my willpower not to turn and study Medina's reaction. Instead I play with the collar of Mateus's shirt like I have roughly four brain cells. According to our decided backstory, I'm his girlfriend *du jour* and my English isn't great, so very little about this conversation would interest me. Of course, every syllable matters.

The pause is palpable, though. To Mateus's credit, he maintains a stellar poker face. An easy, patient confidence as Medina ponders his reply.

"What would be the nature of this meeting?"

Mateus chuckles softly. "I have a feeling you know."

"Soloman deals in many different areas. I'd like to narrow it down before I bring it to him for consideration."

I attempt to tamp down the excitement welling inside me. The acknowledgment of Soloman's existence by someone with ready access to him has me almost salivating. God, I wish Medina was Soloman and I could end this right now. Punish him for the hell he's brought on our lives.

"Very well. I have…" Mateus twists his lips into an uneasy smile. "I have a problem I would like to *extinguish*."

"And where does the problem live?"

"The problem doesn't stay in one place too long. Buenos Aires. Rio. Ibiza. He's not always easy to keep a finger on."

Immediately I'm impressed by Mateus's ability to describe our imaginary target. I'm almost intrigued to learn more about him.

"Sounds like he's in your neck of the woods. Why seek us out here?"

Mateus pauses again briefly. I hold my breath and pray he has a ready answer for this too. I've never seen Mateus flustered or off balance. My inherent trust in his abilities goes to war with a crippling fear that everything could go horribly wrong.

"I'm seeking Soloman out because this is very personal and very important to me. I would like it handled quickly, professionally and, above all, discreetly. That is not always such an easy request to make in one's own backyard. At least not without repercussions."

"Understood. How did you get my information?"

"You weren't so difficult to find."

"Generally, I'm not. But finding a channel to a man like Soloman is." Medina takes a swallow of his beer, but he's anything but casual now. He went from easygoing to painfully direct the second Soloman's name was uttered.

Mateus maintains a stone face. "Is it me you underestimate or my relationships?"

I don't love the challenging turn the conversation is taking, so I sigh heavily and study my nails, preparing myself to pitch a bored girlfriend fit as soon as I need to.

"Neither," Medina answers briskly. "But Soloman doesn't take meetings with just anyone. You need a reference."

I pull my phone out of my purse to check my messages.

"No phones." Medina levels his sharp blue eyes at me.

My heart beats like a barrel drum in my chest as we linger in the standoff for several seconds. I don't have to act pissed off, because I am.

"Not now, *querida*," Mateus whispers to me in soothing Portuguese.

"Are you almost done? I'm hungry," I reply in the same tongue, dropping my phone back into my purse.

"Soon, *querida*. We're taking care of some business. Then we can eat."

"You promised it would be quick. This is boring," I whine.

"We will. Five minutes. I promise."

"Is there a problem?" Medina interjects.

Mateus pauses, seeming to collect his thoughts. "If it's a reference you need, you're welcome to seek one out. My secrets are few, and I honor confidences. If you feel this is a worthwhile undertaking, you know how to reach me. Money, of course, is not an object. Now"—Mateus brings my hand to his lips and gives it a warm kiss, as if he's exercising infinite patience tolerating both of us—"if you'll excuse me. I've promised Jazmín a night out."

He stands and brings me up with him.

"It's been a pleasure, Mr. Medina. I do hope to be hearing from you."

TRISTAN

I give Mateus and Isabel a head start back to the Fontainebleau. Medina lingers in the booth, drinking his beer for several minutes before making a call. The exchange is brief. So is the next call he makes. Unfortunately I'm not close enough to make out the conversation. Finally he finishes, pays the tab, and leaves the hotel moments later.

I catch a glimpse of Townsend outside smoking a cigarette, pacing the hotel driveway, looking like a deranged degenerate. I don't relish the idea of taking him back to the penthouse and introducing him to Mateus, who has already gone above and beyond. And while I don't know the details of the meeting yet, I'm hopeful the outcome will be a second meeting—one with Soloman. Townsend's reasons for being here could not be further from the mission. He's emotional and too impulsive for this, but I don't have much choice other than to bring him with. If I have any chance of controlling him, I'll have to keep him close.

Twenty minutes later, Townsend and I are on our way to the penthouse. The elevator deposits us on the top floor and the doors glide closed behind us, leaving us to our palace in the sky. The opulence of the place seems to momentarily distract Townsend from his angst.

"Nice place," he mutters, looking around the living room with round eyes before Ford suddenly appears.

Townsend barely gives him a glance as he takes another step inside.

"Wait up. Who are you?" Ford creates a barrier with his massive hand on Townsend's chest.

"The name's get the fuck out of the way."

Ford doesn't waste a second moving the barrier forward, pushing Townsend until he's pressed against the wall. "Wrong answer."

Townsend snarls at the man who could snap him like a twig. He looks to me, but I'm disinclined to help him. I don't want him here at all, let alone spouting off to everyone in sight. He's been intolerable since the second he showed up. If Ford can teach him a lesson, all the better.

Finally Townsend seems to relent, unfisting his hands, no doubt realizing the fight he's picking is unwinnable.

"My name is Killian Townsend, and I'm traveling with this ugly fuck for the foreseeable future, so you may as well get used to it."

Ford slides his gaze to me.

"Other than his bad attitude, he's fine."

"He's your responsibility." He points to me like it's law.

I sigh. "Unfortunately, yes."

Ford casts one last warning glare at our unwelcome guest before releasing him. Townsend slips to the side and shifts his shoulders like he's shaking off the test of manhood. I get that the news about Jay has him in an especially foul mood, but for everyone's sake, I hope it lifts.

"Where's Mateus?" I ask Ford.

He motions toward the patio, so I go and Townsend follows.

Mateus and Isabel are sitting at one of the tables chatting quietly when we arrive.

"How did it go?" I ask.

Isabel visibly tenses at the sight of Townsend by my side.

Mateus rises. "I think it went well. Did you make a friend?"

"I'm not a friend," Townsend snaps.

Mateus lifts an eyebrow and looks at me.

"This is Killian Townsend. He's with the Company."

"Formerly," he corrects. "Free agent anyway. Also none of your fucking business."

I resist the urge to roll my eyes at his antics. "He's going to help us with the Soloman situation, after which I've agreed to assist him with a separate matter." I look to a worried Isabel, wishing I could explain more, but it'll have to wait. "What happened with Medina?"

"He was cagey." Isabel stands and crosses her arms tightly over her chest. The motion is defensive, like she's protecting herself from something. "Paranoid and protective when it came to access to Soloman. But I don't think he suspected anything. Mateus played it off well."

"And Isabel was a most convincing distraction. He would have pushed me for answers I didn't want to give had she not been there. It was the right decision to bring her."

I'm relieved to hear it but no more thrilled about her roleplaying as someone else's lover. Still, progress was made.

"I saw him making calls after you left. Hopefully one of them was to Soloman."

Townsend lights a cigarette and starts walking around the deck, surveying all the amenities like he's the one who paid for them.

"Is he staying?" Mateus asks quietly. "And if so, should I be concerned?"

"He's coming off some bad news. Just a little punchy is all." I brush the back of my fingers over my cheek briefly. "He'll be fine, but I'd have Ford keep an eye on him. He may not look it, but he's lethal in his own right."

"Very well." He looks to Isabel. "You should get some sleep. If we get the call we want, tomorrow could be a long day."

She comes to my side, catches my hand in hers, and leans her body against me like she needs the contact. She's barely been out of my sight all day, but I can't deny the relief that comes with being close to her again.

"Townsend," I call out.

He halts his tour and turns his head.

"Ford can show you your room for the night. Try not to be an asshole."

He flips me off as he exhales a plume of smoke. I laugh to myself and we go inside, disappearing into the privacy of our room. The second the door closes, Isabel strips her dress off unceremoniously.

"I thought you were going to let me unwrap you." My tone is teasing, but under it I'm dead serious.

She answers with a tired smile, tossing the garment to the floor. "Sorry. I'm just coming down from the adrenaline spike of the meeting, I guess."

"Sounds like everything went smoothly. Did something else happen?"

She drops to the edge of the bed and slips off her heels. "No, it was fine. We both kept our cool and put on a convincing show, I think. I'm just stressed it wasn't enough. Medina was really guarded. It was hard to tell what he was thinking and act dumb at the same time. I just hope I didn't screw it up somehow. That was our one shot."

She goes for the strap on her thigh. I stop her, shift her up the bed, and climb over her, trapping her hands on either side of her head. Her eyes glimmer as she stares up at me.

"If it's not enough, we'll come up with a plan B. In the meantime, I don't want you losing sleep over it, all right?"

She exhales softly. "Okay."

I release her hands and move down to unfasten her strap. Carefully I slide the knife and strap off, planting a kiss on the inside of her thigh before putting everything away on the bedside table.

"What about Townsend? He showed up out of the blue?" she asks.

"He was following Medina. Punched me first chance he got and let me know it was for Jay. He's going after Crow unless I can talk some sense into him."

She sits up sharply. "Are you serious?"

"Did you see him?" I gesture toward the closed door. Somewhere on the other side of it, I'm certain Townsend's still wearing down a path with his embittered pacing. "He's manic. He's a goddamn mess over this. I guess he and Jay were closer than I thought. Honestly, I don't know if he's going to be able to let it go until he gets his hands on Crow."

"That complicates things." Her voice takes on a listless quality.

"When he's gambling on me being able to find him, yeah, it does."

8

ISABEL

I wake up to an empty bed and the quiet murmur of voices beyond the bedroom door. I dress quickly and go to the living room, where Tristan, Mateus, and Townsend are all gathered. It looks like they're in the middle of an intense strategy session, judging by their pensive stares and the empty coffee cups littering the table.

I scrub my fingers through my mussed hair. "What's going on?"

Tristan rises from the couch and comes to me. "Medina called first thing this morning."

My heart lurches. "And? Did we get the meeting?"

"We got something else."

Townsend leans back into the couch and props his feet on the table. "Hope you've got more than one party dress, cupcake."

I glare at him. "Don't call me that."

Tristan releases a tense sigh. "Ignore him. And you don't have to do this if you don't want to. It may be too dangerous. Correction, it *is* too dangerous."

"Tristan."

Mateus shoots him a hard look that's immediately returned.

"What? What is it?" I ask, desperate to be clued in.

"He didn't confirm a meeting, but he's invited you and Mateus to a yacht party being held tonight. Soloman should be there."

"And who else?"

Tristan shrugs. "I have no idea, but Townsend and I are going to head down to the marina soon to find out more. It's supposed to leave around eight, just after sunset."

"Okay, he'll be in public. Surrounded by people. We knew this was his MO."

Tristan lets out a caustic laugh. "Yeah, we weren't expecting him to be on a goddamn boat. I'm struggling to think of a worse setup for a hit."

"But Mateus and I will be on the boat."

"Ford too," Mateus adds. "One security detail is permitted."

"Doesn't matter," Tristan says. "Even if you get a window to take him out, you've got no escape route. You're on a boat in the middle of the ocean with a bunch of witnesses."

I go to the couch and pour myself the cup of coffee I badly need to get my brain in gear for this conversation.

Townsend shifts his boots to the side and slides the tiny pitcher of creamer my way. I take it without making eye contact.

"You're welcome," he mutters.

Go to hell, I answer silently.

I ignore him and try to wrap my head around this development. "This may be our only chance," I say. "We have to try to make it work."

"Everyone who gets on the boat needs to be prepared to make the hit," Townsend says.

Tristan takes the seat beside me. "Mateus can't be implicated, and I'm pretty sure this isn't what Ford gets paid for. That leaves Isabel, who may well be recognized." He rubs his forehead vigorously again. "We shouldn't force this. We can wait for another meeting."

"Tristan, we've already agreed. The time is now."

Mateus's voice is firm, which gives me hope. The Medina meeting worked. We can pull this off too.

I take a sip of my coffee and set it down. "Okay, let's say we go to the party and nothing happens. We don't get an opening. The worst-case scenario is Soloman sees me and recognizes me, right? It's a party on a yacht, so there should be a lot of people. I don't have to stay on Mateus's arm all night, or at all. I can mingle and talk to other people while Mateus has his meeting. Or I can find someplace to hide out until the boat docks again."

"You don't have to go at all," Tristan says.

I pause a moment. "What if you came too?"

"Seriously? You think they won't recognize either of us?"

"They're not going to check IDs, right? Just names. Why can't you go as Ford and wear a disguise or figure out how to stay out of sight until the right time?"

He shakes his head slightly. "This is fucked."

Townsend drops his feet to the carpeted floor. "Now that we've got the cast of characters down, let's talk about execution. Gun's not going to work. There's likely to be security of some kind, plus they're fuckin' loud and someone's bound to see you pop this guy. Let's rule that out."

"Agreed," Tristan mutters.

"I think I can be resourceful," I say.

Townsend meets my eyes. "I think we can agree on that also, so we'll leave that option open. Now, option three and my personal preference: poison. It's just a matter of when, where, and how long you want it to take."

For the first time since he's reemerged into our lives, I'm interested in what he can bring to the equation.

"And if," Tristan adds, "*if* one of us gets an opportunity to slip him something."

"Well, it's a fuckin' good thing we have options, right? Anyway, you want this to go down quickly? Or are we going for a slow death in, say, three months?"

"I would think it should be fairly quick," I say.

Townsend nods. "That gets my vote too. More problematic in the short term. No doubt we'll have a scene and some confusion and the whole matter of getting everyone off the boat. But I'm sure I don't speak only for myself when I say I'd like to be rid of this guy sooner rather than later. I prefer aconite. Few drops in his drink, and he'll be heaving his guts out in about twenty minutes. That's when you'll know it's started working."

Everyone's quiet for a minute, taking in Townsend's proposal.

"Do you have enough for each of us to carry some?" I ask.

He shoots me a crooked smile. "Never leave home without it."

TRISTAN

The party is eight hours away, and the plan is only half-baked. Townsend and I are pulling up to the marina while Mateus takes Isabel out to shop for something yacht-appropriate. Whether I actually let her get on the cruise will have to be a game-time decision. For now, I'm going along with it. Townsend's push to keep our options open has merit, because once things start to unfold, our options could narrow very quickly.

We walk from the parking lot to the marina and down the pier with the most impressive yachts docked along it. I could stop and ask questions at the main office, but my hunch is we'll find the vessel here.

"What's it called?" Townsend asks.

We slow at the stern of the second yacht docked. I point to the dark serif lettering stroked with gold on the back. *King's Ransom.*

Townsend coughs out a laugh and taps a cigarette from its pack before tucking it behind his ear. "That's fuckin' ironic."

"I think that's the idea."

"Can I help you with something?" A man comes from behind us in a stiff white crew uniform.

I shoot him a friendly smile, something I save for Isabel and people I need to manipulate. "Hi. I'm working security on the cruise tonight. I was hoping to get some information so I can coordinate details for my client."

He looks Townsend over hesitantly before returning his attention to me. "Sure. How can I help?"

"About how many people are you expecting?"

"I believe there are sixty passengers on the guest list, give or take."

"And where are you going?"

"The plan is to cruise for a few hours with a short stop at Fisher Island to drop some people off before we dock here again."

"Perfect. We'll see you around eight."

"My pleasure, sir."

"Who owns the boat?" Townsend interjects as I'm about to turn and leave.

The man hesitates a moment before replying. "The *King's Ransom* is owned by Mr. Simon Pelletier."

"Does he ever go by Soloman?"

The man opens his mouth to speak. Flustered, he snaps it shut again quickly.

Townsend's riding a dangerous edge again, pushing my tolerance and risking discovery when we need to lie low and maneuver carefully to position ourselves for the hit. The crew member's already given us the answer we need, so I pat Townsend's shoulder, signaling him that we're leaving.

Townsend winks before he turns. "Thanks for your time."

We scope out the rest of the marina and walk back to the car. "You think you can tone it down a little? I know you're in a mood, but I'm about to put Isabel on that boat, and it'd be great if no one suspected anything before I did."

Townsend lights up his cigarette. "When are you going to reach out to Crow?"

"When this is done. You can't smoke in my car."

He takes a long drag and tosses it before we get in. I start the engine, and we get on our way.

"I want you to set something up before this goes down with Soloman. If you don't make it, I'm out of luck."

"Not exactly a vote of confidence, is it?"

"Not sure if you've noticed, but I don't exactly have a sense of humor about it. Someone's going to pay for what happened to her."

"You really want to put your life on the line for this? How does Jay feel about that?"

He looks out the window, not answering. My guess is she's not thrilled. What's done is done. If she cares about him, she's not going to want to lose him over this.

"The sooner you make the call, the sooner I'll be out of your hair, mate."

"He's not likely to take a meeting out of the blue. With Soloman out of the picture, though, that's news that will pique his interest. The minute this is done, I'll set something up. You know how these mob families work, though. If you manage to get to him, he's probably got a hundred cousins who are going to want to come after you."

"Let them," he snaps, murder in his eyes all over again. "Let them fuckin' come after me."

I shift my focus to the road. There's no reasoning with him. Maybe that's how vengeance goes. I should know, since I've made good money killing people in the name of revenge. But I've never carried the stuff myself. Nothing I've ever done has been infused with the kind of hatred that chills the air between Townsend and me.

Hell, he's the one who wiped my memory. I should want to kill him, but I don't. He was doing a job, same as all the ones I did. We're two puppets in the same fucked-up play. And if he wants to sell his soul to revenge, that's his choice.

We park, and Townsend heads toward the entrance while I type out a text to Crow.

Need to meet soon.
Give me a time and place.

When we arrive at the penthouse a few minutes later, the living room is filled with shopping bags. Isabel is trying on a pair of nude, studded slingbacks out of a Valentino box when she notices me.

"Mateus went all out, huh?"

She stands and rests her hands on her hips. "I bought it all. I mean, he insisted of course, but I wasn't putting this on his dime. Even if sliding my card through the machine nearly gave me a stroke. Do you like them?"

"You're wearing those on a fuckin' boat? You planning to fall overboard and bringing Soloman with you?"

She shoots Townsend a narrow look that makes me smile. "Why don't you stick to what you're good at and get out of my face?"

"Sure thing, cupcake." He walks to the patio, leaving us alone.

"He really gets under your skin, doesn't he?"

"I'm going to have an aversion to needles for the rest of my life, thanks to him. Sorry if I'm not over it just yet."

She turns and pulls out a scrap of a dress from one of the bags. It's low cut and almost the same color as her skin. "I think I'm going to wear this."

Envisioning her in it is already driving me crazy. Selfishly, I want to see her wear it, but the idea of anyone else enjoying the view makes me feel a little homicidal.

"You're going to look naked."

"I'm going to blend in. The last thing I need is to make myself a neon target."

Of course, she wouldn't need to worry about blending in if she weren't there at all. The alternative is staying back with Ford and Townsend, which poses its own problems.

"Are you sure you want to do this?"

She flashes her gaze to mine, hitting me with an unflinching look that answers before her words do. "I'm in this with you, Tristan."

I try to release the tension that's building up as I imagine her, dressed to kill, walking right into the lion's den like it's her job. And it's fast *becoming* her job. I realize that now. I can't hide her away, and I can't hold her back. She doesn't like the sidelines, and she's unlikely to stay there even if I insist on it. We're going to have to do this together, whether I like it or not.

9

ISABEL

When we arrive, the fading sunset glints off the high-rises overlooking the marina. As we near the yacht, I'm relieved to see a crowd of people already forming on the top deck. Tristan said around sixty people, but it's a huge vessel. If people are gathering in one spot, this won't be an intimate affair, which should at least give me a chance to fly under the radar. I fiddle with the pendant on my necklace as Mateus, Tristan, and I wait behind another couple ready to come on board. I exhale a nervous sigh and send up a quiet prayer that everything goes to plan.

A few minutes later, the three of us have been checked off the list, scanned for security, and step on board. Dressed in black and his face obscured behind sunglasses and a dark cap, Tristan takes off first.

The second he disappears from view, I start to worry.

It'll always be this way. Until all the people who want to hurt us are gone, we'll always worry when one of us has to leave the other. I can't get hung up on it right now, though. I force my thoughts to the task ahead of us.

"Let's go up," Mateus says, gesturing for me to lead the way.

Together we climb two flights of stairs and pass a dozen more people before we finally arrive at the heart of the party. People are talking everywhere in small groups. Music is playing just loud enough to make their conversations murky. Pink and blue lights bathe the bright-white couches in color and add to the party atmosphere.

I seem to be in good company, judging from the other women in the crowd dressed to the nines, a few of whom don't look old enough for the drinks in their hands. Everyone lurches a little when the boat undocks and we start to make our way out to sea. A few people holler and clink their glasses to mark the occasion.

We catch two glasses of champagne from a passing server just as Medina emerges from the crowd and walks toward us. His expression is unexpectedly warm and inviting. I can't ignore the hit of relief seeing someone familiar, even if he's essentially a stranger.

"Mateus. Jazmín." He croons our names like we're old friends. "I'm so glad you could make it."

Gone is his careful demeanor from the night before. Something's changed. I'm curious to know what it is, but making small talk with him isn't part of the plan. Instead I lean into Mateus and manage a small smile. Even a high-maintenance girlfriend has to be excited about a yacht party.

"Thank you for having us," Mateus says for both of us.

Medina lifts his glass. "To new friends."

Our flutes make a pleasant tinkling sound—a celebration of this budding relationship that's built on lies and promises death. As we drink, Mateus's earlier request goes unspoken, but I sense we can all feel it. Mateus wouldn't have bothered to come if he didn't expect a meeting.

Medina clears his throat before he speaks.

"Good news. Soloman flew in this afternoon. He's still getting settled and taking care of some other business, but he's looking forward to meeting you. I'll be sure to find you when he's ready."

Mateus's lips curve into a satisfied smile. "Perfect."

"I have to say hello to a few people, if you don't mind. Please enjoy the party and make yourselves comfortable."

Mateus thanks him again, and the man disappears to the lower deck. The plan was to split up, but I squeeze Mateus's hand because I'm not totally ready to part ways yet. He turns his head and gives me an answering squeeze.

"You're good," he says softly. "You've got this, *querida*."

The term of endearment helps me steel my nerves. As Tristan would say, there's work to be done. Somehow with that thought, I find my resolve. "What do you say we mingle?"

"I'm ready when you are."

I ready myself to take my first tentative steps into the crowd when a woman with long black hair down to her waist approaches us. Her body is draped with a flowing sheer dress wrapped loosely over a shimmery gold bikini that barely covers her ample breasts. With a glass of wine dangling from her fingertips, she somehow manages to look both runway and yacht-party ready at once.

"Welcome to the party. I don't think I know you."

"Mateus da Silva."

"Oh, you must be a new friend of Simon's. I'm Athena Pelletier, his wife."

She extends her free hand, which he kisses warmly in true Mateus fashion.

I swallow over my shock. If Soloman is Simon Pelletier, as Tristan informed us earlier, that means Soloman has a wife. Why had that never occurred to me before? Maybe because as of yet, he doesn't have a face to me. He's a myth. A legend. Not a flesh-and-blood human being with a wife.

Athena's cheeks flush a little before she glances over to me.

"This is Jazmín," Mateus says, releasing her from his grasp.

"My God, you're gorgeous. Come, let me introduce you to the girls." She slides her gaze to Mateus. "As long as you don't mind. The boys usually like to work first and drink later. We like to drink first and dance later." She punctuates her plea with a carefree laugh that's almost infectious.

The breezy way she classifies everyone brings some levity to my nervousness. She's not the devil. She's just married to him. I can work with that.

Mateus plants a peck on my cheek. "Go have fun, *querida*. I'll be close."

I watch him leave to join another group when Athena links her arm into mine and we begin to walk the other way around the perimeter of the deck.

"So where are you from?" She takes a sip of her wine and swings the glass lazily to her side.

"We're from Brazil."

"Oh, how wonderful."

"Do you live here?" I ask.

She laughs again. "We're citizens of the world. We live *everywhere*." She emphasizes the last word like it's almost a hardship. "We travel a lot for Simon's work. I stay back in New York a lot of the time, but I wasn't going to pass up a trip to Miami this time of year. We love taking the boat out."

I smile like I can relate to anything she's saying. She's probably as disconnected from what her husband really does as she is from anything outside the bubble her wealth affords her. But it's too tempting not to ask.

"What exactly does Simon do?"

Her eyes widen a little, but the rest of her face doesn't move, which seems unnatural. "Oh, you know, a little bit of everything. The people here"—she gestures with her glass like it's her pointer finger—"are into everything. Tech, banking, real estate, *politics*."

She sticks her tongue out a little, like the last one grosses her out. My guess is politicians comprise the lowest economic rung she's willing to socialize with.

"What about you? Tell me about you. No wait, let me guess." She takes another big gulp of wine and looks me over. "You're not tall enough to be a model, but you have the face for it. So you must be an actress. Yes, that's it."

I laugh at her half insult, half compliment. "I'm just Mateus's girlfriend. My story isn't that interesting."

Not as interesting as your husband's.

She rubs her shoulder against me like we're already close friends. "Nonsense. I'm sure your story is so interesting. Come on, let's show you off to everyone."

She talks quickly, but her words are meaningless. I think she's half drunk and totally disconnected from reality. Still, I play along and pretend to be excited that she's being nice to me. Seconds later, she drops me off with a small group of women before excusing herself. After a quick round of introductions, I realize Athena has grouped me with the other girlfriends, which I'm immediately grateful for. They're quiet and spend most of the time on their phones. Violet, the blonde next to me, is surveying the crowd, though.

"Those are the wives," she says in a tone that reeks of envy.

I follow her gaze. Athena's not with them, but their style matches hers. They're a little older than us. Still provocatively dressed but in ways that are decidedly more expensive. They glitter with obscene diamonds and thick watches, as if they'd ever need to know what time it is.

"Who are you here with?" I ask Violet.

"Ramsey Paulson. His family owns the patents for a bunch of medical equipment."

"How does he know Simon?"

She shrugs. "They're in this rich-guy club. They do a lot of things together."

I bite my lip and try to calm the intrigue spiking through me. "A club?"

She nods, still staring intently in the direction of the wives.

"There are eleven of them."

TRISTAN

Most of the party is clustered on the upper deck and sky lounge at the very top. I notice a few other security details as I roam the main and lower decks to get a sense of the layout and game-plan ways to get the hell off the boat. Then I need to find Soloman.

I duck into one of the interior rooms—an empty but spacious living area that matches the opulence I've already seen. Everything is pristine and new. The plush carpeting silences my journey to the other side of the room, where two slick double doors lead to more interior cabins. I pause at the juncture when I hear voices on the other side.

They're low and hard to make out. I drop to one knee and withdraw a tiny wireless camera from my pocket. It's shaped like a long, flat ribbon and has a camera at one end. I slide it carefully under the edge of the door and open an app on my phone to pull up the video.

I move it around until I get the best angle. The room appears to be an office or conference room of sorts, with a small round table surrounded by four bucket seats. On the other side of it stand two men. One is Javier, who swiftly disappears out the door, leaving the other man alone. He's tall, dressed head to toe in a crisp white suit. His hair is cut short but is pure silver. The only contrast on him comes with the thick, black-rimmed glasses he wears.

He lowers into one of the chairs and brings a cell phone to his ear. I press mine to the door to hear better.

"What's the situation?" he asks without a greeting. He pauses. "*Still* no word?" He whips his glasses off. "I don't care if their job is to disappear. I want you to fucking find them. Do you understand me? The clock is ticking on this." Another pause. "Call me when you have news."

He puts the phone down on the table, takes a handkerchief from his jacket pocket, and proceeds to clean his glasses—silently, rhythmically, and for what seems like too long to achieve the task. He only stops when there's a knock at the door.

He replaces his glasses on his face and looks forward. "Come in."

Javier appears again, flanked by a face I know well. Mateus.

The man in white rises to his feet with a tight smile. They shake hands as Javier disappears through the door again.

"Mr. da Silva. May I call you Mateus?"

"Of course. And you must be King Soloman."

He laughs. "My friends call me Simon. Please, have a seat."

Mateus obliges, taking the adjacent chair. "This is a beautiful boat. Truly magnificent."

"Thank you." Simon smiles. This time seems more genuine. "It used to be owned by a Saudi prince, under a different name of course. We took a meeting on it a few years ago, and I admired it so much, he decided to offer it to me in lieu of payment for my services. I heartily accepted."

"Sometimes it can be a challenge to find joy in such abundance."

"This is true." Simon pauses, cants his head to the side a couple degrees. "Where do you find your joy?"

"In winning." Mateus's answer is so swift it can't be mistaken for anything but the truth.

This makes Soloman smile wider. "Very good. I suppose that is why you've done so well. Your business is quite impressive."

"You've done your due diligence."

"Of course. I'd love to help you out with your problem, but these are delicate matters to pursue without a little familiarity between parties. I must say, though, your reputation is perhaps one of the most impeccable I've encountered."

Mateus lets out a small chuckle but doesn't answer.

"That means you're either very good at keeping secrets hidden or you're very good at staying out of trouble. Which is it?"

"A measure of both."

Simon stares at Mateus like he's trying to read him. "What's the name of this problem of yours, then?"

"Are you accepting?"

"I can't accept until I know his name. You have to insulate yourself from the task you're asking me to carry out. I have relationships to protect as well. There are seven billion people in the world, and you'd be surprised how many of them know each other."

"In this rarefied air, I'm certain many do."

"Precisely."

A long pause stretches between them. I don't know what Mateus will say any more than Simon does. Something has to be said, though. Someone has to be named.

"His name is Lucas Barcelos."

Simon pauses thoughtfully. "I don't recognize the name."

"I doubt you would. He was at his peak thirty years ago before civilian government was restored in Brazil."

"Why him?"

"Does it matter?"

Simon folds his hands on the table and leans forward with interest. "It does. Context is important to me."

A long moment passes between them. I find myself holding my breath, waiting for Mateus to answer him.

"My sister and I were orphaned at a young age, forced to raise ourselves and make the most of what was left to us. My parents were activists whose voices were silenced in the most permanent and violent way. Barcelos was a regional commander at the time. It was his decision, but he never faced his crimes, thanks to the amnesty laws that were passed some time later. He's since retired and now lives a quiet, peaceful life, traveling with his family, rich off the spoils of war. I'm certain he has long forgotten the lives he destroyed, but I have not forgotten him."

I exhale a silent breath. Shit. After Mateus's joke about having a list of expendables, I didn't expect this. He'd told me the story of his parents' murder before, but he'd never mentioned Barcelos. He's been holding on to this grudge for as long as I've known him and, even knowing what I do, chose not to name the man who destroyed his family. Why?

"Thank you." Simon's tone is even, respectful of the gravity of what's been shared. "I understand the nature of things now."

"Will you do it, then?"

"There are some internal checks that we typically run, but I can say with almost complete confidence that this is something we can help you with."

"I'm glad to hear it. Just let me know the fee—"

"I don't think that will be necessary."

Mateus pauses. "I'm not asking for a favor. Name your price."

"Not a favor. I'd like to think of it as a gesture of good will. An invitation."

"An invitation? I've explained my request."

"And I have a request for you as well. Your business is very interesting to us. Even more so is the way you do business. It's very clean, and I like clean."

"Who is *us*?"

"Allow me to explain. You've been so kind as to tell me some of your story. I would like to share with you a little of mine."

Mateus turns his hand, a gesture for Simon to continue.

He pushes his glasses up his nose. "If you've found me, you already know what I can do for you. It may not surprise you to learn I've been doing this for many years, quite successfully. It wasn't always this way. You've risen to the top of your industry in your country. To achieve that kind of steep climb, you have to reach far and wide to grasp every opportunity that presents itself. I did this too. I cast a wide net and connected with a lot of people. When you start brokering lives, though, there's value in a small circle—one that both serves you and protects you. One that can move each of its members forward by sharing our advantages and knowledge and influences in just the right way."

"Raw ambition will only take you so far," Mateus says.

"Exactly. At some point we learn to work smarter, not harder, and part of that is surrounding oneself with others who share this philosophy. It's no longer about seeking those highly coveted favors from those above you or creating distance from the people below you. It's about being among true equals, captains of industry who can open doors for each other that no one else can. Suddenly the race to pull ahead of the competition becomes laughable it's so easy. The unified power of us is unmatched. It's infallible."

"Infallible?"

Simon folds his fingers together more firmly. "Together, we're untouchable. The kind of thing you're asking for is a small request. A pittance. Something that's easily granted to our members."

"What exactly are you offering?"

He pauses.

"Mateus, I would like to invite you to be a part of that circle."

10

ISABEL

When I casually press her, Violet rattles off the names of a few more members of the "club," which I immediately commit to memory. But she's new to this. She and Ramsey have only been dating for a few months, and the social calendar is set to ramp up over the summer. If all goes to plan, she's hoping to get a ring by Christmas. As rapt as I am with her strategy to lock down the billionaire of her dreams, I have a nagging urge to find Mateus. Now that night has fallen and the alcohol has been flowing for an hour or so, the party on the deck seems busier, and I haven't seen Mateus since Athena escorted me away.

If he's in the meeting with Soloman and has an opening to give him the aconite, then timing is everything. As soon as it's done, we're supposed to meet Tristan on the lower deck. The more minutes that pass, the edgier I get.

I excuse myself with Violet and take up the search. Not finding Mateus on this level, I meander downstairs. A smaller group lingers there. I scan their faces.

In an instant, my whole body freezes. My heart plunges into my stomach. I can't move, but I need to. He's right there, so close, chatting with some other men in suits with a lowball in his hand. I recognize his expensive watch, smooth scalp, and charming smile.

Then his cool blue eyes meet mine as if I'd called his name out loud.

Vince.

I turn and walk as briskly as I can manage toward the back of the boat. Maybe he's drunk and so engrossed in his conversation that he didn't see me. He wouldn't recognize me that quickly, would he? A woman emerges through a side door, which I realize is a bathroom. I duck in to hide and lock the door.

I brace my hands on the counter and catch my breath. My heart is flying.

The chances of Soloman recognizing me existed, but we'd never met in person. I spent hours on Vince Boswell's arm the night we met. He put his mouth on me. He beat me. Despite his promises to Tristan when held at gunpoint, he definitely still wants me dead. Mine isn't a face he'll soon forget.

I pull my phone out of my pocket and call Tristan. It rings endlessly. Every second he doesn't answer sends my panic climbing.

My hands are shaking. I need to calm down. Maybe I'm freaking out for nothing.

Bang bang bang.

I slap my hand across my mouth to keep from screaming.

"Isabel, is that you?"

Oh my God. Oh fuck.

I'm trapped in here. Worse, I'm unarmed. I scan the bathroom for anything I can use. Tristan's shiny knife wouldn't make it through security, and while I committed to be resourceful, I'm currently coming up short.

Bang bang bang. "Open the door. I know it's you. Open the fucking door!"

I open the cabinets. Toilet paper, towels, soaps. Nothing. Nothing I can use. I'm shaking badly now. All the adrenaline is doing is pushing the tears that have evaded me for days into my eyes. Pure panic. I run my hands through my hair, close my eyes, and breathe. Just breathe. Think.

Vince's next words are a little more measured. "Listen, I just want to talk to you."

Yeah, right.

When I open my eyes, I'm staring at the floor...and at a pair of shoes that could be deadly if wielded with enough force. Just then my phone vibrates. Tristan.

I press the phone to my ear as I slip off my shoes.

"Boswell is here." My voice is shaking now too.

"What? Vince?"

"I'm locked in a bathroom on the upper deck. He saw me. He's outside the door."

"Shit. Okay. Listen, Mateus is almost done with Soloman. We have to move. Can you get Vince to take you to the back of the boat?"

I will my heart to slow down, but it just won't. "You can't come get me?"

"He's not going to hurt you and cause a scene with all these people around. If I go up there, there's going to be a scene."

"What if he doesn't go with me?"

"Then fucking kill him."

With my shoe.

Breathe.

"Leave your phone on," he says. "I'm coming your way right now. If he pulls anything, I'll be there in thirty seconds. Go now before he talks to someone."

I drop my phone in my purse and clutch my shoe like it's a life preserver in a stormy sea. I open the door, ready to use it, but Vince is suddenly gone. When I step out, I see him walking toward the front of the boat. He's going back to the party. If he tells anyone I'm here, it's over.

"Vince!"

He pivots. The look he gives me morphs from satisfied to ruthless in seconds. A fresh shot of panic works its way through me, making my stomach knot and my palms sweat. I turn and start walking quickly toward the back of the boat, an easier task in bare feet. I don't have to worry about whether he's following me. I can hear his loud footsteps gaining on me. I get to the back and grab the railing to the stairs that will take me to the lower deck.

But I only make it a few steps before Vince grabs my wrist.

"Get back here," he growls, yanking hard on my arm.

The motion throws me off balance, and I lose my footing on the stairs. The weight of my body and his angle above me is too much. He lets me go, and I stumble down the rest of the way, landing at the bottom with a painful cry. He rushes down and pulls me back to my feet like I'm a ragdoll.

My shoes. Shit, I've got nothing in my hands but the starchy white fabric of Vince's shirt. Slamming me against the wall, he brings his face too close to mine. In a moment of pure panic, I see Bones. I can taste the muzzle of his gun on my tongue. I can feel the emptiness in his soul because I recognize that same emptiness in the man before me.

"Gotcha," he sings, a smug smile forming on his face.

I shift my leg to knee him in the crotch, but he flattens me against the wall and quickly pins my wrists. "Not this time. This time you're going to give me everything I want. And then I'm going to finish you for good. Kolt's already forgotten about you anyway. You should see the girl he's fucking now."

I close my eyes and get ready to head-butt him, anything to interrupt his hold on me. Then suddenly it loosens. I open my eyes as he grunts, his eyes suddenly round with fright. His fingers go to his neck and claw at the fine rope that's cinched around it. Tristan's face is beside his, his features hard and strained as he gradually pulls Boswell away from me while holding the rope tight.

Vince thrashes his limbs around to no avail. His efforts are both wildly desperate and lacking strength, a horrible combination. He's losing the fight. He's dying.

"Look away," Tristan says.

But I don't. I can't. I'm riveted by the slow failure of Vince's attempts to save himself. I'm intoxicated by the sudden relief of being free of him. The threat of him. The violence he promised me. All of him.

His flailing stops completely, and when his body goes limp and crumples to the floor, Tristan holds him there a moment longer, ensuring it's done.

Finally, he releases the rope, rolls it up, and stuffs it into his pocket. Only then does it dawn on me that Tristan's killed a man, and he wasn't even our target. We're still on a boat in the middle of the ocean. This wasn't the plan.

"What do we do with him?"

"No better place to lose a body than in deep water."

TRISTAN

I check our location on my phone. We're still miles out from our planned stop at Fisher Island. I want to be long gone before the yacht gets near land anyway. Except now I have a body to deal with, and Mateus still hasn't shown up. That could mean anything.

After Soloman's noble speech about the Company's design and purpose, Mateus had little choice but to tentatively accept the invitation. I would have done the same just to end the conversation. Thankfully the initiation called for drinks, at least one of which hopefully had enough aconite in it to put Soloman in his grave. But I couldn't stick around to watch it happen. After Isabel called, I had to get out of there. If I could hear them, they could hear me.

Fucking Vince Boswell.

I curse his existence as I look around for something to weigh his body down with.

In the far back of the yacht is a huge unlit garage filled with boat toys. Inside it is a lifeboat and two jet skis. I take the anchor from the lifeboat and tether it to his body using the rope that cut off his air supply.

"Where's Mateus?" Isabel asks, her voice still quivering.

Her dress is ripped, and her knees are skinned. I wish I could go to her and comfort her, but time is of the essence. I need to get rid of Boswell before someone notices he's gone and starts looking for him.

"He should be here soon."

I freeze at the sound of footsteps coming down the stairs. I pull Isabel to the side with me so we're hidden in darkness.

"Tristan." Mateus's voice is a harsh whisper.

Relieved, I step out and Isabel follows.

"We're here."

His brows knit tightly when he sees Boswell's lifeless body behind me. "What happened? Who is that?"

"Boswell. He recognized Isabel. It didn't go well for him. What happened with Soloman? I overheard the whole thing until you started to get drinks going. Did he take it? Is it done?"

He shakes his head. "No."

Dread fills me. Suddenly I feel like I'm the one being dropped into deep water with the weight of this anchor lassoed around my entire being. I could have killed Soloman myself. I could have walked through the door and done it in a matter of seconds. He was right there.

"I didn't give it to him. I could have, but… Well, you heard him. You heard the proposal."

My jaw falls a fraction. "Mateus… No."

"I all but said yes already. And once I'm inside, we'll know everything. All their vulnerabilities. All their plans."

This is a nightmare.

"Mateus, they'll destroy you if they find out."

"They destroyed you!" His jaw tightens. Fire flashes in his shadowed gaze. "They robbed you of your life, Tristan. They used you and twisted you to whatever ends they saw fit. And then I set you on this path."

"You had nothing to do with it."

"Isabel told me. You had to kill to save Karina, and then you knew what you were capable of. I brought this on you, and I will see it through. I will make it right."

I'm stunned. So thoroughly that I can't recalibrate our plan for several seconds. I glance around at the jet skis and the outline of the door in the side of the boat that will give us an escape route. I turn back to Mateus.

"I have to get Isabel out of here."

"Go then. Take her, and I will deal with the rest."

I take in a breath and pull my thoughts together. "The boat will be three people short when it gets back to the marina. You need to get off at Fisher Island before they do a final count. Otherwise they might realize it's Isabel and me and link it back to you."

"It's a private island. You have to know people..." He rubs his forehead. "All right. I'll make some calls. I'll figure it out. Go now. Before there are suspicions."

The sound of the yacht's engine goes an octave lower. We're slowing down, and I have no idea why. I slam the switch that opens the boat's garage door. It lifts open with a low hum I hope no one hears. When I look back, Mateus is already gone.

Soon Boswell will go out to sea, and Isabel and I will be on our way. Hopefully she can forget what she saw here. The look in her eyes as I finished Boswell off has a knot forming in my gut already. It's the same feeling I get whenever she gets a glimpse of the man I've become— the killer in me who even now can't bring himself to feel an ounce of regret for this loss of life.

I roll the body closer to the opening and give it a hard shove into the water. The boat is still going fast enough that he's out of sight seconds later, taken under immediately by the extra weight.

I see lights in the distance, and the yacht slows down even more. There are half a dozen boats docked up ahead. I exhale a sigh of relief. This is just a stop on the cruise. Slowing down means I can get us out of here because the choppy waves crashing into the garage are already evening out.

Boom.

Isabel screams and jumps at the sound that seems to rock the whole boat. Then another and another, followed by celebratory hollers on the decks above us.

Streams of colorful lights dance on the uneven water. Fireworks.

Thank you, Jesus.

The engines cut, and the sound of the anchor dropping is almost deafening.

I get on the jet ski and motion Isabel toward me. "Get on," I shout. With a little shove into the water, we'll be out of here.

She jumps on, and I position her arms around my middle. "Hang on to me."

She hangs on tight, then lets go suddenly. "Oh wait."

"Wait?" I take my fingers off the throttle.

She jumps off, runs toward the stairway, and returns a few seconds later with her shoes hanging around her wrist.

"Are you kidding me?"

"Sorry. They were really expensive. Let's go."

The second she locks her arms around my torso, I gun the engine, launching us into the water. The next wave of fireworks masks the zing of the engine as we lurch forward into the darkness and zip toward the brightly lit Miami skyline.

11

ISABEL

I look back to the yacht several times until it's just a pinprick of light with the others glowing against a black night. I'm relieved to be gone, but I won't rest easy until Mateus is back on land and safe too. I press my cheek to Tristan's back and let my body absorb the shocks of the jet ski as we skim the water's surface on the journey back to land. Tristan seems to know exactly where to go, navigating us back to the marina, which is dark and mostly quiet. We ditch the jet ski and head for the parking lot, where Ford is waiting for us with a car.

When we get there, Townsend is leaning against the side of the vehicle, blowing plumes of smoke into the humid air. He pushes off when he sees us, his expression growing serious.

"Where's Mateus?"

"He's still on the boat," Tristan says.

"What the fuck happened to you?" He looks me over. "Did you take care of Soloman? Is it done?"

"We didn't get an opening," Tristan says quickly as we slide into the back seat of the car.

We share a silent look. He's lying. He's protecting Mateus.

Townsend slams the passenger door.

Ford meets our gaze in the rearview mirror. "Back to the hotel?"

"Drop us there and come right back for Mateus," Tristan says. "They're going to drop him off at Fisher Island. He'll probably take the ferry over from there."

"If you didn't knock him off, why'd you bail?" Townsend presses.

I lock my mouth tight, unsure how much Tristan wants to share. Mateus said Soloman offered him a proposal. Sickness roils inside me because I'm afraid I know what it might be.

Tristan takes out his phone. The screen casts a bright glow on his face. He taps out a message, but I can't see it. "We ran into trouble with an old associate. He recognized Isabel, so we had to take care of him. The party won't miss us. They would have missed Mateus, so we split up."

"Fuck," Townsend mutters. "Now what?" He turns in his seat. "We had a deal, you know. You dropped the ball, but you still owe me a meeting. I'm not sticking around to watch you screw things up again."

"I haven't forgotten," Tristan snaps.

Ford drops us at the hotel and doubles back for Mateus. When we get to the penthouse, Tristan makes a beeline for the executive desk. He scribbles on a piece of paper and hands it to Townsend, who frowns as he reads the scrawl.

"What's this?"

"It's a strip club in New York he likes to go to. He'll be in a private room in the back."

"Good." Townsend's mouth sets in a determined line. "That's all I need."

Tristan holds his stare a moment. "Are you sure you want to do this?"

"You've got enough to worry about, mate. You shouldn't be worrying about me."

"I'm not worried about *you*."

Townsend's expression is taut. "I'll be fine. She'll be fine, all right?"

"Whatever you say." Tristan shrugs like he doesn't care, but I know better. If anything happens to Townsend, Jay will be unprotected, which isn't a responsibility either of us is eager to take on again.

Without another word, Townsend turns and leaves. After the elevator doors close behind him, I walk out to the deck and stop at the edge. The ocean is dotted with a few lights shimmering in the distance. I silently wonder if any of them are the *King's Ransom*. Are they on their way to the island now? Has the party escalated the way Athena seemed to think it would by the end of the night?

Tonight was nothing like I expected. For the first time since all of this began, the Company took on a face. The members of the "club" and the people in their circles live in a world unto themselves, apart from the rest of us. They play by a set of rules driven by the need for power and wealth and consuming the best of everything. At least we have a glimpse of who we're dealing with.

If Mateus had dropped the aconite into Soloman's drink, maybe everything could have ended tonight. We'll never know. But now I fear this journey is far from over.

Tristan comes beside me. "You okay?"

I'm not. I'm reeling again, my thoughts spinning wildly between fear and regret and renewed determination. But I don't tell him any of that.

"I'm worried about Mateus."

"He texted me a few minutes ago that everything's fine. No one knows Vince is missing yet. He connected with a friend who owns a place on the island. He's all set."

I exhale a weighty sigh. "Thank God."

He squeezes my shoulder. "He'll be all right. Everything's going to be all right. It's a booze cruise. It'll probably be morning by the time anyone realizes Vince is missing."

"What was the proposal?" I peer up at him. "He said they offered him something."

Tristan's jaw tightens. He doesn't have to say it. I already know.

"Damn it. Why?" I drop my head into my hands. "Why did he do it, Tristan? Now we've missed our chance. This is my fault. I shouldn't have said what I did. He made a comment at the bar about you wasting your talents. I wasn't thinking. I just wanted to defend you. He doesn't understand what you've been through or what this means."

Tristan pulls me against his chest. The tears I've been holding on to for too long stream down my cheeks with my quiet sobs. He hushes me and kisses the crown of my head.

"Isabel, listen to me." He touches my chin and tilts my gaze to meet his. "How much do you think Karina's life was worth to Mateus when I found her? Before they were even lovers?"

I wince. "I don't know."

He brushes my tears away gently. "Mateus could have settled the debt years ago. Every time I asked for something, he took care of it, no questions asked. The penthouse in Ipanema would have been more than enough, but he insisted it wasn't. Taking us into his house in Petrópolis. The jet to Panama. Dozens of other times, he was there to help me in a pinch. This isn't about the debt or Karina. This is about Mateus and me, and nothing you could have said would have probably changed the course of this."

I swallow over the knot in my throat. "Do you really believe that?"

"Mateus paid his debt a long time ago. This is something else. This is personal. I just figured with something this important, I could get him to finally admit we were square. Then he had to go and up the ante."

"Does he realize who they really are? These are crazy rich and dangerous people."

"Mateus is crazy rich, and I wouldn't mess with him either. He may not be old money, but he's got something they want. If anyone can do this, it's him." He pauses, and something shadows his gaze. "There's something else."

The knot of anxiety that's been growing inside me all night tightens a little more.

"What is it?"

"He gave them a name."

TRISTAN

It's two in the morning when the elevator dings and Mateus's figure appears looking only slightly worn down, like maybe he just spent the past five hours attending a fabulous party hosted by vultures masked as socialites.

"*Bom dia.*" He goes to the bar and pours himself a strong drink before sinking into the accent chair directly across from me.

"Morning. Glad to see you got back in one piece."

"I didn't end up at the bottom of the ocean, so I suppose I should consider myself lucky." He takes a substantial swallow of his drink and sighs audibly. "Isabel is sleeping?"

I nod. After I got her calmed down and cleaned up, I treated her wounds from the encounter with Boswell. Even as she began drifting off to sleep, I couldn't keep from touching her, kissing her gently, as if somehow I could erase what she went through tonight. Every time I think of his body crushed against hers, I'm grateful I killed him, even if she had to see it. He'll never hurt her again. He'll never take what he wanted from her.

"How is she?"

His question pulls me from my murderous thoughts. For all my unease over their pretend closeness, I know Mateus's concern for her is genuine.

"He banged her up a little. She fell down the stairs, but she's okay. A few bruises and scrapes. Could have been worse."

He nods wordlessly.

"How did it go?"

He flips his hand. "Soloman got the answer he wanted, and for all he knows, so did I. There was little left to do but drink and watch the party. I met a few of the others, but it was loud. Everyone was distracted. More people came on at Fisher Island. A few left. It was chaos. Too much alcohol. If they had a count, I doubt it was an accurate one."

"That's a relief."

"So now we watch and wait."

I would have rather watched and waited from a place of knowing that Soloman was dead, but things are different now.

"You went off script."

His jaw hardens. "I did what I felt was best."

"That's not what we discussed. The plan was to kill Soloman. To end this. Now we're back at the beginning."

"We're at the beginning of something bigger. You knew killing Soloman would set something off that you couldn't control. You know nothing of his reach. His power. His resources. Yet you wish to be free of it."

"This wasn't your call."

He lifts his brow. "No? Am I only your pawn?"

"This was about a favor."

He laughs and takes another swallow of his drink. "That favor is ancient history and you know it."

His casual confirmation crystallizes what I ignored for too long— something I never let myself believe because the prospect of friendship and loyalty in my world felt less and less possible the deeper I fell into this life. But here we are. Bound by something more than an agreement. We're bound by the years between us.

"You don't have to do this," I say. "There's still time to back out."

"Maybe I want something from it too. Has that occurred to you?"

"If it's about Barcelos, you know I can take care of that. All you had to do was ask. Hell, you *know* me."

"Let him die by the hands of monsters. You, Tristan, are no monster. I saw the heart in you before I enlisted the soldier in you. You're brilliant and lethal, but it was your heart that brought Karina out of there alive."

I wince and look to the side, where beaming blue lights make the pool glow. I'm not sure what to do with those words or the feelings they inspire.

"I've never given you a reason to think more of me," I mutter quietly.

"You're wrong. You sell yourself short. You always have, and here we are, fighting the monsters who made you believe this is all you were ever worth. A mindless killing machine." He leans forward, and I meet his eyes, which are burning with something I can't name. "I have never known someone so alone in the world as you, Tristan. But now... Now you have Isabel. Your miracle. She sees your heart and your darkness. She stays because she's in love with you."

"I haven't given her much choice."

"I don't think she's given you a choice either."

I don't answer. He has no idea how strongly we're bound now, but he's on the right track. I bend myself forward and slice my fingers through my hair with a groan. Like always, everything is a goddamn mess. Two steps forward, one step back.

"We'll beat them. Trust me. I know these kinds of people. Their confidence is always what brings them down. I'm not like them."

I look up. "But you are."

He shakes his head. "Money is nothing. It comes and goes. Power is the same. When you come from where I come from, you take nothing for granted. They take it all for granted. Infallible." He laughs. "That's when I knew. They are living a delusion, Tristan. Their vulnerabilities exist like everyone else's. And as close as I will be, I will find them."

"What about Karina? You put her in danger getting mixed up in this. If they find out what you're doing, she'll be at risk."

He spins his glass on his knee. "She'll be safe. I'll be sure of it."

"And Isabel?"

He arches an eyebrow. "Jazmín? She was temporary, like most of the women there. No one will wonder why she was by my side one moment and gone the next. They'll wonder more why I don't have someone new every time they see me."

"When do you see them next?"

"Soloman will contact me when Barcelos is taken care of. Then we'll see where it goes from there."

I have no choice but to accept the path he's put us on. At least with Boswell gone, I have one less target to worry about. But Soloman was the prize. I want him gone with an irrational dedication now. It isn't revenge that fuels this desire to take him out of the equation. Or is it?

If Morgan Foster bought me a first-class ticket to the front lines and Jay took the wheel on my life as an assassin, where does Soloman fall in it all? Morgan's crime was loving his daughter too much. Stripped of her power and place in the Company, Jay is as vulnerable as any of the marks I took out.

But Soloman is the master of monsters. Monsters like me.

12

ISABEL

"Are you going to eat that?"

Tristan pushes his plate to the center of the table, and I fork the rest of his *foie gras* to mine. It disappears quickly, even as I try to savor each tiny mouthwatering bite. We're at a little French restaurant in South Beach, which is just intimate enough that Tristan seems to be enjoying himself. He seems relaxed even, a smile playing at the edge of his lips as he watches me sample each course.

With Mateus gone, we've had the penthouse to ourselves for the week. And while I know Tristan is more than content to stay cooped up in our palace in the sky, I was happy when he insisted on taking me out tonight. Knowing our time in Miami is coming to an end, I was hoping to see more of the city before life took us elsewhere.

"You still haven't told me where we're going next."

He swirls his wine glass by the base. "That's because I don't know. I'm waiting on Mateus, and he's waiting on Soloman."

"Have you heard from Townsend?"

He smirks a little. "I moved his meeting around with Crow a few times. So he's stuck in New York for a couple of days until I let him know Crow's gone out of town unexpectedly. My guess is he'll go back to wherever he's hiding Jay, and maybe she'll talk some sense into him."

I make a tsking sound. "If he finds out you're meddling, he won't be happy."

"He's already not happy. He needs time to get his emotions under control."

"I can't disagree with that."

"I can hardly blame him. I'd be the same way if it had been you. I'd be a madman trying to make it right somehow. When Boswell had you in that hotel room in New Orleans, I thought I was going to lose my mind. When I saw him hit you…" He works his jaw. "I'd never felt like that before. It's a miracle I didn't kill him then. In hindsight, maybe I should have."

The waiter comes and drops off a new course and pours more wine to pair with the meal. If he overheard the tail end of Tristan's sentence, I hope he's not thinking of calling the authorities on us.

"Does it bother you," Tristan asks once we're alone again, "what happened with Boswell? The things you saw?"

I focus on my food, investigating all the little ingredients accenting the two hunks of grilled Spanish octopus on my plate. All the while, Tristan's question lingers between us. Does it bother me? Does the vision of him forcing the life out of someone who wanted to kill me haunt me? Does it change the way I feel about him?

"Isabel." He says my name gently, with a hint of pleading.

I look up into his tortured gaze.

"I don't want you to think the worst of me, but I realize you probably should."

I put my fork down and weigh my words. Somewhere between our brushes with death, inside the slivers of time when I can breathe and think and let myself really feel everything that's happened, I've started to reason some of it out. It's been a quiet conversation with myself, one that's not nearly over.

"I think that when you're surviving, the rules change," I finally say.

"I don't have the luxury of being bothered by death anymore. I can't take for granted that keeping Boswell alive would have cost me my own life. Surviving has nothing to do with some arbitrary moral code. It has nothing to do with passing judgment on myself or anyone else for the things they do. I want to live. It's that simple. So as long as there's someone out there who wants me dead, I'll do whatever I need to do to protect us. The fact that you'd do the same reinforces the instinct."

He pauses. "I wish it weren't this way."

"It won't always be. And if it is, then so be it... One life, one chance, right?"

I couldn't have known then, when I'd inked those words onto my ribs, that this is where life would take me. That this journey with Tristan would forever change my path and mark my soul in ways far deeper than any imprint on my skin. Still, the words are a constant reminder to push past my fear. To both live and survive. To take chances I've been taught my whole life not to take.

We don't talk anymore about Boswell, and when dinner ends, Tristan takes us to our next stop. A surprise. Our life is full of surprises, and not always good ones. But I have an idea of what to expect when Tristan's trying to make up for our bad days. He knows a few things that can make me forget everything else.

"I asked the bellman, and he said this is the place to be tonight," he says as we pull up to the valet.

Story is deceivingly plain on the outside. Set against white stucco, its simple signage is illuminated by a soft pink light and framed by palm trees. We bypass the long line, and one of the managers takes us inside, where the music is already vibrating the walls. A show of lights beam across every surface of the nightclub.

I can't suppress the buzz of excitement that hits me as we're led to our secluded table on a higher level, giving us a view of the action in every area of the club below while offering the privacy Tristan enjoys. Even though our bellies are full of French food and good wine, the primal energy of the club changes the mood. The DJ's beat is infectious, a nonstop rhythm that seems to build on itself. I'm itching to dance and lose myself in the music.

By the time the cocktail waitress brings us our own bottle of Leblon and a lifetime supply of limes, the crowd is already thrumming with bodies on the dance floor. The second she leaves, I take advantage of the privacy, grasp Tristan's face in my hands, and kiss him the way we do when we're alone. I hold nothing back, and judging by his roaming hands, neither does he. The spinning lights glint in his eyes when we break away. Something else is there too. Heat and love and the unmistakable thrill of being here, living and feeling it all together.

TRISTAN

I hold the cachaça on my tongue and relish the slight burn as Isabel offers me the best view. Rolling out the red carpet tonight to watch her run her hands all over her body and bounce to the rhythm of the music in our little private corner of the club is possibly the best idea I've ever had. She's long past holding on to her inhibitions, and I'm not far behind. At least when it comes to keeping my hands off her.

I stand, come up behind her, and place my hand low on her belly to press us close. Never missing a beat, she slides her hands into my hair and weaves her body against mine. We sway together in a slow dance designed for one thing—to drive me straight out of my mind. After watching her dance for hours, no way will I last this way.

"You ready to go back?" I ask when the song transitions.

She twirls seductively in my embrace and answers me with a kiss that quickly goes from sensual to hungry. I push her back until she's against the railing, no longer moving to the music but responding to my touches. A slow slide up the back of her thigh. A possessive squeeze over her hip. I exhale harshly. Need her. Now.

I pull back and take in her lusty gaze. Her swollen lips. The way her cocktail dress accentuates everything I already love about her body.

She lifts a finger. "Give me one minute. I'll be right back."

The bouncer who's been manning our area escorts her to the ladies room on a higher level, guiding the way with his flashlight to the area reserved for patrons of the private sections. I scan our table and grab her purse, making sure we have everything to make a hasty exit. Her phone lights up in her purse when I open it.

Somehow in the blur of filthy thoughts I'm having about her, the words on the notification cause me to do a double take.

New Email from Kolt Mirchoff: Re: Please read.

The fuck.

I swipe it open and start reading his latest reply.

Will you meet with me? I'm staying at my place in Cambridge. Or I can come to you. Just let me know when and where.

Love,

Kolt

My focus is laser-sharp now as I scroll down to read his original plea and her reply. *Make me believe it.* I clench my teeth to the point of pain.

My thoughts fly as I process a fast sequence of emotions: rage, jealousy, and a strong dose of suspicion that Kolt is trying to lure her to Boston to fall into another one of Boswell's traps.

I look up. Isabel's nowhere to be seen, so I return to the screen and type a reply.

Meet me at the Black Rose on State Street on Friday night.

I send the message and immediately delete his and mine so she won't know anything about this exchange. I drop the phone back into her purse and look up when a dozen huge plumes of smoke eject into the air on either side of the dance floor, causing a loud uproar of celebration.

I fixate on the never-ending show to distract me from the flood of resentment and anger threatening to take over our night. She should have told me... *Make me believe it.* What the *fuck* does that mean?

When she returns, it takes all my willpower to act normal. I take her hand and we leave. The car ride is tense. I catch her eager hand on my thigh and hold it in the center space between us. I don't need the distraction when I'm this dedicated to my new mood. We ride up the elevator in silence, and by the time we make it to the penthouse, I'm seconds from blowing my cover and calling her out on her exchange with Kolt.

I go to the bedroom and tear off my collared shirt. She follows behind me.

"Tristan, what's wrong?"

"Nothing."

A pause. "Did I do something wrong?"

"No," I answer brusquely.

"I thought we were having a good time there."

"I'm glad you had fun." The sentiment is flat.

Of course, I am glad she had a good night up to now, but I'm a million miles away from where we were moments ago. I'm deep in a tornado of frustration. So deep that when she skims her smooth palm up my back, I react without thinking it through. I turn, catch her wrist, and haul her hard against me. I fist my fingers in her hair and ravage her mouth until I'm certain I've poured every ounce of feeling in me into the act. She releases a needy whimper and claws at my skin with her blunt nails, which only makes me ache to drag my teeth all over her. To mark her and make her feel me, all this need and fire. Revenge may still be a distant concept, but jealousy is solidly in my wheelhouse.

She's breathless when we break apart. "What the hell, Tristan?"

I answer by tossing her onto the bed. She bounces, and her dangerously high heels dig into the expensive bedspread. I crawl over her, ready to bury all these feelings by burying myself in her.

I yank her dress down and hike it up in one motion. She reaches for my belt and struggles with my zipper, rushing with me now toward the climax we both need. Seconds later, still half dressed, I'm driving into her. Something between a scream and a desperate moan tears past her lips, again and again, until it feels like we're tearing each other apart. There's nothing sensual or romantic about it. It's feral, and the raw nature of it feeds the animal in me who needs to make her mine. Mine and only mine.

I'm tempted to make her say it. But it feels wrong and desperate. Plus she'd say anything when we're like this…this close…climbing fast and hard.

She brings her hand to my face and stares into my eyes, holding me there through the storm of our bodies coming together.

"I love you," she rasps.

I wince because I'm falling off the cliff. Even that can't keep me from challenging her, pushing her to say it again until I can't ever doubt it. "Do you?"

"Yes… I do…"

"Then say it like you mean it."

Her eyes flutter closed. "Oh God…"

I'm seconds away from coming, so I give her everything I have left. Every ounce of my strength and power into her until she moans my name into the air—a long sound that stretches out until we're both wasted from the rush.

We don't move for a long time. She drags her heel up the back of my pant leg and plays with my hair lazily.

"I love you," she mumbles. "I really do."

When I pull back, her eyes are nearly closed. I get us cleaned up and tuck her into bed to crash from what turned into a very long, eventful, and unexpected night. Once she's dozing, I slip into the living room with her purse.

A new notification lights up the screen. I swipe it open and read the short reply from the man who's either trying to steal my girl or get her killed.

I'll be there.

Continue The Red Ledger with

REVENGE

Coming Soon

ALSO BY

MEREDITH WILD

THE RED LEDGER

Reborn

Recall

Revenge

THE HACKER SERIES

Hardwired

Hardpressed

Hardline

Hard Limit

Hard Love

THE BRIDGE SERIES

On My Knees

Into the Fire

Over the Edge

ACKNOWLEDGMENTS

While writing a novel often feels like being trapped on an island by myself, it does in fact take a village to pull it all off. I'm very blessed to have had the incredible support of so many people along the way.

My heartfelt gratitude goes to…

…my husband, Jonathan, who read every sentence and provided hugs, enthusiasm, and ideas whenever things felt hopeless.

…my awesome children, who accepted the sacrifices of time I had to make, including much of their summer. I promise to make it up with lots of cupcakes, snuggle sessions, and your college tuition.

…my sprint ladies, Angel Payne and Victoria Blue. Thank you for your friendship and always giving me a place to go for much-needed motivational pushes and venting. Maniacs!

…the Waterhouse Press team, who had little choice but to tolerate my painstaking writing pace on top of an intense production schedule. I hope you'll forgive me one day.

…my editor, Scott Saunders. Thanks for pretending like my deadline was no big deal when I couldn't deal with one more iota of pressure. You're the best.

…my mom, who was always there for late-night cheerleading texts and reminders to recharge and take some "me" time along the way.

…Kika Medina, who whipped my Spanish into shape on short notice, and Cleida Roy and Carol Sales, for your input on all things Brazil and Portuguese.

…my Team Wild rock stars, Company 11 Assassins, bloggers, beta and ARC readers! Thank you for loving this story so much and making the writing journey a blast, even on the most trying days.

I look forward to sharing *Revenge* with you very soon!

ABOUT THE AUTHOR

Meredith Wild is a #1 *New York Times*, *USA Today*, and international bestselling author. After publishing her debut novel, *Hardwired*, in September 2013, Wild used her ten years of experience as a tech entrepreneur to push the boundaries of her "self-published" status, becoming stocked in brick-and-mortar bookstore chains nationwide and forging relationships with major retailers.

In 2014, Wild founded her own imprint, Waterhouse Press, under which she hit #1 on the *New York Times* and *Wall Street Journal* bestseller lists. She has been featured on *CBS This Morning* and the *Today Show*, and in the *New York Times*, the *Hollywood Reporter*, *Publishers Weekly*, and the *Examiner*. Her foreign rights have been sold in twenty-two languages.